Murder Is Academic

Murder Is Academic

A Cambridge Mystery

Christine Poulson

Thomas Dunne Books
St. Martin's Minotaur ⚑ New York

M Y S
POULSON

www.minotaurbooks.com

ISBN 0-312-31807-3

First published in Great Britain by Robert Hale Limited,
under the title *Dead Letters*

First U.S. Edition: April 2004

10 9 8 7 6 5 4 3 2 1

My thanks to Elspeth Barker, Peter Blundell Jones, Frank Falco, Sue Hepworth, Carola Hicks, Avis Poulson, Amanda Rainger, Jonathan Waller and Kit Wright for comments and encouragement. I am also grateful to East Midlands Arts who sponsored a report from an anonymous critic to whom I am much indebted.

St Etheldreda's College – if it existed – would be located near Cambridge University's School of Veterinary Medicine on Madingley Road. Its organization is idiosyncratic: unlike other Cambridge colleges, it is split into departments. However, idiosyncrasy and even downright eccentricity aren't uncommon in Cambridge, so this seems a permissible liberty.

Prologue

Presentiment is that long shadow on the lawn
Indicative that suns go down;
The notice to the startled grass
That darkness is about to pass.

Emily Dickinson

It's hard now to remember what first struck me as not being quite right, but I think it was the garden sprinkler.

I certainly wasn't concerned when no one answered the doorbell. After all, it was a lovely day, so Margaret might have taken her work out into the garden. It's only with hindsight that everything seems to have been leading up to the moment that split the day like a seismic shock, opening up a gulf between past and present. If I'm to tell this story, if I'm to get it all clear in my own mind – and after all that's why I'm writing it: to make sense of the crazy events of the past year – then I must try to get it right.

So: the garden sprinkler. As I walked down the path, I heard the gentle swishing without being able quite to identify what the sound was. Then I turned the corner of the house and saw the water falling in slow, rhythmic veils. The ground underneath the sprinkler was sodden, the grass almost submerged. It must have been on for hours, all night probably. You'd have to know Margaret as well as I did to understand why that was odd. She ran a tight ship

7

in college and it was the same at home. I'd often thought it was just as well that Malcolm was fanatically tidy, too. They would have driven each other mad otherwise.

A little gust of wind threw a handful of droplets onto my bare arm, and raised goose-bumps. I shivered and looked around the garden. At the far side of the garden by the pool was an overturned chair with papers scattered around it. A few more papers were lying on the lawn. I made my way towards the nearest one. When I read the bold print on the top sheet, I positively yelped in surprise and protest.

University of Cambridge Tripos Paper, it said, and, underneath, 'The Nineteenth Century Novel'. Attached to it by a tag were about a dozen pages of big, loopy writing.

It was one of the exam papers I had come to collect.

I snatched it up and ran towards the pool. And then I saw what hadn't been visible from the other side of the garden. At the near end a layer of papers floated like water-lilies on the surface. There must have been thirty or forty of them. Thick as the autumnal leaves that strew the brooks in Vallombrosa, I thought. Incongruous quotations tend to dart into my mind at moments of crisis, but perhaps Milton's description of the rebel angels destined for Hell wasn't as incongruous as all that. If those papers didn't represent souls exactly, they did represent student lives: three years of work, a degree, a future career. Paradise lost indeed. Not to mention the hell that was going to break loose when the examining board found out about this. I just couldn't believe Margaret had been careless enough to let this happen. Careless? That didn't come near it. This was a crime, right up there with seducing the students or cooking the college books. Worse perhaps. You could probably get sacked out of hand for it.

All this flashed through my mind in the time it took me to run in through the conservatory door and bellow for Margaret. Then I rushed back to begin gathering up swathes of papers from the pavement before another gust of wind could sweep them into the water. I dumped them on the white cast-iron table by the pool and anchored them with a wine bottle that was standing on it. Then I lay on my stomach, the chill of the stone striking up though my thin summer dress, and plunged my hands into the water. I winced at the sudden cold. Most of the papers had drifted towards the middle of the pool out of reach. The few I did manage to scoop up were sodden, the pages stuck together and the writing blurred into illegibility. I could have wept.

I'd need some kind of implement to get the rest out. I scrambled to my feet and gazed around the garden, cursing Margaret's tidiness. There wasn't a rake or a hoe in sight. Then I saw the wooden clothes prop standing against the wall of the house. I grabbed it and rushed round to the other side of the pool, hoping I could push the papers to the side using the forked end. I misjudged the weight. The end of the prop landed with a splash among the papers and disappeared below the surface. I groaned and tried to pull the prop back. It seemed to catch on something. Without thinking, I gave a great tug.

As the prop came free, I staggered back. There was a strange heaving in the water. The papers rocked in the swell.

A hand, white and bloated, thrust itself up through the litter of papers.

Chapter One

'Are you sure you don't want me to come with you?' Stephen asked.

'Quite sure, thanks. After all, you hardly knew her.'

'All the same ... for moral support ...?' He pulled out cautiously to overtake a flock of students on bicycles. 'It's not too late for me to ring the office.'

'No, truly. I'll be OK. Why don't you pull over here? Look, there's Merfyn. I'll walk the rest of the way with him. You know what it's like trying to park in the centre of Cambridge.'

He indicated and pulled in by the Bridge Street entrance to St John's College. I leant over to kiss him goodbye. The smoothness of his shaved skin and the familiar smell of soap were comforting. He didn't take his eyes off the road. Instead of turning to kiss me, he leaned his head against mine, pressing his cheek hard against my lips.

'Are you sure this is a good idea?' he said. 'I'm sure everyone would understand ... under the circumstances ... and you know what the doctor said ...'

'Stephen! We've been through all this!'

Behind us an impatient taxi driver was sounding his horn.

'OK, OK,' Stephen said. 'Give me a ring when you want me to collect you.'

I struggled out of the car. As I straightened up, a wave of dizziness swept over me. The ground swayed beneath my feet. As Stephen's glossy black Audi was carried away by the flow of traffic, I felt a surge of panic. Why hadn't I let him come with me? I felt an absurd impulse to run after him, bang on the side of the car, but already the car was disappearing round the corner. For a moment I seemed to see myself from the outside, a pale woman with red-rimmed eyes, dressed in a dark suit and a wide-brimmed straw hat with a black band, stranded on the kerb in the midst of a chattering stream of students, shoppers and tourists.

I felt a hand on my arm and looked round to see Merfyn standing next to me.

'Are you all right, Cassandra?'

As he spoke I felt something knock against me from behind. Involuntarily I took a step towards him and Merfyn put his hands on my arms to steady me. I caught a whiff of an old-fashioned cologne smelling of lime.

'Ah, *scusi*,' someone murmured.

'Bloody language students,' Merfyn said.

I turned and glared at the gaggle of students who were giggling and shrugging as they made off down the street. The next instant my eyes were prickling with tears. I put a hand up to my mouth.

Merfyn looked at me with concern. 'Here, take my arm. The service doesn't start for another twenty minutes. We can sit for a while on one of those benches in All Saints Garden.'

He steered me through the crowd.

'It used to be town and gown,' he said. 'Now it's town and gown and the whole bloody world. D'you know, the other day I counted seven different languages just from walking between the market and Jesus Lane? French, Italian, German, something Scandinavian, Spanish, Japanese – and do you count American as a foreign language? I think I do.'

We reached the sanctuary of the little park. It's just a triangle of land opposite the chapel of St John's College, mostly gravel with a few ornamental trees, a couple of silver birches, a cherry tree or

11

two, and something exotic that Stephen had once told me was a maidenhair tree. Round the sides were stalls selling handmade jewellery and pottery and prints of old Cambridge. A couple were just leaving one of the benches set around the central flower-bed. I sank down in their place and Merfyn joined me. He leaned back, stretched out a pair of long legs and crossed them at the ankle. He was wearing a suit of ivory linen, rather crumpled and old-fashioned in cut. He would only have needed a cane and panama hat to look as though he'd stepped out of a short story by Somerset Maugham. You'd never guess that he'd been a working-class boy from the Welsh valleys: thirty years in Cambridge, twenty of them at the college where we both worked, had virtually worn away his accent. I always felt that he was one of the older generation although he was only fiftyish to my late-thirties. It was partly that he had three grown-up daughters, partly that he had been something of a mentor.

We sat and watched people walking past with their shopping or their guidebooks. Students on bicycles wobbled over the uneven cobbled road. A couple of giggling Japanese girls were taking photographs of each other against the Gothic window of the chapel.

'All right now, Cassandra? Merfyn asked.

'Better, yes. I think the sedatives are making me feel woozy.'

'You're probably still in shock and no wonder ...'

His voice trailed tactfully away. I realized that he probably had only a rough idea what had happened. I hadn't been able to bring myself to describe it in detail to anyone in college.

He took a handkerchief out of his pocket, shook out the sharply ironed folds and mopped his forehead.

'God, it's hot. Feels all wrong for a funeral, this kind of weather.'

'Everything about it feels wrong.'

'You haven't heard any more ...?'

I told him what Malcolm had told me the day before, that the

12

police thought Margaret had probably hit her head diving in and the inquest wouldn't be for at least another five or six weeks. 'The end of July at the earliest.'

Merfyn sighed and shook his head. 'It's very hard on him. They'd been together since they were students, hadn't they?'

'He's torturing himself for not being there when it happened.'

The police had eventually tracked Malcolm down to a hotel in Cardiff where he had been on business connected with his computer software company.

'How are the paper conservators getting on?' Merfyn asked.

Margaret had been in the water for at least twelve hours and the exam papers had had all night to distribute themselves around the garden. I didn't want to think about that, but I couldn't help myself. I saw the colours of the garden gradually changing to grey, a chilly little wind starting up, ruffling the papers, slowly turning over the pages, gaining enough strength to tumble them off the table. I saw the papers rolling across the pavement, settling on the surface of the water like great flakes of ash, concealing what lay beneath …

I slammed shut that door in my mind.

'The papers are going to be more or less OK,' I told Merfyn.

'Bloody good job they all write in Biro. I hate the stuff, but if it had been ink … Of course, the real question is what the hell are we going to do about the others?'

The police had made a thorough search of the garden. One exam script had been found on a rose-bush in a neighbouring garden, another was wrapped round the steel railings of the sports field at the end of Cranmer Road. Those that had been in the water were laid between layers of blotting paper and taken to the paper conservators at the Fitzwilliam Museum. In all the panic and commotion it was some time before anyone had thought to check the papers against the list of candidates. After that another, wider search had taken place. The house had been searched and Margaret's office in college, but to no avail.

13

At the end of it all, four finals papers were still missing.

'Margaret would have been horrified,' I said. 'That just adds to the sheer bloody awfulness of it all.'

I rubbed my forehead wearily with the heel of my hand, almost dislodging my hat. I'd forgotten I was wearing it.

'You know, I don't think Lawrence'll be able to keep this under wraps much longer,' Merfyn said. 'Some sort of rumour's obviously circulating. One of the third-years came to see me in my office this morning, and another came up to me in the corridor. They'd heard that there might be a problem about getting their degrees.'

'What did you say?'

'I told them to go and see Lawrence. He's the bloody Master after all. Why the devil didn't he come clean about those exam papers straight away?'

'He's still hoping that we'll find a way round it.'

'Not very likely now, is it?'

'You know, Stephen thinks the students might well have grounds for suing the college.'

'Trust a lawyer to think of that,' Merfyn said grimly. 'You'd better ask that boyfriend of yours not to make that opinion too widely known.'

I frowned at him. 'Of course he won't.'

Merfyn glanced at his watch. 'Come on, time to get going.'

We made our way down Trinity Street in the full glare of the afternoon sun. By common accord we paused outside Heffer's bookshop window to look at the display. Travel books with brightly coloured covers; Bill Bryson, Colin Thubron, Bruce Chatwin. It looked cool and dim inside. All those books, all those other worlds just waiting between the covers, I thought. For a moment the temptation to go in and lose myself among the shelves was almost too strong.

Merfyn put his hand on my arm. We moved on.

I said, 'You know, I used to think you could find the answer to

14

everything in books, but there are times when even literature can't help.'

Merfyn gave me a look of enquiry.

I hesitated, not quite sure how to put it into words. 'There are terrible, senseless deaths in literature, of course ... Greek tragedy, *King Lear*, lots of modern novels ... but somehow, it's not completely senseless, is it? And that's because it's in a work of art ... it's stirring, moving.'

'Cathartic, yes. You come out of the theatre thinking that life is terrible, but it's wonderful, too.'

'That's just it. But when it's ordinary life, when it really happens, it's not like that at all. There isn't any meaning. It's just a big fat nothing, as the students say. An emptiness. I still can't really believe that it's happened. I mean, she was only forty. It's like a bizarre conjuring trick.'

'Now you see her, now you don't.'

'That's it. One moment, they're there, absolutely normal; the next, they're gone, and you can't understand how it could have happened. They can't have just disappeared. You keep looking around ... wondering where they are.'

Merfyn nodded sympathetically, but before he could speak we were separated by a group of American tourists who were being led by a tour guide down the middle of the street. When we again managed to fall into step together, the moment had passed, and we walked along in silence.

We emerged from the narrowness of Trinity Street in the broader space of Market Square. On the right, the newly cleaned Senate House was a dazzling bone-white in the sun. On the left was Great St Mary's, the medieval university church, to which other people in dark clothes and hats were also heading.

It wasn't until we were walking up the flagstone path to the porch that Merfyn said, 'You may have something there, Cassandra.'

'How do you mean?'

15

'The conjuring trick. When the magician makes someone disappear, they don't really disappear, do they?'

'Of course not.'

We paused at the threshold to the church. I looked sideways at him, puzzled. He was frowning thoughtfully. I couldn't think where this was leading.

'So?' I said.

Merfyn seemed about to say something, but at that moment a group of people coming up the path behind us forced us to move on. He shook his head as though he were dismissing an irrelevant train of thought and stood aside to let me go first into the church.

Before I could say anything else, a black-coated usher came forward to show us to a pew. The funeral was about to begin.

'With the death of Margaret Joplin we at St Etheldreda's mourn a greatly valued friend and colleague. She had been with us for ten years, six as head of the English department ...'

Lawrence had a surprisingly sonorous voice for such a small man. I couldn't really see him from where we were sitting near the back of the church, but every word was clear and distinct.

The service was nearly over, thank God. All through it I had been thinking off and on of what Merfyn had said. I glanced at him. He was leaning forward with his hands clasped between his knees. With his beaky nose in profile and his thick black hair spiked with silver and standing up on the crown of his head, he looked like a benign bird of prey. What had he meant? There hadn't been any doubt that it was Margaret in the pool, even though ... but I didn't want to think about those moments after I had dropped the clothes prop. He couldn't know about that, no one did. I felt a flutter of panic in my stomach.

I tried to focus on the here and now, to anchor myself in the present, where there was nothing to fear. I looked around the church at the mass of mourners, filling not only the pews, but the Jacobean galleries above. And there was the church itself, the stone, the flagged floor firm under my feet, the glass, the wood. The pew end next to me was decorated with an exquisitely naturalistic carving of a deer. I looked at the tiny ears folded back against the head, the little hoof pawing the ground. I touched it. Its back, cool and smooth under my fingers, was polished by the touch of thousands of other hands over the centuries.

I'd missed some of what Lawrence had said. He was talking about Margaret's academic work.

'Her superb book on Anglo-Catholicism in the nineteenth century novel, published when she was still only in her twenties, established her very early on as one of the most promising literary scholars of her generation. Her recent biography of the Victorian novelist, Charlotte M. Yonge, amply fulfilled that early promise. Literature was her life ...'

And her death. The thought seemed to appear in my head from nowhere, shocking me with its incongruity. And yet ... it was a literary sort of death in a way. There was Shakespeare of course – 'too much of water hast thou, poor Ophelia' – and Milton's Lycidas in his 'watery bier'. I found myself assembling a list. Shelley, too, that poem about Adonis, but the poet himself as well, lost in a storm at sea, his body washed up on the shore of the Mediterranean, an archetypal Romantic death. There flashed into my mind Tennyson's description of the hand that rises out of the lake to take back Excalibur: 'Clothed in white samite, mystic, wonderful'. The poem was on my Victorian poetry course. I realized that I was never going to read it again without thinking of Margaret.

'Yet she was no blue-stocking,' Lawrence was announcing. 'She did not see why the life of the mind should preclude a love of clothes. Her elegance and flair, her intellect and sharp wit, that is what we will remember ...'

I saw again the hand rising out the water, the sun striking a brief dazzling light from the diamond ring on its finger. There was a moment when time seemed frozen. Then, as if it were beckoning to me, the hand slowly turned over and disappeared beneath the water.

Merfyn's words came back to me: 'Now you see it, now you don't.'

'The part she played in the wider Cambridge community,' I heard Lawrence say, but something seemed to have gone wrong with the volume control. At one moment his voice boomed around the church, the next his mouth was moving soundlessly. Little pinpoints of light were dancing in front of my eyes and there was something sour in my throat.

I fumbled for my handbag and struggled to my feet. The church and the congregation were flickering before my eyes as if lit by strobe lighting. Someone was touching my arm. 'Shall I come with you?' I heard Merfyn say, his voice sounding as if were a long way off. I shook my head fiercely and struggled out of the pew, knocking my knee against the little wooden shelf that holds the hymn books. A woman sitting a row or two in front of me looked round and frowned. Other heads were beginning to turn.

The sparks were becoming star bursts. I could hardly see the door. Then the iron latch was in my hand. I struggled with it, it shot up, and the heavy oak door swung open.

I stepped out into the heat of the day. The door closed behind me with a reverberant thud.

Keeping one hand on the wall, I walked round the side of the church to where I knew there was a bench. It's often occupied by a group of sociable drunks, sharing bottles of cider and cans of extra-strong lager. Today, thank God, it was empty. I sank down on it and leant forward, bracing myself with my hands on my knees. My straw hat fell to the ground. My shirt was sticking to my body and I was chilly with evaporating sweat. I focused on the flagstones and concentrated on taking slow, deep breaths. I could see the neck of a brown bottle sticking out from under the bench, and there was the sweet, heavy smell of stale beer.

The church door creaked open. A woman came into view. I

looked around and saw that it was the one who had turned to look at me in church. She was still frowning, but I saw now that it was a frown not of disapproval but of concern.

'Are you all right?' Her voice was surprisingly high-pitched and girlish in its inflexion, but it also had a ring of authority.

'Will be in a minute.'

She sat down next to me, smoothing her skirt over her knees. A flowery scent overlaid the smell of old beer.

The drone of Lawrence's voice ceased. There was a pause, and then the low notes of the organ and the shuffling sound of a large congregation getting to its feet reached us. After a bar or two, I recognized 'The day Thou gavest, Lord, is ended'.

Slowly I sat up. My companion put her hand on my shoulder and briefly squeezed it. For a moment or two I sat quietly, taking in the bustle of the market, people walking back and forth with bags of shopping and children in push-chairs, Auntie's Tea-Room and the Internet Exchange, the blessed ordinariness of it all.

I turned to my companion. Now that I saw her properly for the first time, I realized that she was older than I had thought. Early forties, perhaps. The fair hair had a lot of white in it and her smile brought the lines around her eyes into relief. It was a pleasant face, and a shrewd one.

She fumbled around in her handbag and brought out a packet of Marlborough Lites.

'Do you mind?' she asked.

'No, in fact, could I ...?'

'Of course.'

I took one, and she lit it for me.

I inhaled deeply. The nicotine rush seemed to bring the world into sharper focus. Oh, God, I'd almost managed to forget how good this was. I felt like a schoolgirl who had sneaked out of class to smoke in the lavatories.

'I shouldn't be doing this. Sets such a bad example to the students for one thing.'

19

'Me, too,' she said, 'though it's patients in my case. I'm always telling them they should quit. Sheer hypocrisy.'

'You're a doctor?'

'A GP.'

'Margaret's?'

'No, just her neighbour. Jane Pennyfeather. I live next door.'

'I'm Cassandra James.'

Jane tapped the ash off on her cigarette and looked at me thoughtfully.

'Ah, so it ...'

I took a long drag on my cigarette.

'Yes. It was me.'

She gave a little grimace of sympathy. 'How awful for you. No wonder you need a fag.'

Her matter-of-factness, the intimacy of being alone together, set apart from both the funeral continuing behind us and the bustle of the market place in front of us, even the very fact that she was a stranger: suddenly it was easy to tell her.

'I haven't told anyone ... but I just feel so ashamed ...'

I bit my lip hard, but it was no good: tears were welling up. One spilled over and ran down my cheek into the corner of my mouth.

Jane delved into her bag and brought out a handful of paper tissues. She pressed them into my hand.

'I ran away,' I told her.

In my memory there was nothing between the splash of the pole hitting the water and finding myself by the telephone in Margaret's sitting-room. It was as if I'd been transported there by magic. I rang for an ambulance and the police and went out through the front door to sit on the kerb in the hot sun, head in hands. I was still there when the police arrived. I couldn't go back into that garden where I knew that something monstrous was waiting for me under the surface of the water.

'I feel terrible,' I told Jane, scrubbing at my face and sniffing. I didn't try to get her out of the water. I didn't even look to see if it was Margaret in there.'

Jane dropped her fag-end on the floor and ground it out with her heel. 'It was Margaret all right, I identified the body. And there was absolutely nothing anyone could have done. She'd been in the water for hours.'

'But how could I have been sure?'

She leaned forward and took one of my hands in both of hers. 'Now listen, how long do you think it takes to drown?'

'Ten minutes?'

'Even less than that. The brain can't survive without oxygen for more than a few minutes. I'm sure you knew that she couldn't possibly be alive.'

I thought of the settled silence that had hung over the garden and the house, the sodden exam papers, the water-sprinkler in its pool of water, the brief glimpse of that hand ...

'Perhaps I did.'

'Of course you did,' she said with emphasis.

But still, I thought, why didn't I at least go back to the pool and wait there with her? I was afraid; afraid of Margaret, my colleague and my friend. I didn't want to see what she had become. It wasn't going to be easy to forgive myself for that loss of nerve.

Jane was saying, 'It's survivor guilt, what you're feeling. It's always like that when people die suddenly. I see a lot of it.'

I remembered my conversation with Malcolm.

'Malcolm's blaming himself, too,' I told her.

'Mmm.'

It was as though a cloud had momentarily hidden the sun. It was like a little drop in temperature, nothing much, just a degree or two, but something had changed between us. I looked at Jane, but she had her head down and was rooting about in her handbag again. She brought out a pair of dark glasses and put them on.

'The police asked me about Malcolm being away so much on business,' she said.

'But ... what did they want to know exactly?'

21

In the silence that fell between us, I was aware that it was quiet in the church, too. The hymn had finished.

'They don't think – they can't think – that he was having an ...' I couldn't get the word out. 'Malcolm was absolutely devoted to Margaret!'

'They have to ask these questions. I'm sure it's just routine,' she said, getting to her feet. 'Look, they'll be coming out in a moment. Do you feel up to joining them?'

I nodded.

She bent down and picked up my hat for me.

The church doors opened. The leading pall-bearers emerged, and the coffin with its cargo of wreaths came into view. Malcolm followed it, hands clasped in front of him, head bowed. He was a tall, thin, sandy-haired Scot with that fair skin that marks so easily. Around the eyes his skin was pink and puffy. He had a tendency anyway to stoop, but now he was bending over as though he had been buffeted and bowed by gusts of grief.

I glanced at Jane. She seemed to be gazing at Malcolm, but it was impossible to be sure or to read her expression behind the dark glasses.

Chapter Two

'I just can't believe that Malcolm was having an affair.'

Stephen groaned. 'Look, Cass, I thought we'd already been through this – how many times? Three, four?'

We were sitting on a bench at the end of my garden. It was late on the day of the funeral and it was a glorious summer's evening. In other circumstances it would have been perfect. The faintest of breezes, no more than a stirring of the air, brought the scent of roses and honeysuckle to us. The long spell of hot weather had brought them fully into bloom. The tall, narrow shape of the house was almost black against a turquoise sky, the weather-boarding no longer visible in the twilight. Light was spilling out of the floor-length kitchen window and laying streaks of gold on the channel of water that flowed beneath the house. The house had been built as a granary across a creek where barges could moor underneath to receive grain through a chute.

A dark shape detached itself from the eaves, swooped over the flower-beds and darted down to the surface of the water.

I felt Stephen's arm jerk against mine.

'It's only a bat,' I said. 'They come out for the insects.'

We sat on for a while in silence.

My thoughts plodded round the same old track again and again like a weary old horse.

'Malcolm is the last person ... I mean, they were such a settled couple. They'd been together, what fifteen years? Twenty years?'

'Cassandra!'

'Sorry, sorry. I'll shut up.'

After a minute or two, Stephen said, 'That in itself doesn't necessarily mean much, does it, the length of time?'

I slipped my hand into his and squeezed it. I guessed that he was thinking of his own twelve-year marriage, and the way it had ended four years ago. His wife had left with one of his closest friends.

He sighed. 'You can never really know what's going on in someone else's marriage. Or even in your own for that matter.'

I knew that, of course, and, like Stephen, I knew it from bitter experience. But Malcolm and Margaret ... they had been one of those couples who seemed as married as your own parents, the kind that makes you think perhaps it *can* work after all. I gave a sigh and stretched, trying to ease the ache between my shoulder blades. My eyes were sore and I could feel their shape in my eye sockets. I ought to go to bed, but I was too tired to make up my mind to do it.

'Anyway, aren't you reading too much into what that woman said?' Stephen went on. 'Perhaps it was just a malicious little comment.'

I considered this. 'No ... it wasn't like that. It was more as though she were warning me about something ... or, perhaps not that exactly ...'

My voice trailed off as I realized that Stephen wasn't listening.

He was gazing towards the house.

'Stephen?'

'Wait a minute.' He held up his hand. 'The telephone, I think.'

I had to concentrate to hear it. At this distance it was more like a pulse in the air than a sound.

'Oh, God. I should have put the answering machine on. I can't face talking to anyone now.'

24

'We'll just leave it. They'll probably have given up by the time we get back to the house.'

It was impossible to talk knowing the phone was ringing on and on. We sat and listened in silence until at last it stopped.

It was almost completely dark now, and the evening was growing chilly.

'Come on,' Stephen said, standing up. 'We're not going to get anywhere tonight. We're just going round in circles. Let's go to bed.'

He pulled me to my feet and we made our way hand in hand up the garden along the creek. It was almost as broad as the house, but it was silted up now and flowed sluggishly.

While Stephen stayed in the kitchen to clear away the dinner things, I went up to bed. The first flight of stairs opens straight on to the big, low-ceilinged room that comprises all of the first floor. I really must get round to putting up some more bookshelves, I thought, just as I did every time I came up those stairs. But that day I seemed to see the room with fresh eyes. There were white painted bookcases under the long, low window seats and in the alcoves on either side of them, but it wasn't enough. There were books everywhere; stacked under my desk, lined up on the window seat, piled all round the edges of the room and up the stairs. Stephen had offered to do some DIY, perhaps I should take him up on it. But this was a familiar thought, too, and I knew I never would. I didn't want to let him that far into my life, not yet anyway.

My cat, Bill Bailey, was asleep on top of some books arranged in two adjacent piles: the complete works of Thackeray. When I clicked my tongue at him, he opened sleepy slits of eyes and got to his feet. He stretched, arching his back and yawning. The tower of books swayed. With an air of unconcern, he turned round, positioned himself in exactly the right place, carefully lowered himself down, and curled up again.

I went on up the steep oak stairs with its rickety handrail to my bedroom on the second floor of the house. The air was heavy with the accumulated heat of the day. I opened a window to let a current of cooler air flow. Resting my arms on the sill, I gazed out across the fens. The window on the other side of the room looked out onto the little city of Ely several miles away, standing proud of the plain and topped by the floodlit towers of the cathedral. But from this window the only signs of human habitation were the tiny scattered lights of a few distant farmhouses. The vast fields and the long straight drainage channels that ran to the horizon were covered now with a darkness as soft as velvet, and above them stretched the huge East Anglian sky, pricked by a few stars. Down in the garden, white roses glowed. The light from the kitchen illuminated a tangle of green water-weed just below the surface of the creek. The kitchen light went off and the creek, too, was absorbed into the night.

Stephen clattered up the stairs. Then his footsteps were muffled by the rug on the bedroom floor. There was a click as he switched on the bedside lamp and a warm yellow light suffused the room. I didn't turn round. I felt his hands on my shoulders. He said nothing, but slowly began to press his thumbs into the sore places of my upper neck. I sighed and pressed my shoulders back against his hands.

He said, 'I'll understand if you'd rather I didn't stay tonight. I know you sleep better when I'm not here.'

'And you've got work tomorrow.'

'Could get up early.'

I hesitated. We didn't usually spend the night together during the week.

'It doesn't have to be ... it could be just for company,' he said.

I twisted round and looked into his face. He slipped his arms around my waist.

'Sure?' I asked.

He nodded. I reached up and stroked the dark hair that was just beginning to show threads of silver. His arms tightened around me. I relaxed into his embrace. His lips touched mine and at that instant, as though the contact had triggered an alarm, the telephone rang.

We stood there, frozen. Then I stepped back.

'Hell and damnation,' Stephen said.

As I moved towards the phone by the bed, he said, 'Wait. I switched the machine on as I came up. Let's see who it is first.'

Abruptly the ringing stopped and was followed a moment later by my own voice, distorted by the tape and muffled by the floorboards. There was a second or two of silence when I thought the caller was going to hang up, then I heard a sharp intake of breath.

'Cassandra, if you're there, would you please pick up the phone? It really is urgent. It's the exam papers. Look, I'll, um, well, I'll ring back in an hour or so if I can't get hold of Lawrence. There's no answer from his phone either.'

In his agitation he was about to hang up without giving his name. I reached the phone in time, but it wouldn't have mattered anyway. There was no mistaking those precise Kelvinside tones. It was Malcolm.

Forty minutes later, Stephen and I were sitting with him at his kitchen table at his house in Cranmer Road.

The missing scripts were spread out on the kitchen table. The cover sheet of one of them had been torn in half and sellotaped together. There was a piece of avocado skin stuck to one of the others, something that I guessed was red wine on another, and a strong smell of rotting vegetables.

'You are sure that they are all there?' I asked anxiously. 'Every single page? Nothing missing?'

'I think so. I did go through them.'

'I just can't believe we've got them back.' I was light-headed with relief.

Malcolm leaned forward and put a finger on the sellotaped cover sheet.

'I had to stick this back together. And the actual script, that was torn too, but it's all here.'

I began to look through the exam papers.

'Are you really going to ask someone to mark these in this state?' Stephen wrinkled his nose in distaste.

I plucked a piece of wilted lettuce leaf off one of the pages. 'No, we'll have them transcribed. That's what we're going to do with the others, the ones that have been ...' I was suddenly aware of the swimming pool lying only yards away from me in the darkness of the garden.

'Anyway,' I went on hurriedly, 'these don't seem too bad considering that they've been in the dustbin.'

'They had some newspaper wrapped round them,' Malcolm said.

'When is the rubbish collected?' Stephen asked.

'Tomorrow morning.'

We contemplated this narrow escape.

I stole a glance at Malcolm. He had changed out of his dark suit into jeans and a crumpled shirt. His hair was tousled and there was a dusting of pale stubble on the lower half of his face. The lines around his mouth and nose were deeper than I remembered, but had I ever really looked at him before? For me he had always worn a label: 'Colleague's husband: kind, reliable, not very interesting and out of bounds anyway'. Was there something I hadn't noticed? Certainly that Scottish accent was very attractive and although I didn't really like fair men myself ... He looked up and his eyes met mine. I looked away in confusion. I thought, It's the day of Margaret's funeral and I'm sitting here at her kitchen table, wondering whether I fancy her husband.

'But where are my manners?' Malcolm said. 'I haven't so much as offered you a cup of tea? Or perhaps a brandy, Cassandra? You look as if you need it.'

'Tea would be great.'

Malcolm got up and put the kettle on.

'Are you going to take the papers home with you, Cassandra?'

'I think, just to be on the safe side, we'd better take them round to the college and get the porter to lock them away.'

Malcolm turned and leaned against the sink with his legs crossed at the ankle as he waited for the kettle to boil. None of us spoke. It wasn't a comfortable silence. I didn't want to catch Malcolm's eye again. I fixed my gaze on the second hand going round on the kitchen clock. It was one of those ultra-modern ones; just a white disc, no numbers, and a stainless steel surround like a porthole. It matched the rest of the expensive, streamlined kitchen. Eleven forty-five. I found myself yawning, but it was as much from nervousness as tiredness. There was something I had to say.

'How do you think—'

'It must have been—'

Malcolm and I had spoken at once.

'Sorry,' I said. 'Go on.'

'I don't know how this could have happened, Cassandra. Margaret was so careful, meticulous even, about anything to do with work. All I can think is that the exam papers got in amongst the newspapers by accident. She put them in the bin without realizing that she'd picked up the scripts along with the newspapers.'

The click of the kettle switching itself off was loud in the silence.

'I suppose that could have happened,' I said doubtfully.

Malcolm busied himself with tea bags and mugs.

Out of the corner of my eye I was aware of Stephen tapping his fingers very gently on the table.

'All the same, there is something a bit odd here, isn't there?' he said. 'How was it, I wonder, that the police didn't find them when they searched the garden?'

His voice was perfectly pleasant and sympathetic, but there was something in it that I hadn't heard before.

Malcolm put down three mugs of tea on the table, and sat opposite me.

'They were down between the black plastic bag and the side of the bin,' he explained. 'It was a fluke that I found them myself. When I pushed the rubbish down to make room for more, I saw the edge of one of the papers sticking up.'

'Also,' I reminded Stephen, 'we all assumed that the papers had blown away. Probably no one thought to look in the dustbin.'

There was a short silence.

Then Stephen said, 'You know, Cass, it's time I took you home to bed.'

I looked at my undrunk mug of tea.

'Don't worry about that,' Malcolm said.

'I am terribly tired,' I admitted.

We all stood up. Malcolm emptied our mugs into the kitchen sink and left them there. He wouldn't have done that in Margaret's day, I thought. Looking around the kitchen I saw other signs of her absence: crumbs on the table, a dirty tea towel crumpled up on one of the work surfaces, an unwashed frying-pan on the hob.

Malcolm packed the papers in a plastic carrier bag and handed the bag to me. He ushered us out of the kitchen and we walked ahead of him down the hall. I glanced back and saw that he was pressing his lips together in an effort to keep control. The skin round his mouth was white and his face was a mask of misery.

I turned and put my hand on his arm. 'Malcolm, are you going to be all right?'

He pulled a handkerchief out of his pocket and blew his nose vigorously. 'I'll be OK. My sister's here with me, actually. She went to bed before you got here.'

'Well, if there's anything I can do ...'

I gave him a hug. I only came up to his chin and the narrow bony back felt strange beneath my hands after Stephen's solid, stocky body. He gave me a quick awkward squeeze.

'I'll give you a ring in a day or two,' I said.

As Stephen started up the engine of the car, I looked back at the house. Malcolm was framed in the light from the doorway. He raised his hand in farewell.

We drove down Cranmer Road in silence. It was as if we didn't want to speak within sight of the house. We turned left into Grange Road. The long, narrow street was dark and almost deserted. There was just one couple, with their arms around each other, loitering outside the rugby ground. The big houses that were set back along the road were muffled by shrubbery and mature trees, and the streetlights were dimmed by the dense canopy of leaves.

Stephen said, 'So what do you make of that?'

'I don't know what to think.'

'Can you imagine Margaret dumping those exam papers in the bin even by accident? Can you imagine her taking so little care of something so important? And why was she putting newspapers in the bin? I noticed a box of them in the corner of the kitchen, obviously waiting to be recycled.'

I looked down at my lap. I had both hands on the bag of exam papers, almost as if I thought they might fly off into the night if I didn't keep tight hold of them.

I shook my head. 'No, I can't. But what else could have happened?'

Stephen shrugged. 'She did it deliberately? A breakdown of some kind?'

'Breakdown? Margaret?'

'Perhaps she'd been drinking. That might explain how she ended up in the pool.'

With the suddenness and vividness of a slide throwing an image onto a screen, I saw the cast-iron table in Margaret's garden, and remembered securing the exam papers down with a wine bottle. I tried to remember what it had felt like in my hand. I didn't think it had been empty, but I wasn't sure. I'd never seen Margaret even a little bit drunk before, but perhaps that would explain the accident ...

Stephen said, 'What that woman said to you outside the church – what if Malcolm had been having an affair and Margaret had found out?'

'But ... Malcolm ... he seems so upset ...'

'You're not thinking, Cass. Of course he's upset. If it's true, he'll be eaten up with guilt. And, besides, even if there was someone else, it wouldn't necessarily mean he didn't love Margaret, would it?'

He slowed down to turn into Madingley Road.

'It's all balls to think that you can't love two people at once,' he added.

He was right, of course. A wave of fatigue swept over me. It was all too much. I wanted to put my head on the dashboard and go to sleep.

'Will the university want to conduct an inquiry into what happened to the papers?' he asked.

'Mmm, probably not, now that they've all been recovered.'

'They might at least want to tighten up their procedures for dealing with the papers in future.'

My eyes were closing, my body beginning to let go ... I woke up as the car bumped over a sleeping policeman in the college drive. I could only have been asleep for a minute or two, but I got the impression that I had missed something important.

' — pretty intensive questioning, I imagine,' Stephen was saying. 'At the very least, they'll be entertaining it as a possibility. I think you should be prepared for that, Cass.'

My stomach flopped over. I sat up as if I'd been prodded. The plastic bag began to slither off my knees. I slapped a hand on it.,

'Prepared for what?'

Stephen pulled up outside the porter's lodge. He turned to look at me, his face pale in the darkness of the car. He put his hand on mine.

'For the possibility that it wasn't an accident, that Margaret might have committed suicide.'

32

Malcolm's fe
staircase ahe
Stephen and I
back to the h
The college p
home – provisi
needed before t
  Malcolm paus   white-painted plank
door.

and laid in orderly rows. The desk held only a
parent case of floppy disks, a black and red
pens and pencils, and a framed photog
The room was full of the light an
afternoon. The distant sounds of
game – sporadic clapping and
ness inside the house.
Malcolm walked o
graph.
'I didn't kno
I followe
Malcol
had

'Actually, this is the first time I've been up here since ... well, it was so much Margaret's domain ...'

'Would you rather I ...?'

'No, no, got to face it sometime.'

He lifted the wooden latch and pushed open the door.

It was a long, low room tucked under the eaves of the house. The rambling red-brick house had probably been built for some turn-of-the-century don. This must have been the servants' quarters. More recently it had been Margaret's study. The window at the front looked out onto Cranmer Road and a side window looked onto the playing fields of Corpus Christi College. The room was sparsely furnished and immaculately tidy. There was a *chaise-longue*, a swivel chair and a desk with a table at right angles to it. On the table were piles of papers, neatly squared off

33

omputer, a trans-
cquer tray containing
ph.

sleepy heat of a summer's
young men playing a boisterous
cat-calls – only accentuated the still-

er to the desk and picked up the photo-

she had this up here,' he said.
him and stood by his elbow. The photograph showed
and Margaret against a backdrop of cliffs and sea. He
his arm around her shoulder. The wind was pulling at their
hair and clothes. They were laughing and squinting into the camera.

'Last year in Cornwall,' he said.

He lowered himself heavily in the chair, his eyes still on the photograph. Then he turned his face away, but not before I had seen that his eyes were full of tears. To give him time to recover, I leaned over the table and began to leaf through the papers.

A few moments later I heard him sigh, and out of the corner of my eye I saw him push his chair back from the table.

He said, 'Cassandra ... about the exam papers ...'

I turned and leaned against the table.

'It's all right,' I said. 'They've been marked now. It's all been a bit of a rush – well, that's an understatement – but we're not much behind. The results will be out by the end of the week.'

He nodded. 'Lawrence told me on the phone. That is just such a relief, but that's not what I meant. I wanted to say: the other night ...'

He hesitated.

Oh, God, I thought, he's going to tell me something I'd rather not know.

'I wasn't myself,' he said finally, 'or I'd never have thought that

34

Margaret could have put those papers in the bin. She'd never, ever have been so careless. I think I know what must have happened. After the accident, when the wind blew everything off the table, some of the exam papers must have got mixed up with the newspapers when they were blown across the garden. They could have ended up against the dustbin. That could have happened, couldn't it?'

I thought about that. Newspapers on table, exam papers on table. I saw them tumbling together across the lawn, becoming entangled. Well, why not?

'That could have happened,' I said slowly. 'But then ...?'

'How did they get inside the bin? I wondered about that for ages. Then I thought, there must have been a lot of people around the place – after you called the police.'

I nodded. The garden and house had been swarming with people.

'Thinking to be helpful, one of them might have dumped the newspapers in the dustbin. Not knowing that the exam papers were inside, obviously.'

I considered this. I wanted to believe it. It was improbable, yes, but was it as improbable as the idea that Margaret had done it? I thought of the woman I had known for the last five years: meticulous, orderly, self-disciplined.

Malcolm's eyes met mine. He had pale blue eyes, the sort that often go with sandy hair. As he looked steadily at me, I felt myself blushing as if he could somehow have overheard the conversation Stephen and I had had in the car.

He looked back at the photograph.

'I've known Margaret since we were both eighteen,' he said. 'I met her on my first day at university. She was my first girlfriend. My only girlfriend. There's never been anyone else.'

There was a pause. He went on gazing at the photograph.

It occurred to me that already I was forgetting exactly what Margaret looked like. In the photograph she had a hand up to her hair. It was very short and bleached. She had worn it like that for years. Sometimes it had given people the wrong idea, made them think she was laid-back and easy-going. They didn't make that mistake for long. It seemed to me that just as my mental image of her was beginning to blur, so I had been losing touch with my sense of her as a person. It seemed so obvious now. The idea that Malcolm could have been unfaithful, that Margaret might have killed herself: this was just a paranoid fantasy of the early hours. I'd been suffering from shock and exhaustion, and as for Stephen: it just showed what a cynical breed lawyers are, and, of course, he didn't know Margaret and Malcolm as I did.

'You're right,' I said. 'That must have been what happened.'

Malcolm nodded, without taking his eyes off the photograph.

After a few moments he squared his shoulders as if bracing himself to move on.

'I'll leave you to it, shall I, Cassandra?' He glanced at his watch. 'I did say I'd drop in at the office sometime this afternoon. Just for half an hour. Would you mind?'

'Of course not. You go ahead.'

'Thanks.'

He touched me briefly on the arm and turned to go. His footsteps were loud on the bare floorboards of the stairs. I heard the distant thud of the door closing and went over to the window to watch him get in his car and drive off.

Now that Malcolm had gone, the room seemed strangely empty. There was an air of expectancy about it as if Margaret had just stepped out and would be back any moment. I realized that I was standing with my head cocked, that I was actually listening for footsteps on the stairs. I shook my head impatiently. But, all the same, I swung the swivel chair round so that my back wasn't to the door.

I looked through the papers, sorting them into college business and Margaret's personal research. It didn't take long. Everything was in apple-pie order. I stowed the relevant papers in my briefcase and stood up. I arched my back, stretched, and gave a yawn that almost dislocated my jaw. I was *so* tired. What to do until Malcolm got back? I thought of going down to the kitchen and making myself a cup of tea, but I didn't like the idea of roaming around the house alone.

The *chaise-longue* against the wall caught my eye. I kicked off my shoes and sat down. I plumped up one of the cushions, laid down and put my head on it. As I shifted about, trying to get comfortable, I felt something sharp dig into the back of my neck. I sat up and felt the cushion. There was something inside, something familiar with a hard narrow ridge. I unzipped the cushion cover, pushed my hand inside and pulled out a handful of computer disks.

I found myself smiling. This was exactly the kind of thing I did myself. I had caches of back-up disks hidden both in my office and at home against the day when some laboured-over text should disappear into computer limbo, or the day when a burglar would take my computer and all my floppy disks. I fanned out the disks as though they were playing-cards. They had labels; Yonge book, Mrs Gaskell article, PhD thesis.

I plunged my hand back in to make sure that I had got everything, and brought out a creased manila envelope, its sides bulging. I took it over to the table and tipped out the contents: twenty or so smaller, white envelopes addressed in a large, spiky hand to Dr Margaret Joplin at her college address. The top left-hand corner of each was marked *Private and Confidential*. I opened one. Inside was a single sheet of A4 paper. It was a letter dated 16 January and headed 'The British Library'.

'*Darling, darling, darling,*' I read.

Instinctively I spread a hand over the letter as though someone might be looking over my shoulder.

There was a tiny sound from somewhere deep down inside the house. I got up and went over to the door. I opened it and looked down the stairs, listening intently. The house was heavy with silence.

I glanced at my watch. Malcolm couldn't possibly be back from his office yet. I walked over to the window that looked onto Cranmer Road. The space where his car had been parked was still empty.

I returned to the desk and skimmed the page:

... supposed to be concentrating on medieval manuscripts ... can't think of anything except you ... memories of that last evening we spent together ... in a glow of happiness ... what it was like to be in bed with you, kissing, touching, stroking ... Nothing has ever been a greater surprise – and nothing has ever been more wonderful ... so much in common ... so right and inevitable ... too soon to see how things will develop ... back next week ... living for the moment when I can take you in my arms again ... marvellous and funny and strange ... ever felt that I was so much myself before ...

Always, always, yours,

Lucy

The name seemed to leap off the page.

I felt as if someone had punched me in the solar plexus. I groped for the edge of the desk and lowered myself into the chair. I put my head in my hands.

There had been infidelity all right – another woman even – I had just been looking in the wrong place.

Lucy was a student, a postgraduate in my own department, and she had died several months ago. When exactly had that been? Mid-April? Yes, it had happened just before the beginning of the Easter term.

I fumbled with the letters, searching for the one with the latest postmark. It was dated 7 April and had been posted in Derbyshire. I took the letter out of its envelope. It was soft and creased from being handled and re-folded. In one or two places the ink had run. I looked closer. Tear-stains, I guessed. The letter began abruptly and the writing rushed headlong across the page.

38

My love, I can't stand this concealment any longer. I know that you have got a lot to lose – so have I, for that matter – and that other people will be hurt by our decision, but it's too painful to go on like this, snatching odd moments, worrying about whether anyone will see us together and guess. I want to sweep all that aside and come out into the open.

There has never been anything like this for me, and I want to seize this happiness with both hands. I can understand that you might not want to stay in Cambridge when it all comes out, but couldn't we start again somewhere? Oh, please, please, please, my darling, be brave and make up your mind.

I hope that while I am up here for a few days you'll have time to think things through, and to realize that what we have is too good to be corroded by secrecy and lies. I love you, and want to be proud of my love, and to stand by your side in the light. One night soon, I want to lie in bed with you, breathing in your warm, sweet scent, knowing that we will still be together in the morning and every morning to come as long as we live.

You'll keep everything I've written safe, won't you? I want you to have everything of mine that I most value: all of my life and all of my love.

Lucy

I got up and walked over to the window. I watched the trees and the sky, the cars parked on the quiet street. I noted with detachment that cumulus clouds were massing in the sky to the north. The good weather that had lasted so long was on the turn.

I felt a surge of anger. A student, Margaret had had an affair with a student! It was so much at odds with my idea of her that it was like a personal betrayal. How could I not have suspected, not have noticed that something was going on? Of course, I hadn't been looking … Now I *did* look; I searched my memory for clues, for hints. There was nothing.

39

It was all too bizarre to be true. I seized on that idea. Perhaps it was all a fantasy, an obsession on Lucy's part. Don't people sometimes become convinced that a person they hardly know is in love with them? It's a recognized illness. But no: the way the letters had been hidden, the creases in them, the tear-stains. It was true all right.

I felt the twinge of an unfamiliar emotion, something that didn't seem appropriate. What was it? To my surprise I realized that it was envy. The way that Lucy had loved Margaret: did anyone feel like that about me? Stephen? I didn't think so. I certainly didn't feel like that about him.

I rested my arms on the windowsill and gazed down into the street. It took me a moment to take in what I was seeing, but when I did, my heart seemed to miss a beat.

Malcolm's car was in the drive.

I turned back into the room. Lucy's love letters were spread out over the table. Even from ten feet away her scrawling signature seemed to stand out from the page with a cabbalistic power. Surely no one could enter the room without their eye being drawn instantly to that single word. It seemed to shriek out the whole story of Margaret and Lucy's love affair.

And the door was still open.

There was a moment of crazy indecision; I didn't know whether to move towards the door or the table. Footsteps coming up the stairs decided me. I headed for the table.

A few seconds later Malcolm appeared in the doorway.

Chapter Four

'My goodness, it's hot in here,' Malcolm said.

I turned from the desk and leaned back on it with my hands spread out behind me. We stood there for a few moments, regarding each other from opposite sides of the room, like figures in a painting by Edward Hopper.

Malcolm walked across to the window, glancing at me as he went.

'You look quite flushed, Cassandra.'

'It *is* hot,' I agreed. I could hardly hear my own voice for the blood pulsing through my head.

As my eyes followed him across the room, I caught a flash of white on the edge of my vision, down where my right hand was resting on the desk. Without taking my eyes off Malcolm I pushed the envelope behind my back.

He opened the catch of the casement window and pushed it open.

'Not that this'll make much difference,' he said. 'It's nearly as humid out as it is in. Wouldn't be surprised if there was thunder on the way. How are you getting on?'

He looked round the room as if seeking signs of progress. His gaze settled on the computer disks that were still lying on the *chaise-longue*.

'Oh, those are just some back-up disks that I came across,' I said hastily.

'Ah.' He nodded.

There was a pause. I groped for something to say, but my mind was a complete blank.

Malcolm said, 'I really came up to see if you wanted a cup of tea.'

'That would be lovely, yes.'

At least that would get him out of the room.

'Shall I bring it up here?' he asked.

'No, no. I've nearly finished. I'll be down in ten minutes or so.'

Still he lingered.

'I'll, mmm ... I'll get on then, shall I?' I said.

'Yes, of course, sorry. It's just that there's something I've been wanting to ask you. Margaret didn't make any formal arrangements about a literary executor. She did make a will, of course, we both did, but neither of us really thought that ... there was no reason to think ... and I don't know exactly what there is in the way of unfinished work.'

For a short while I didn't quite grasp what he was saying, and he must have misunderstood my look of incomprehension. His eyes slid away from mine. He looked embarrassed.

'Perhaps I shouldn't have asked. You're probably too busy. It's just that Margaret thought highly of you ...'

'Sorry, Malcolm, of course: you'd like me to see if she left anything that can be published?'

'Would you mind? I can't tell you how grateful I'd be.'

'Yes, I mean, no, no, of course I wouldn't mind.'

'Well,' he gestured towards the door, 'I'll go and make the tea then.'

He got as far as the threshold. I closed my eyes and let out the breath I had been holding. When I opened my eyes he was still there, standing on the top step with one hand on the door frame.

Go on, go on. I stared hard at his back. Perhaps I could force him out by sheer willpower.

He turned round. Without a word, he strode straight towards me and reached past me to pick something up. He was so close that I could see the weave of his cotton shirt and I caught a whiff of his shampoo. I gulped. He straightened up and stepped back.

He had the framed photograph in his hand.

'Just thought I'd like to have this downstairs. Now I really will leave you in peace.'

He left the room.

I stood there for a bit with one hand flat on my chest, waiting for my breathing to return to normal. When he had had the time to get down to the kitchen, I gathered up the letters and put them into a zipped pocket inside my briefcase. I didn't know what I was going to do with them, I just knew that I wasn't going to leave them here. I picked up the computer disks and the draft of an article that I'd found on the table and put them in my briefcase, too. For some absurd reason this made me feel I was committing less of a felony. After all, if I was Margaret's literary executor, I had a right to take things away, didn't I?

Downstairs in the kitchen, Malcolm was sitting at the table, looking at the photograph propped up against the teapot.

I made a show of looking at my watch.

'Would you mind if I didn't stay for tea after all? If I leave now, I might miss the worst of the rush hour.'

'Of course, if you're sure. Are you all right Cassandra?' he said, looking at me doubtfully.

'Oh, yes, yes, I'm OK, just a bit tired, that's all. Oh, and by the way, Malcolm, I've got some of Margaret's research material. I'll try to have a look at it soon.'

'No hurry,' he said, getting to his feet. 'I'll come out to your car with you. Give me that.'

He stretched out his hand. Before I knew what had happened, he had taken the briefcase. As we walked down the hall, I couldn't have been more conscious of that case if I'd known Malcolm was carrying radioactive uranium. I had to make an effort not to snatch it away from him.

As he opened the front door, Malcolm said, 'You know, Cassandra, I've been a lucky man.'

I didn't know what to say. Fortunately a response didn't seem to be required.

'Yes,' he repeated, standing back to let me out, 'very lucky. Over twenty years of happy marriage. It's a long time. A lot of people never have that, I mustn't ever forget it.'

'She was a remarkable woman,' I said. That certainly was true.

Outside the air seemed denser, as if it were pressing my clothes to my skin. My scalp prickled with the heat. In silence we walked round the sweep of the drive to the car, our feet sinking into the gravel. I unlocked my Renault and Malcolm put the briefcase onto the back seat. I pecked him on the cheek and got into the car. It reeked of hot plastic and the steering wheel was almost too hot to touch.

Glancing at my wing mirror as I drove, I saw Malcolm still standing at the kerb. The next time I looked he had gone. As I waited for a break in the traffic at the junction with Grange Road, I looked again and saw the tiny figure of Jane Pennyfeather emerge from her garden gate and turn into Malcolm's drive.

As I drove north-east on the A14 towards Newmarket, I tried to reconstruct the past in the light of what I had discovered. Had the affair been serious? Yes: with Margaret, it couldn't have been otherwise, and there was the evidence of what Lucy had written, too. I thought back to when Lucy had died. We'd all been upset, of course, but had Margaret seemed more upset than the rest of us? I remembered the energy that she had put into establishing a memorial fund. Perhaps she had managed to channel her grief into that. It was deeply disturbing to think that this emotional drama had been played out under my nose and that I had been totally unaware. Did Malcolm know? All my instincts told me that he didn't.

44

As I swung into the lane that leads to the Old Granary, I realized that I had driven the eight miles from the A14 on autopilot. I couldn't remember any of it. I parked by the gate and got out of the car. The hundred tiny sounds of the countryside – the rustlings, the birdcalls – that I usually hardly noticed were conspicuous by their absence. I looked up at the trees. Not a leaf was moving. A sullen yellow light bathed the garden. The clouds that I had noticed earlier in the day now filled the sky to the north and they had darkened to a dingy gunmetal grey.

Bill Bailey came bounding down the garden path, greeting me with a loud mew. I picked him up. He squirmed out of my arms and ran up the path ahead of me. When I opened the door, he brushed past my legs and sprinted into the kitchen as if he, too, were conscious of the coming storm. I closed the door and leaned against it, savouring the relief of being home.

In the kitchen Bill Bailey was sitting by the fridge, his eyes fixed intently on me. I poured a saucer of milk for him and a large whisky for myself, and went over to the floor-length window. I stood for a while, watching the water flowing lazily out from under the house. That running water had always seemed such a friendly thing; for the first time I wondered if it would be possible to drown in it. It was only a couple of feet deep, but didn't I remember reading somewhere that you could drown in only a few *inches* of water?

I continued to watch from the window, whisky glass in hand, but I wasn't seeing the rippling water any more. I was seeing a winter's day in Sheffield over five years ago, one of those days when snow shuts down the city early. I remembered every detail of that journey home: big, watery flakes of snow melting as soon as they hit the windscreen; Billie Holliday on the cassette player, *'I've got a man, crazy 'bout me'*, she sang with that catch in her voice, *'He's funny that way ...'* The narrow road that led down to our house was steep. I had skidded as I turned into it. The car easily recovered, but the temporary loss of control gave me a jolt.

I crept down the hill in first gear, turned into the driveway and parked. I struggled out of the car with my briefcase. Bill Bailey, little more than a kitten then, was sitting on the doorstep, mewing piteously, his long hair plastered to his body. I scooped him up with one arm and felt him shivering. I fumbled with my key in the lock, my fingers already feeling numb. The lock clicked and I began to push the door open. It met resistance and I was puzzled for a moment until I realized that the chain was on. Then I was puzzled again. It was usually only put on at night, it was part of Simon's locking-up routine. I put my finger on the doorbell and kept it there. When there was no answer to the second ring, I trudged round to the back door and let myself in. I dumped my briefcase on the kitchen floor and went into the hall. I heard movement upstairs and looked up to see Simon at our bedroom door, wearing a towel, as though he'd just got out of the shower. So that was why he hadn't answered the door. My face broke into a smile that froze when it met the lack of response on his. It was as though I had caught a stranger's eye in the street. Then he took charge of himself and made an effort to override the shock of seeing me, but it was too late. At the very moment that he reached behind him to close the bedroom door, Samantha appeared at his shoulder. She was wearing my dressing-gown.

The marriage had limped on a little longer, but really it had ended at that moment when I stood looking up the stairs. Something had been lost that could never be recovered. A few months later, I had been offered the job in Cambridge and I had accepted.

A roll of distant thunder brought me back to the present. I thought of handing Lucy's letters over to Malcolm, of his face, at first uncomprehending, then pale and stricken. 'I've been a lucky man, I mustn't ever forget that,' I heard him say. I thought of the letters being produced at the inquest.

I took a box of matches from the shelf by the hob and went upstairs to the big study and sitting-room that takes up the first floor.

I went over to the hearth and opened the heavy iron door of the wood-burning stove. I put the letters in a rough heap inside and set a match to them. I sat down on the tiled hearth and watched the tiny flames eat round the end of an envelope. Where they touched the paper, the edges of the flames were a clear azure blue. Then with a rush, long yellow and orange tongues of fire engulfed the pyramid of letters. Soon all that was left of the love between Margaret and Lucy was a handful of grey flakes. 'And into ashes all my lust,' I thought. I'd loved that poem by Andrew Marvell when I was an undergraduate. How did it go on? Yes, that was it: 'The grave's a fine and private place, But none I think do there embrace.'

I went over to the telephone.

It took a long time for Stephen to answer. 'I've only been home about ten minutes. You got me out of the shower.'

'Can you come over right away?'

'Are you all right?'

'Yes. Can you come?'

'Forty minutes?'

'Fine.'

It was only six o'clock, but a murky twilight was descending and it was growing dark inside the house. I took a bottle of Chablis from the fridge. In the bedroom I cleared a stack of books off the bedside table to make room for the wine and glasses. The heat at the top of the house was stifling, the air heavy and stale. I pulled the pins out of my bun and shook my hair free, running my hands through it close to my scalp. I opened the window: a blast of cold air came in. After a few seconds I closed it and stood gazing out towards Ely. Thick curtains of rain were sweeping across the plain. The outline of the cathedral became blurred and then disappeared. There was a flash of lightning overhead, rapidly followed by a roll of thunder that cracked like a whip. Huge drops of rain began to fall, at first slowly, then more urgently, thrashing the leaves on the trees and pock-marking the surface of the stream.

Stephen's car turned into the drive. I raced down the stairs to let him in. As he ran down the path, the skies opened. It was if someone was emptying buckets of water over him. He plunged through the door, gasping and pushing his hair back. I slammed the door behind him as if the storm might follow him into the house. Water was streaming off him. He kicked off his shoes, peeled off his sodden jacket and dropped it on the floor. We stepped into each other's arms. Leaning against him, eyes closed and my face pressed against his shoulder, I breathed in the familiar citrus scent of his cologne mingled with wet, freshly laundered shirt. The dampness soaked into my shirt and made me shiver. I pulled away and got a towel from the kitchen.

We climbed the first flight of stairs with our arms wrapped around each other's waists. The second flight was narrowed by the books I'd piled on either side of each tread. We went up single file, Stephen towelling his hair as he followed me.

Sheets of rain were sliding down the bedroom windows. The view out across the fens wavered, dissolved, reformed.

I left my clothes where they fell and got into bed. Stephen did the same. I poured the wine and handed it to him.

'I thought you were saving this for a special occasion..'

'Isn't every day a special occasion?' I raised my glass. 'To "days of wine and roses".'

Stephen touched his glass to mine.

' "They are not long ...",' he said, 'Isn't that how it goes? Tennyson?'

'Ernest Dowson. One of the poets of the decadence.'

Stephen picked up a handful of my hair and held it up to the light. Red and gold strands glistened among the brown.

'There's something decadent about making love to a woman with hair down to her waist. Have you ever thought of cutting it?'

I looked into the familiar face: the hazel eyes with their heavy lids, the slightly aquiline nose.

'Never,' I said. I leaned across and pressed my lips to his. His arms tightened around me.

48

A little later, a wine glass rolled off the bed. I heard it crack as it hit the wooden floor, but it was too late.

I awoke with a jolt. For a few moments I couldn't think where I was or what time of day it was. The bedside light was on. Beyond its circle of light the room was dim. The clock on the bedside table said five to ten. Next to it was a half-full bottle of wine and one empty wine glass. My mouth was dry and I was heavy with sleep. I pulled myself up against the pillows. My hair was everywhere, stuck to my back, netted over my breasts. I gathered it up in both hands and pushed it back over my shoulders. Clothes were strewn around the bed, some of them Stephen's. The day came back in a rush: Margaret's study, the letters, the storm, the urgent love-making, and afterwards our bodies stuck together with sweat.

A distant clatter of pans and a droning noise, which I recognized as Stephen singing, told me that he had gone down to the kitchen to start cooking.

I got out of bed and opened the window. The wet garden glinted in the light from the house. The rain had sharpened the scent of the flowers and there was a delicious freshness in the air. In the deepening twilight only Bill Bailey's white paws, chest and muzzle were visible as he strolled down the garden path.

I poured myself a glass of wine, got back into bed and pulled the sheet up over my breasts. Presently, I heard Stephen coming up the stairs. He appeared in the doorway with a tray. He was wearing only a tea towel knotted round his waist.

'You know, you're in pretty good shape for a man of your age,' I said.

'Why, thank you. I can cook, too. Here we have penne with anchovies, olives and capers.'

He put the tray in the middle of the bed and clambered in next to me. We ate in ravenous and appreciative silence. When we had finished, Stephen moved the tray and pulled me towards him. I put my head on his shoulder. He shifted round to kiss me, but I put a

49

hand on his shoulder to hold him off.

'I want to ask you something. How easy do you think it would be to drown yourself in a swimming pool? On purpose, I mean.'

'Ah. So that's the lie of the land? I thought there was something up. Well ...'

He lay back, looking at the ceiling as he thought this over.

At last he said, 'I think it would be difficult, that's assuming you could swim. And Margaret could, I assume?'

'She was a good swimmer.'

'Well, you'd have to overcome a powerful physical instinct for survival. Drink or drugs could do it. Of course the pathologist will have checked for those in Margaret's blood.'

'That'll come out at the inquest, won't it?'

'Yes, but it still wouldn't prove that she'd killed herself. It might just be that she fell in accidentally and was too drunk to get out again.'

Stephen shifted round so that he could look into my face. 'But why are you asking? There's something you haven't told me, isn't there? Have you found out that Malcolm *was* having an affair?'

I turned my face away.

'There is something, though, isn't there?' he persisted.

'You won't tell anyone?'

'Cass! I wouldn't have lasted long as a lawyer if I didn't know how to be discreet.'

'I know. OK.'

I told him about the letters.

He let out his breath in a long sigh.

'Oh dear, oh dear, oh dear.'

'You don't sound very surprised.'

'I thought there was more to this than met the eye. I just didn't know what. Do you think Malcolm had any idea?'

'I'm sure he didn't.'

'You know, it's amazing what people can keep secret. One of my first jobs when I qualified was acting for a woman who had just discovered that her late husband had another wife – and child – tucked away for the last ten years of their marriage. Neither of them knew a thing about the other.'

I was longing for a cigarette. Lying in bed talking: this was one of the times when I missed smoking most. I realized that I had made a mistake having that cigarette on the day of Margaret's funeral. I rolled over, took a packet of extra strong mints out of the drawer of the bedside table and offered one to Stephen.

As he took it, he said, 'What folly though, keeping those letters. It's amazing the way that people will hang on to incriminating evidence.'

'They were all she had left of Lucy.'

'You said she was dead. What happened exactly?'

'Climbing accident, in the Peak District.'

'Do you think there was any chance of her leaving Malcolm?'

I sat up and rested my arms on my raised knees while I thought about this.

'Doubt it, really. She was so down on that sort of thing – people breaking up their marriages. And the scandal: her successful career here, the kudos of it, it all meant such a lot to her.'

'Would it have been such a scandal? People are more enlightened than that, aren't they – especially here?'

I considered this. 'Well, in a way they are, of course. Academically there is a lot of focus on homosexuality, and it's sometimes quite confrontational: Queer Theory is the latest thing – yes, it is really called that! And there are plenty of gay dons, there always have been, but it's very much a male thing and there's still quite a lot of misogyny around. Running off with a woman, and a student, at that ...'

'So she was on course to destroy both her private and her professional life.' He pursed his lips and shook his head. 'When sensible people make a mistake, they often do it big-time. Pity she didn't destroy those letters.'

'But lucky I found them and did it for her.'

In the silence that ensued there was a thin, high wail like the cry of a baby. I got up and opened the bedroom door. Bill Bailey stalked in. When I turned to get back into bed, I saw that Stephen had propped himself on his elbow. He was staring at me as though I'd just lobbed a hand grenade into the bed.

'What?' I said.

He went on looking at me with an expression of exaggerated incredulity.

'WHAT?'

He flung himself back onto the pillows. 'How could you do that, Cassandra?'

'You've just said yourself she should have destroyed them.'

'But she didn't,' he said, emphasizing every word. 'She did not destroy them. And it wasn't your place to do it for her. What did you do, burn them?'

I nodded. 'Stephen, I couldn't let Malcolm see those letters. It would tear him apart.'

'It wasn't up to you to decide that, Cassandra. They were evidence that should have been put before the coroner.'

'Evidence of what? You said yourself that it'll be difficult to tell if Margaret committed suicide. Why should Malcolm suffer more than he already is? He's the innocent party in all this.'

'As far as you know,' Stephen said grimly. 'Suppose he got wind of the affair and gave Margaret a helping hand into the pool?'

I stared at him. 'You don't really think that.'

'How the hell do I know?'

'But … no, he wouldn't …'

At the sight of my stricken face he relented.

'Oh, well, probably not. You said he was away on business, didn't you? The police will have checked that out. But even so … And another thing, how can you be sure that you're the only one who knows about this?'

This stopped me in my tracks. 'It was a secret. Lucy said so in her last letter.'

'Really, Cassandra, for an intelligent woman, you are remarkably stupid sometimes. For all you know Lucy could have had a string of jealous lovers. She might have married, too, like Margaret!'

Chapter Five

From a bench outside the French windows of the Senior Common Room, I could hear a murmur of conversation from within. The end of term lunch of salmon and mayonnaise, strawberries and cream was over and I had slipped out with my cup of coffee. The storm of the previous night had cleared the air and the fine weather had returned. The carefully tended garden with the trees, its shaved lawns and its flower-beds spread out before me in the sunshine. When I came for my interview at St Etheldreda's, I had been charmed by the domestic scale of its neo-Georgian revival architecture, and red brick and white paint, like an immense doll's house. It was comforting to think that so many students and teachers had wandered in this garden for so long. The size of the copper beech testified to that. Probably it had been here before the college.

I leaned back, closed my eyes and let the sun soak into me.

First thing that morning I had gone into the college registry and got out Lucy Hambleton's file. I looked at the next of kin box: Angela Hambleton. It was scrawled in a casual hand, one that was familiar to me from the letters. I felt a pang at the sight of that routine entry, which she little suspected would one day be needed. I skimmed the rest of the form. There was nothing to suggest she had ever been married. I noted that she was twenty-eight, a mature student in fact. I remembered now that she had been a bit older than the normal postgraduate. That made me feel a bit better about her relationship with Margaret. I saw she had been working as a qualified librarian at Durham University before being accepted to do a PhD at St Etheldreda's, working under Alison Stirling, our specialist in sixteenth and seventeenth century literature. Because Lucy wasn't working on the nineteenth century, I hadn't had much to do with her. I looked at the photograph attached to the form: a narrow, bony face with a nose that was very slightly crooked, shoulder-length dark hair swept back from her face. Her chin was tilted up a little: there was something confident, even challenging, in her expression. The knowledge that she had less than a year to live added a poignancy, a kind of innocence to the photograph.

A shadow fell on my face. I opened my eyes.

'You look as if you need a drink.'

Alison was standing next to me, holding two glasses of wine. I squinted up at her. She was one of those big women who suit being a little overweight.

'Are you OK?' she said.

'Mmm, just came out to be on my own for a few minutes. The social effort was just too much.'

'Know what you mean.' She made a face. 'Still, I suppose it wouldn't have done to cancel the end of term party. Want me to leave you alone?'

'No, no,' I patted the bench next to me.

She handed me a glass and sat down.

'At least it means the year's over, and what a hell of a year it's been,' Alison said. 'First, Lucy – one of the most promising post-grads I've ever supervised by the way, tragic waste – and now Margaret. Makes you think, doesn't it?'

I shot a sideways glance at her. She had lifted her face up to receive the sun. Her hair fell back from her forehead. She was nearly fifty, but her hair was still so dark, nearly black. There was just one white streak, so striking that you might have thought she'd dyed it.

55

'*What* does it make you think?' I asked.

'Well, you know, *carpe diem* and all that, gather ye rosebuds while ye may. We none of us know how long we've got.'

I relaxed. It wasn't likely that she knew about Lucy and Margaret, but just for a moment I had wondered ...

'Too true,' I said.

Alison looked at me with an expression so consciously sly that it was comical.

'So, how about you and that boyfriend of yours, Cass?' she said. 'You've been hanging about long enough. Why don't you get married? How old is he, forty? Just right for you. No point in hanging about, especially if you want to have children.'

She was a little drunk, I realized. I was feeling light-headed, too, less from alcohol than from tiredness.

'There's just the small point that he hasn't actually asked me. A technicality, I know ...'

'Oh, come on. If you gave him the *slightest* encouragement ... I've seen the way he looks at you when he thinks no one's looking. Don't look at me like that, you know I'm right.'

I had a mental image of Stephen sitting up in bed with an outraged expression in his face. We had made things up, but our goodnights had still been cool. I had decided I wouldn't ring him for a few days.

'I don't think we're all that well suited, to tell you the truth. Anyway, I've got no intention of getting married again. Twice is enough, too much even.'

'Twice? Oh, yes, I'd forgotten. But the first time: that was when you were a student, wasn't it? Just boy-and-girl stuff. A false start.'

'To lose one husband may be regarded as a misfortune; to lose two looks like carelessness.'

Aiden emerged from the other French windows further down the façade. With an air of manifest relief he took a packet of cigarettes out of his jacket pocket and lit up. I found myself wishing that some of the smoke would drift my way.

I was about to beckon him over to bum a fag off him, when Alison shook her head and frowned at me.

I was amused. 'You really don't like him, do you?'

'I know we needed new blood in the department, but why did Margaret and Lawrence have to choose Aiden?' she grumbled.

'That book on Coleridge – very impressive. And he's popular with students.'

'Too popular. Thinks he's a cross between Lord Byron and Jack Nicholson.'

I smiled. He did look a bit like a young Jack Nicholson.

'He does have a certain louche charm.'

His hand went to his hair in an automatic smoothing gesture. He did this so often that it seemed as though it might account for his receding hairline.

'I asked him why he always wears black – such an affectation,' Alison said.

'A lot of young people do that.'

'He's not that young – must be at least thirty. Anyway, he said, "I'm not in mourning for my life, if that's what you're thinking", and he positively leered at me.'

'Leered? How very Edwardian! Pity he hasn't got a moustache to twirl!'

Alison laughed. 'Oh, I know I'm an intolerant old bat, but I do like the students to be students and the members of staff to be members of staff. I've seen him in the bar, surrounded by giggling girls. I only hope he's not sleeping with any of them – or all of them.'

Lawrence appeared at the French windows a few feet away.

How much had he heard, I wondered.

'Ah, Cassandra, there you are,' he said, his tone carrying the implication that it was quite unreasonable of me to be sitting here in the sun when he had been searching for me inside. 'I wonder, could you spare me a few minutes? In my office?'

*

57

'I want to offer you the position of Acting Head of Department.'

Strangely enough, this possibility hadn't occurred to me before. I'd never thought of myself as an administrator, and if I'd thought at all about who would replace Margaret – and my feet had hardly touched the ground since she died – I'd just assumed that after a decent interval her job would be advertised. Of course, it could take months to get the right person, so it made sense that someone would be in charge in the meantime, and why shouldn't that someone be me? I had a much stronger publication record than either Merfyn or Alison, and I was senior to Aiden, who'd only been with us a year. But still, there was something I didn't understand here. It was more to do with Lawrence's manner than his actual words.

'So ... just for a few months, until we find a replacement?'

Lawrence was sitting in a high leather chair behind a huge mahogany desk, and I was sitting in an armchair on the other side. The arrangement, intended to disguise the fact that he was several inches shorter than me, actually made me more aware of it. It was warm in his office, but he hadn't unbuttoned the jacket of the pinstriped suit he always wore.

'A little longer, say a year? There'll be a few hundred a year on your salary, of course.'

I didn't say anything.

'And perhaps a grade up the scale. I can't really offer you more than that,' he said, misinterpreting the puzzled expression on my face.

The gleaming surface of his desk was bare except for a pad of paper and a silver propelling pencil. He picked it up and began to slide it up and down between his fingers.

'But – a year? I don't understand. We'll have someone in place before then, won't we?'

What he said next was even more unexpected.

'As the only department that doesn't teach a language, the English Literature Department has always been something of an anomaly. And a relatively recent one at that.'

58

It was true that the college had always specialized in languages. The English department dated only from the 1950s when the place had been run by a power-mad literary critic intent on founding an empire. St Etheldreda's had been founded in 1920 by a manufacturer of patent foods and pills as a memorial to his only son, killed in the First World War. He had intended to promote internationalism by educating the future wives and mothers of the nation in the language and cultures of other countries.

Lawrence leant forward, hands clasped in front of him on the desk. The pale blue eyes looked into mine. He was waiting for a response.

'You surely haven't called me to discuss the history of the college?' I said.

'Quite right. It's the future of the college that I have to consider, rather than its past, Cassandra. As you know, the next Research Assessment Exercise takes place in approximately eighteen months' time. Our future funding is absolutely dependent on our performance. By this time next year, I want absolutely every single academic in this college to be able to contribute publications of some significance for our submission to the RAE.'

'Ah.' The penny had dropped.

'I see we understand each other.'

Lawrence opened a drawer in his desk and took out a folder. 'A few months ago I requested members of staff to submit details of their publications to me as a dummy run. You will remember doing that yourself, Cassandra.'

He pulled out a single sheet of paper and held it out to me.

'This is Alison Stirling's submission.'

There were a couple of book reviews and an article for a middlebrow journal, *Writers and their Times*.

'Woefully inadequate, you'll have to agree. And as for Merfyn ...' He spread his hands in a gesture of dismissal. 'Worse than inadequate: embarrassing. It used to be possible to build a whole career on a book that hadn't been written. No longer.'

'This really isn't fair,' I protested. 'They're both excellent teachers, first-rate in Alison's case.'

'That doesn't cut any ice with our lords and masters these days, unless it's backed up by publications. I can't give you more than a year to turn things round.'

'And then what?'

Lawrence shrugged.

I gaped at him. 'You can't do that!'

'I think you'll find that the board of trustees will back me up. Of course, we'd be sorry to lose you and Aiden Frazer, fine academics both of you, but—' He shook his head. 'Two out of four, it just isn't enough.'

I was having difficulty taking this in.

Lawrence said, 'Do you accept my offer, Cassandra?'

He leant forward, hands clasped, and looked into my eyes. I needed time to think. I shifted my gaze. My attention was caught momentarily by a flicker of light at the edge of my vision: the Virginia creeper around the casement window sifted the sunlight into dappled patterns on the carpet. A perplexed bluebottle was throwing itself against the window and buzzing fiercely. Lawrence cleared his throat. My moment of indecision had gone on too long. I thought of Merfyn and Alison, who had a sick husband dependent on her. They were both pushing fifty and neither of them would ever get another job. Even for me it would be touch and go. I thought of my bank balance, my mortgage and my book-laden house out in the fens. Academic life is like a game of musical chairs these days; every now and then someone takes a chair away. I couldn't risk being the one left standing when the music stopped.

'I'll do it.'

'You'd better move into Margaret's office so that you'll have Cathy at hand.'

Cathy! Why hadn't I thought of her? She was struggling alone to raise a teenage daughter and was as vulnerable as any of us.

'What about Cathy? Would she also have to go, along with the rest of us?'

Lawrence shook his head. 'Secretarial skill is transferable. She could be deployed elsewhere in the college.'

As I was getting up to go, another thought struck me.

'Did you tell Margaret that you were thinking of closing the department?' I asked Lawrence.

There was a pause. He pushed his chair back into a patch of sunshine. The strong light behind him blurred his features so that I couldn't read his expression.

At last he said, 'Not in so many words. But she would have been a fool if she hadn't realized that the writing was on the wall. And, whatever else she might have been, Margaret was no fool.'

'Why didn't Margaret tell me what was going on?' I asked Cathy.

It was the following day and we were sitting over a cup of coffee in Margaret's office. The night before, I'd slept twelve hours and woken up feeling as if I'd been under an anaesthetic. I still felt groggy. Cathy didn't look too good either. She was pale and her eyes were bloodshot. I'd never seen her so subdued. Even her dark, springy hair seemed flatter than usual.

'I think she was trying to get Alison and Merfyn up to speed first,' Cathy said. 'And that was starting to happen. At least, I know that a couple of weeks ago Alison gave Margaret an outline for an article that she thought she might write.'

'Every little helps.'

The cornerstones of our RAE submission would have to be Margaret's biography of Charlotte Yonge, I thought, and my own book on Victorian poetry that was nearly finished.

'And then there's Aiden,' I said, thinking aloud. 'No problems there.'

Cathy seemed about to say something, then she shook her head.

'What's up?' I asked.

61

She shook her head. 'Margaret did say something about Aiden. I can't quite remember what, but I know she thought there was a problem.'

I'd have to look into that.

'But Alison and Merfyn know what the situation is?'

Cathy nodded. 'She put a rocket under them. I don't know exactly what she said, of course, but I saw Merfyn when he came out: he looked a bit shaken up. He was supposed to come and see her again before the end of term.'

'When exactly?'

Margaret's office diary was lying on the desk beside us. Cathy reached for it and flicked it open. She ran her finger down the pages for the previous week.

'Oh,' she said.

I gave her a look of enquiry. She turned the diary towards me and pointed to the entry.

3.30 p.m. on the previous Friday.

The day of the funeral.

The entry had been made in Margaret's own neat hand. After it, in brackets, she'd written *with first chapter of book.*

I sighed. 'I'd better find out what's going on.'

'I'll ring him and ask him to come and see you, shall I?'

'No, no, I'll do it. I don't want him to feel that I'm ... well, that I'm ...'

'Pulling rank?' She looked at me quizzically.

'I want to tread carefully.'

Cathy pushed her glasses up onto her hair, got to her feet, and collected the coffee mugs. She stood there hesitating and frowning. I wondered what she wanted to say. She'd worked closely with Margaret, and had probably known her better than anyone else in the department. If anyone had known what was going on between Margaret and Lucy, it would have been Cathy.

She put the mugs back on the table, but still didn't speak.

'What is it, Cathy?'

62

'Would I still be kept on if, you know, if things came to the worst? Margaret told me that I'd be OK. She knew I was worried about Hannah – with her still being at school – and I don't get much from her dad in the way of maintenance.'

'Sorry, of course, I should have mentioned that earlier. The college would keep you on. Lawrence said so. You'll be all right, I promise.'

When she had gone, I let myself have a few minutes to gather my thoughts. Margaret's office was a spacious room on the first floor of the college. The sun was striking through the Venetian blinds onto a deep red Persian rug. That wasn't college issue, nor was the single painting on the wall, an abstract of red, black and white squares. I'd have to take them round to Malcolm, along with her other personal possessions. There wouldn't be much. Unlike most academics – my office was a chaos of books and paper – Margaret was a minimalist. I opened the desk drawer. There was a box of Tampax, a toothbrush in a case, a small tube of toothpaste, a packet of Fisherman's Friend, and nothing else. The desk was almost bare, too. The only decorative object was a small round black lacquer box containing paperclips. I looked at it more closely. On the lid was a painting of a woman swathed in white furs standing in a sleigh pulled by a dappled horse. The strong, clear colours – red, yellow, orange – stood out sharply against the black background. It looked like an illustration to a fairy tale, but I couldn't quite think what.

With an effort I turned my attention back to the matter in hand. What was I going to say to Merfyn?

When I'd first met him about fifteen years ago, he was a dashing young lecturer with a penchant for wearing cloaks and fedoras, and I was a humble research student. I was in awe of him. He'd recently published some groundbreaking articles on the supernatural in Victorian fiction and was known to be working on an important book on the subject. He seemed light-years ahead of me, in a different league altogether. He'd been something of a mentor. But over the years there'd been a gradual shift in our positions. Merfyn's book didn't appear – and people stopped expecting it to. When my own book on Victorian women poets was published, I suddenly realized that I hadn't just drawn level with Merfyn, I had overtaken him. Merfyn still talked as though the book would be finished one day, but I didn't really believe it any more and I wondered if he did.

Putting this discussion off wasn't helping. I punched in the number of Merfyn's extension, cravenly hoping that he wouldn't answer or that, if he did, he wouldn't be free. But he did, and he was; he would come straight round to my office.

When he arrived, he was wearing the same linen suit, even more crumpled, that he had worn on the day of the funeral. I gestured towards two armchairs on either side of a coffee table. He sank into one and placed a decrepit briefcase at his feet. I took the chair opposite.

There was a moment when neither of us seemed to know what to say.

'How's Celia?' I asked. Merfyn's wife was a high-flying civil servant in the Home Office.

'Oh, fine. She's always complaining about her minister, but she loves it all really.'

'And the girls?'

'Oh, fine, fine.'

There was a short silence.

I took a deep breath, but before I could plunge in, Merfyn said, 'I don't suppose you'll feel that congratulations are in order, Cass, under the circumstances, but for what it's worth, I'm sure you're the right person to take over from Margaret.'

'Thanks, Merfyn. Yes, it's something of a poisoned chalice. You know, we really have got our backs to the wall.'

He nodded. 'The RAE, yes, I know.'

He delved into his case and pulled out a bulging blue cardboard folder. He presented it to me with a flourish.

64

'I think this will relieve your mind to a certain extent.'

Pulling out the top page, I saw it was headed 'Chapter One'.

'What's this? It's not ...?'

Merfyn was beaming all over his face.

'It is? It's your book? But that's ...'

For a few moments, words failed me.

'It's, well, what can I say? It's just great!'

'No need to hide your amazement,' Merfyn said. 'I'm pretty surprised myself. And my publishers must have despaired of it years ago. I'll have to break it to them gently, they might have a collective heart attack!'

I read out loud the title of the first chapter. ' "*Is there anyone there?*" *Spiritualism in the mid-nineteenth century.* Wow! How much is there here?'

'First four chapters. I'll push on with it over the summer. And I've got a few weeks' study leave in the Lent term next year. I've got masses of material, some of it partly written up. I've never quite been able to work out how to put it all together until now. It could be finished in the spring if I really go at it.'

I flipped over the pages of Merfyn's typescript, reading a sentence here and there.

'This looks absolutely fascinating. Didn't people like Ruskin and Tennyson and Browning attend séances in the 1860s?'

'Absolutely right. They really took it seriously. Of course mediums were often exposed as charlatans, but not always by any means. Have you heard of the American medium, John Dunglas Home?'

I shook my head.

Merfyn leaned forward, clasped his hands between his knees and prepared to give me a little lecture. 'He took London society by storm in the 1860s. The most extraordinary things happened at his séances; the room vibrated, objects flew about, people were chilled by cool breezes, music was produced by invisible instruments. On one occasion, reputable witnesses claimed to have seen him float in through a first-floor window.'

'Some sort of hypnosis?' I hazarded.

'Perhaps. Or maybe some sort of superior conjuring trick.'

Absently, I went on turning the pages. Hadn't I heard him say something like this before? Something about a conjuring trick? When had that been?

'Actually,' he was continuing, 'in Home's case, no one managed to prove that he was a fraud.'

A picture was forming in my mind: Merfyn and I pausing on a threshold, about to move from the brightness of a sunny day into a dim interior.

'One has to approach all this with an open mind. Just occasionally, the evidence is extraordinarily compelling. In fact ...' His voice trailed away.

When had that been? And what exactly had he said to me?

Merfyn was asking me a question.

'What was that?' I asked.

'I said, have you ever been to a séance, Cassandra?'

I shook my head.

'You don't believe that ... well, that something of us could survive after death?' he asked.

'I don't say that exactly. But surely the whole spiritualism thing – mediums and séances – that's all phoney isn't it?'

With an air of decision Merfyn sat up straight and said, 'Can I confide in you, Cassandra?'

Oh dear, I thought. When someone asks you that, it's never really a question, is it? He scarcely paused for breath, before plunging on.

'That's how my writer's block was cured, Cassandra. At a séance.'

'At a séance?'

My voice carried more disbelief than I had intended. Merfyn flushed.

'I might have known you'd react like this. Conventional academic thinking is so blinkered. Are you going to let me explain, or are you just going to shoot me down in flames?'

'OK, OK. All right, go on.'

'Look, I was desperate. I'd had so many false starts with the book, given up so many times, and then Margaret told me that I was jeopardizing the future of the department, so I *had* to produce something.'

'But why did you think going to a séance would help?'

'I thought I might begin the book with a description of a séance. I was as sceptical as you are. I thought it might be a way in, that's all. To begin with, nothing happened. There were one or two messages for other people – breathtaking in their banality, to be perfectly honest. And then something quite different happened.'

Merfyn narrowed his eyes in concentration, as if he was visualizing the scene.

'What?' I said. 'What happened??'

'The medium started groping around the table. One of the others seemed to know what she wanted. There was a pen and some paper in the middle of the table. He pushed it towards her and then, well, something extraordinary happened.'

Despite my scepticism, I was sitting on the edge of my seat.

'She pushed it towards me,' Merfyn said, 'and the man sitting next to me nudged me to let me know that I was meant to pick it up. Then, well, it's difficult to describe, but I seemed to slip into a kind of trance, my hand started moving of its own accord, and I just found myself writing, on and on. And when I'd finished there were several pages. What I'd got was the beginning of my book, more or less as it is there.'

He gestured towards the folder that I was still holding on my knee.

I stared at him, speechless.

And it was at that precise moment that there was a knocking sound, scarcely audible. A gentle rat-tat-tat. Merfyn's eyes widened. My mouth went dry. Neither of us spoke and then it came again, a little louder. Our heads swivelled towards the door.

The handle turned, it slid open, Cathy's dark curly hair and then her face appeared round the edge of the door.

'I'm frightfully sorry, I wouldn't have interrupted you, but I've got Lawrence on the line. He needs to know immediately if you can attend a meeting for departmental heads at ten o'clock on Monday morning.'

'OK, don't worry, tell him that's fine.'

She closed the door.

Merfyn caught my eye and grinned. I couldn't help grinning back.

'I don't know what the hell I thought that was,' I said. 'But, look, Merfyn, this isn't a laughing matter, is it? What exactly are you trying to tell me? Where does the medium come into it?'

'Oh, she's just the channel,' he said. 'You must have heard of automatic writing.'

'So you think someone else, someone who's dead ...?'

He nodded. 'And from various hints that he's dropped, it's pretty clear who it is.'

'So ...?'

'I think it's Sir Arthur Conan Doyle.'

Was he pulling my leg? One glance at Merfyn told me that he was entirely serious.

'You really mean to tell me that you think Sir Arthur Conan Doyle is dictating your book to you?'

Merfyn looked uncomfortable. 'Not exactly that, that would be cheating really, wouldn't it? It's more like a collaboration. I've done all the research, he helps me to put it all together, get it down on paper. It's not really so surprising, Conan Doyle was a fervent believer in spiritualism, you know. He wants to make sure I get things right.'

We sat in silence as I tried to work out the implications of this. There had been a pair of women writers at the end of the nine-teenth century – Somerville and Ross, was it? – didn't one of them claim that they had gone on writing together after the death of the other? I felt a powerful resistance to the idea and the more I

68

thought about it, the more problems I could see. There was the question of academic detachment, for one thing. If the book turned into a polemic in support of spiritualism, no reputable academic publisher would touch it with a bargepole. I fingered the blue cardboard folder, which was still on my lap.

'Perhaps we could meet again when I've had a chance to read this?' I said.

'Of course, of course.'

I tried to imagine explaining to Lawrence how Merfyn had at last come to write his book. And what if it became more widely known? I could already see the tabloid headlines: 'Elementary, my dear Watson!' Oh, God, what would that do for the future of the department?

'Does anyone else know about this?' I asked.

'Only Celia.'

'Let's keep it that way, shall we?' I said.

He was halfway to the door when I remembered the occasion that Merfyn had spoken to me about a conjuring trick. It had been outside the church on the day of Margaret's funeral, and he had been referring to my discovery of Margaret's body. Now you see her, now you don't. It was as if a cool hand had brushed the back of my neck. In spite of the warmth of the room I found myself shivering.

'Merfyn,' I said.

He stopped and looked round.

'Merfyn, you're not still doing this, are you? Going to séances, I mean? It was just a one-off, wasn't it?'

'Well, actually, I did go again. Just once or twice. What's the matter? Why are you looking at me like that?'

'You wouldn't ... Margaret ... you haven't ... You wouldn't try to ...?'

'Margaret? No, I haven't. I wouldn't – and anyway, I haven't been to a séance since she ... well, since she died.'

Then something seemed to occur to him. He stood thinking for a moment or two.

'You know, they say that people who've died a sudden or violent death, those are just the sort of spirits who tend to remain earthbound.'

I stared at him. 'Merfyn, please tell me you won't try to contact Margaret. I don't believe for a moment that you could, but please don't even try. Promise me.'

The very thought was repugnant.

He hesitated.

'Promise me,' I insisted.

'All right. But you know, Cassandra—'

'What?'

'I'm not promising that I won't ever go to a séance again. And if I do, what's to stop *her* from trying to make contact?'

Chapter Six

'Checkmate.'

'What? No, no, it can't be.' I surveyed the chessboard. 'Oh, Lord, so it is.'

'You know, Cass, I just don't think you've got your mind on this,' Paul said. 'You usually give me a better run for my money.'

He began putting the chess pieces back in the box.

'You're right. I'm not feeling my best.'

I was feeling out of sorts in a way that was difficult to put my finger on: tired, lethargic, a bit of a headache. I realized that I hadn't felt really well since the day I'd found Margaret's body – a couple of months ago now. Surely I couldn't *still* be suffering from shock?

Paul wedged the chessboard and box of pieces under one arm and made his way across the room, shifting his weight awkwardly from one piece of furniture to the next. I knew better than to jump up and help. He was a small, wiry man with a lot of nervous energy and it had hit him hard when multiple sclerosis had forced him to retire from his job as a researcher in the university's chemistry laboratories. That had been a year ago.

He put the chess things away and sank with a sigh into a chair. The table next to it was piled with a jumble of books and cassettes: a biography of Darwin rubbed shoulders with *The River Café*

Cook Book. He fumbled among them and brought out an oilskin bag and a packet of Rizlas.

'I expect having to go to the inquest has taken it out of you,' he said sympathetically. He began the smoker's ritual of the roll-up.

'You're not kidding.'

I had been the first to give evidence. Then I sat listening with a dry mouth to the reports from the police and the pathologist, fearing that Margaret's affair with Lucy would after all come to light, or even – absurdly – that someone would get up and denounce me for having burned the letters.

The pathologist had found no water in Margaret's lungs, but apparently this was by no means uncommon in death by drowning When water comes into contact with the vocal cords, the muscles around the larynx go into spasm and the breathing reflex is inhibited. Death is caused by suffocation. Margaret had died quickly and painlessly. The contents of her stomach and the level of alcohol in her blood suggested that shortly before her death she had eaten a meal with which she had drunk a couple of glasses of wine, but no more than that. There were no signs of heart disease or history of epilepsy. Bruising on her right temple was severe enough to have induced temporary unconsciousness. She had been wearing a swimming-costume. The coroner, a balding, middle-aged man, concluded that Margaret had probably hit her head while diving into the pool, suffering a glancing blow to the head, which had rendered her unconscious. She had been a healthy woman in the prime of life with everything to live for. He felt justified in bringing in a verdict of accidental death, and offered his condolences to Margaret's husband and family. He directed a sympathetic half-smile towards Malcolm and began shuffling his papers together. There was a scraping of chairs as people got to their feet.

I felt relief and exhilaration.

I made my way to where Malcolm was sitting. I noticed that he had just had his hair cut; there was a little scattering of tiny red-gold strands on one shoulder of his dark suit. The attempt at smartness was touching.

I put my hand on his arm.

'Thank you, Cassandra,' he said.

'What for?'

'For giving your evidence so calmly. It can't have been easy.' He took my hand and squeezed it hard. 'I'm glad it's over,' he said.

At that moment I knew that I'd done the right thing.

After all that worrying, it was all over. But I still felt so tired.

I let my eyes wander around the back room of the little terraced house in Newnham. The floral patters of the sofa and armchairs had faded to a soothing dimness and one entire wall was lined with books. Paul was lying back, eyes closed, the hand that held his cigarette dangling loosely over the arm of the chair. The French windows were open onto the narrow strip of garden. Alison was weeding the herb-bed close to the house. The scents of thyme, rosemary and mint mingled with Paul's cigarette smoke. The perfumed air seemed to fill my head. I gave a yawn so wide that my eyes filled with tears.

Alison straightened up. She put her hands in the small of her back and stretched. Brushing some soil off her skirt, she stepped into the house, and sat next to Paul. He opened his eyes and smiled at her.

'I haven't had many afternoons in the garden this summer, I can tell you,' she said. 'I've been slogging it out in the university library.'

'Bless you,' I said.

'Oh, I don't mind really. I'm quite enjoying it. I ought to have written up this piece of research years ago. And anyway we've all got to do our bit. How's Merfyn getting along?'

'Fine, I think,' I stifled the twinge of anxiety that I felt whenever I thought of him. I had read the opening of his book and it had seemed a model of scholarly detachment, but that didn't mean I was happy at the way it came into being.

With an effort, I got to my feet. 'I'd better be off. I need to do some shopping. See you in a fortnight, Paul. I'll get my revenge then.'

It's a pleasant walk into the centre of town from Newnham. As I strolled across Lammas Land recreation ground I was only half-conscious of the sounds of a warm August day: the thud of tennis balls, a man calling a dog, the cries of small children. I was reflecting on the way that trouble so often comes from the direction that you least expect. I had dreaded the inquest for weeks, but it had been over in less than an hour, and Lucy's name hadn't even been mentioned. I'd been worried about Alison and Merfyn, but at least they were trying to get some writing done. And now I was wondering whether I should be even more concerned about Aiden. I'd taken it for granted that there wouldn't be a problem – he'd been appointed on the strength of his research record after all – but when I looked at his list of publications, I understood why Margaret had been concerned. There was nothing dated later than the previous year, and no reference to forthcoming publications. Probably he was working on another major book. That could take *years*. All the same, Lawrence wasn't going to like it, and the really maddening thing was that I hadn't been able to get in touch with Aiden to discuss it. He seemed to have gone to ground after the end of term. I left memos in his pigeon-hole; they stayed there. I rang his house several times a week; there was never any answer, and his mobile was always switched off. I was getting more and more annoyed. He should have let me know if he was going to be away on holiday or was pursuing research elsewhere.

I was standing by the crossing on Fen Causeway waiting for the light to go green and brooding about Aiden, when I realized that I was looking right at him. My eyes had been absently following the figure in a black T-shirt and baggy black tracksuit bottoms for some seconds. He was about two hundred yards away on the other side of the road jogging along the path that led into town by the river. As I watched, he stopped and bent over, hands on knees, to get his breath back. At that moment the crossing light went green.

I crossed the road, ran along the pavement, weaving in and out of pedestrians, and pushed open the metal gate to the path by the river. Aiden was only about fifty yards away. He straightened up and set off at a brisk trot. I yelled his name, but he didn't seem to hear. I jogged slowly after him, my long plait of hair thumping on my back in time to my breathing. He drew away from me and disappeared round the curve of the river.

I collapsed, panting, onto a bench with a stitch in my side. My calf muscles were trembling and my shirt was damp with sweat. God, was I out of condition! Over the last few months I'd noticed my clothes getting a bit tighter, too. It was about time I took myself in hand and got some proper exercise. I sat, catching my breath and enjoying the view. The elders and willows grew so thickly that Fitzwilliam Museum and Peterhouse College on the other side of the river were lost to view. There wasn't a modern building in sight. Short, tussocky pasture dotted with poplars and grazed by black and white Friesian cows stretched out on this side of the river. If you closed your ears to the constant roar of traffic, you could imagine that things had looked much the same for the last hundred years.

I got up and walked on to Granta Place, where the river widens into what was once a mill pond. The paths were crowded here and people were sitting on the grass. There's a place to hire punts and it's always busy. I scanned the crowd just in case Aiden was still there. Through the throng I glimpsed a familiar figure in black. Aiden was at the head of the queue for the ice-cream van. As I made my way towards him, he completed his transaction and walked off down Mill Lane. He wasn't running now, just walking fast, but there were so many people on both the road and the pavement that I couldn't have caught up even if I'd had the energy to run. I followed him to Fitzwilliam Street, where he turned left towards the town centre. It was ridiculous, I knew that, tracking

Aiden through the streets of Cambridge as if I were some kind of secret agent, but my blood was up and I was absolutely determined to pin him down about his research.

August is the height of the tourist season in Cambridge. A couple of times I thought I'd lost him in the crowd, then I would see his head bobbing along in front of me. As I passed the English Teddy Bear Company, I was forced off the pavement by a gaggle of Spanish students. I remembered what Merfyn had said about hearing seven different languages between Jesus Lane and the market. I couldn't see Aiden. I stopped and looked anxiously around. There was a narrow passage to the right, a short-cut down to the market. Had he gone down there? I walked down the cutting and turned left by St Edward's church into Market Square.

Aiden was nowhere in sight.

I was hot and sweaty and crosser than ever. I knew now that he *was* actually in Cambridge; he must have been deliberately avoiding me. I decided to give him time to get home, and then go round to his house. Meanwhile I wandered around in the market, hoping that I might still come across him. I stopped to browse the books on the second-hand book stall. I was inspecting a rather nice edition of Mrs Henry Wood's *East Lynne*, when I happened to glance up: between the polyester dresses hanging on the next stall, I caught a glimpse of Aiden walking swiftly down Market Street. I dropped the book and gave chase.

I emerged from the market just in time to see him disappear into W.H. Smith's.

The ground floor was crowded and it took a few moments before I could be sure that Aiden wasn't there. He must have gone up to the books on the first floor. I ran up the stairs two at a time. At first I couldn't see him here either, but then I spotted his head and shoulders among the aisles of books at the back of the shop. I had him cornered. Something tense and alert about the way he was standing aroused my curiosity. I made my way towards him. He was alone in the aisle except for a woman with a push-chair who was slowly making her way in his direction; a small child was leaning over the side, trailing a large book on the carpet.

I was almost up to him before he saw me. His shoulders jerked back and his eyes widened. I was suddenly conscious of the well-muscled body under the black T-shirt and the not unpleasant salty odour of fresh sweat. Tendrils of black hair were curling over the neck of his T-shirt. His attention flickered to the shelf beside me. My eyes followed his. I took in a couple of titles – *Venus in Furs, My Secret Life* – and jackets in monochrome and sepia showing half-naked women in black leather or corsets, kneeling on cane chairs or reclining on *chaise-longues*. Victorian soft porn. I looked back at Aiden. He was blushing. His hand shot up to his receding hairline in his automatic smoothing gesture.

Then several things happened very quickly. As the woman with the push-chair passed Aiden, her child dropped its book on the carpet. As if in an effort to escape me, Aiden took a step back. His foot skidded on the glossy cover of the book. The woman shouted. In an effort to avoid crashing into the child in its push-chair, Aiden twisted round. Hopelessly off-balance, he tried to right himself by grabbing a waist-high display stand full of books. As I moved forward, Aiden's foot shot out and caught me a glancing blow that knocked my right leg out from under me. I grabbed one of the aisle shelves but my weight carried me on. I slid along it, pushing the books before me. At the last moment I managed to steady myself, but it was too late to stop the books. A dozen fat blue-and-white paperbacks shot off the end of the shelf just as the display stand to which Aiden was clinging toppled over. It hit the floor with a thud that echoed through the store.

There were a few seconds of complete silence. They were broken by the outraged screams of the child whose carelessness had resulted in Aiden lying on top of a crushed display stand, surrounded by copies of the W.H. Smith Romance of the Month.

Chapter Seven

I glanced at my watch. A few minutes after ten; Rebecca was late. Her latest essay, her personal file and my own book, *Introduction to the Victorian Novel*, lay on the desk in front of me on top of a litter of other papers. I leafed through the file. The problems had begun in the previous academic year: work handed in late, poor grades, missed seminars. I wasn't looking forward to my interview with her, but I'd been through this with many students over the years: I knew how it would go and what I could hope to achieve.

I turned round on my swivel chair and looked out of the window. It was the end of the first week of term. The October day was bright and crisp, yet there was something a little sad about the thinness of the sunshine and the quality of the shadows. The lawn was now dappled with yellowing leaves. Yet the beginning of the academic year had also brought a sense of renewal: a chance to begin again.

Margaret's picture and her rolled-up rug were still propped up in the corner of the office – I should have taken those round to Malcolm weeks ago, and I resolved to do it that weekend – but there were no other traces of her in the office. The shelves were overflowing with my books, and the desk was covered in letters, memos and student essays. It was easy enough to take over her office, but how was I measuring up in other ways? I sighed. It was impossible to imagine the cool and orderly Margaret embarking on a chase through the streets of Cambridge ending in one of her colleagues falling flat on his back on the floor of W.H. Smith's. I felt both amused and embarrassed when I thought about it. I hadn't told anyone except Stephen, and I was pretty sure that Aiden wouldn't have spread it around: too much sense of his own dignity. The episode had ended with Aiden promising to produce an outline of his future research. It hadn't appeared yet.

I turned my attention to my book on the Victorian novel and opened it where I had marked a place with a strip of paper, I read a few lines.

The evangelicalism of the first half of the nineteenth century was a potent force in the lives of many writers and thinkers. Even those such as George Eliot and John Ruskin, who rejected the evangelical faith of their childhoods, could not entirely throw off its influence. For George Eliot, duty remained an absolute moral imperative, even when God had become 'inconceivable' and immortality 'unbelievable'.

There was a knock on the door and Rebecca came in. I looked at my watch. Ten minutes late. She caught the gesture, but didn't say anything. I examined her face. Was this just sloppy timekeeping, or a carefully judged gesture of defiance? Probably the latter, but I decided to let it go: better to keep my powder dry.

Rebecca sat down in the chair next to my desk and anchored two curtains of mousy hair behind her ears. We contemplated each other in silence. Her large, smooth freckled face made me think of an egg. She had prominent green eyes with heavy lids. Her mouth was small and pursed, a little sulky in its set.

I picked up her essay and read out the first few lines aloud.

The Evangelicalism of the early nineteenth century was an important force in the lives of many writers and thinkers.

Even those like George Eliot and John Ruskin, who later rejected the Evangelical faith off their childhood, remained under it's influence. For George Eliot, Duty remained an absolute moral value, even though God had become 'inconcievable' and Immortality 'unbelievable'.

'Can you explain to me, Rebecca, how it is that the first page of your essay is virtually identical to the beginning of Chapter Four of my own book?'

I gestured to where it lay open on the desk.

Her eyes flickered away from mine. 'It's not exactly the same.'

'Oh, come on. The odd word has been changed and you've introduced some mistakes in spelling and punctuation, unintentionally no doubt. Nothing more. And this hasn't been the only problem with your work lately, has it?' I gestured towards her file. 'Is there anything you want to tell me? A personal problem, perhaps ...?'

I expected to hear of a broken love affair, an illness in the family, or parents divorcing. She said nothing.

'All right, I'm going to give you one more chance. Go away, put your books to one side, and rewrite this in your own words. I want to see you back here on Monday morning at nine o'clock with a new essay.'

'By Monday!' she burst out. 'I've got rowing practice this afternoon and there's a race tomorrow.'

'Academic work takes precedence over sport, you know that, Rebecca.'

She put a hand on the edge of my desk and drummed her fingers. I let my eyes drop to her hand and then raised them to meet her gaze. After a moment she looked away and removed her hand, but her chin was still lifted defiantly and her small mouth was tight with anger.

The interview wasn't going as I had expected. I was surprised by her intransigence. Students don't mean to cheat as a rule, and they quickly apologize when they realize what they've done wrong. And even if they do mean to cheat, they're usually smart enough to play dumb and put on a show of being contrite.

'If I don't have this essay by next week, and if I'm not satisfied that it's all your own work, I'll have to inform the Master. You could be suspended from the college.'

Finally I seemed to have got through to her. Her lips were still pressed tightly together, but her eyes were brimming. One single tear spilled over and wound its way down her cheek.

'What is it, Rebecca?' I asked more gently. I took a tissue from the box on my desk and handed it to her.

Her face crumpled. The corners of her mouth went down in a grimace. She looked like a child about to have a tantrum. For a few moments she struggled to speak. Eventually a single word emerged.

'Lucy,' she said.

My heart stopped for a moment, and then lurched. Then I thought perhaps she didn't mean Lucy Hambleton. Names go in fashions and the college was full of Lucys, Emmas and Kates.

'Rebecca, you'd better tell me what this is all about.'

'I thought she loved me. She did love me until ... until that woman came along,' she wailed. 'It wasn't fair. She tried to hide it from me. And she'd still be alive, Lucy would still be alive if—'

She was almost incoherent in her anger and misery.

'If what, Rebecca?'

With a visible effort, she got herself back under control. 'If she hadn't come to this rotten place!'

She reached over and took her essay off the desk. In front of my astonished eyes she ripped it in two.

'I'm not going to do this fucking essay Just you try and make me. I can make trouble for you and this bloody college, and don't you forget it!'

She grabbed her rucksack and ran out of the room. I got to the door just in time to see her vanish round the corner of the corridor and hear her feet running down the stairs.

*

'Thanks.'

'What for?' Stephen asked.

'For not saying, "I told you so".'

We were in The Free Press, a small pub in the tangle of little streets and terraces of Regency houses to the north of Parker's Piece. It's a rowing pub, and the wooden panelling is crowded with memorabilia. Faded photographs of young men in blazers looked down on us, and above the threshold of the tiny inner bar, where we were having an early lunch, was the blade of an oar on which the names of a long-gone boat team were painted in white. It was very busy – it always is – but that makes it a good place to talk. No one can hear you above the hubbub.

'I won't say I'm not tempted,' Stephen admitted. 'I've thought all along that someone somewhere probably knew about Lucy and Margaret. It's difficult to be as discreet as all that – especially when you're mad about somebody.'

'I know, I know. I just so much hoped that it was all in the past now and that Malcolm wouldn't have to know.'

'This Rebecca – you think she had something going with Lucy herself?'

'Looked that way. Stephen ...'

'Yep?'

'There's no question of letting Rebecca get away with this. If she doesn't write a new essay, I'll have to report her to Lawrence. I'm wondering if I should get in first. If it's going to come out anyway, better he doesn't hear it from an angry student.'

Stephen said, 'I shouldn't be in too much of a hurry to go to Lawrence. From what you said, it's not clear how much Rebecca knows. And, by the way, Cass, I'd certainly steer clear of saying anything about the letters. If you *were* ever brought to book over those, and I don't see how you could be, then you could always claim you were acting within your powers as Margaret's literary executor.'

82

I was surprised and amused by this pragmatism. 'Is that the solicitor speaking?'

He put on a look of mock solemnity. 'My dear, don't you know you should never do anything without consulting your solicitor? And now, another drink?'

'Better not. I've got to cycle back to college and I'm seeing Merfyn this afternoon. I'll need all my wits about me for that.'

'Coffee then.'

'Not for me, but get me a packet of Benson and Hedges, would you?'

'Cass!'

'Just this once. I absolutely *must* have a fag. Just one. You can keep the rest of the packet for me.'

He raised his eyebrows in a pantomime of reluctant agreement.

'It's the ritual as much as anything,' I explained, when he brought them back to the table. I stripped off the cellophane and shook a cigarette out of the packet.

'Helps me get my thoughts in order.'

He nodded and pocketed the packet. I lit up and took a deep drag. We sat in thought for a few minutes.

'I'm supposed to be seeing her on Monday. She'll have had a chance to calm down by then. I'll try and find out exactly what she meant. If she turns up.'

'She might well be regretting it already. Remember that Tom Lehrer song?' Stephen grinned. ' "Plagiarize, plagiarize, let no one else's work evade your eyes"? You know what amazes me? That she had the chutzpah to crib from your own book!'

I wasn't enjoying my cigarette as much as I'd expected. I stubbed it out without finishing it.

'It's happened before,' I said. 'At least she didn't produce a copy of my book from her bag and ask me to autograph it for her! One student that I was ticking off for something similar actually did that.' I looked at my watch. 'Better be getting back to college.'

'Wait a moment,' Stephen put his hand on my arm. He reached

into his briefcase and brought out something wrapped in tissue-paper.

'I saw this in the antique shop opposite the museum.'

From the way he handed it to me, I could tell it was fragile. It was a shallow, saucer-shaped porcelain bowl decorated with a grainy monochrome print in grey, a little crude but full of charm. A kneeling woman in an empire-line dress that exposed one breast was putting the yoke of a miniature chariot around her neck. The small boy in the chariot was brandishing a toy whip.

Stephen was watching my face.

'It's lovely,' I said.

'I could see it was like the others you've got. "Maternal recreation" you said those prints are called?'

I leant forward and kissed him lightly. He put an arm round me and gave me a longer, firmer kiss. I felt a passionate response that took me be surprise.

'I've got to go back to work,' I said, pulling back and laughing.

As soon as I saw Merfyn I knew that something was wrong. Cathy had let him into my office and he was slumped in one of the armchairs waiting for me. He looked like a schoolboy called up before the headmaster. One leg was twisted round the other and his hands were tucked defensively under his thighs. When I caught his eye, he immediately looked away.

He said, 'I might as well tell you straightaway, Cass, that I haven't got anything more to show you.' The remnant of his Welsh accent was far more in evidence than usual.

I sat down opposite him, trying to disguise my annoyance. 'Merfyn, don't you realize how important this is for the future of the department, and for you?'

'Of course I do.' He was impatient. 'And it isn't as if I haven't been working hard. I've done hardly anything else all summer. In fact I wrote several chapters.'

'So what's the problem?'

84

He didn't reply. As I sat regarding Merfyn, a familiar feeling swept over me, a compound of embarrassment, weariness and a a profound longing to be somewhere else. If only I could close my eyes and open them again to find that I had miraculously been transported to a desert island. Actually, I reflected, it didn't even have to be a desert island. Anywhere would do, anywhere that wasn't here.

Get a grip, I told myself, you're in charge here. I sat up straight, too quickly perhaps because specks of light danced before my eyes and my head reeled. I lowered my head and closed my eyes.

'Cassandra? Are you all right?'

'Yes, yes, I'm fine.'

Merfyn was leaning forward, looking at me anxiously.

'Really?'

'Yes, really. Look, Merfyn, even if *you're* not satisfied with it, I'd like to see what you've produced over the summer.'

The silence between us lengthened.

Eventually he heaved a huge sigh and said, 'If you must know, I've destroyed what I wrote.'

I stared at him.

'It's the truth. I've torn it into little pieces.'

'But – you've got it on disk? Yes?'

''Fraid not. I've deleted it from my word processor.'

I sat back. An image flashed into my mind: a little sheaf of white paper tumbling into the darkness of cyberspace, slowly turning over and over, growing ever smaller, like an astronaut whose lifeline has been severed. Gone for ever. I almost missed what he said next.

'I knew you wouldn't understand.' He shook his head and looked away.

'Merfyn! Look at me!'

His eyes slid back reluctantly.

'You're not going to like it,' he said. 'Conan Doyle told me to do it.'

In fifteen years of teaching, this was the most original excuse for an unfinished piece of work that I had ever heard.

Merfyn was lying back in his chair, legs stretched out, watching the ceiling, apparently relieved to have got this off his chest.

'Are you out of your mind?' I said.

Scarcely had the words left my mouth when I wondered if this was more than a figure of speech. Could it be something pathological here, a syndrome to which a psychiatrist could give a label? Perhaps Merfyn couldn't help himself? Perhaps he just could not finish this book? Was he even a little bit crazy? He didn't look as if he had lost touch with reality, but then what does a person who has lost touch with reality look like? Did I think he'd be gibbering and picking at his clothes?

'Not at all,' he said calmly. 'He came directly through the medium this time. Told me that what I'd written wasn't good enough. Of course, as soon as he said that, I realized. I think I'd probably known it all along. I'll just have to do it again.'

I seized on this. 'So it was the medium who told you.'

'No, I told you, it was Conan Doyle acting *through* the medium.'

'And who is this person, this medium? Does she take money for this?'

'No, she doesn't. She's very strict about that. Ingrid's a perfectly respectable person, a medical secretary, actually. It's a gift she has. She tries to help people.'

I thought this over.

'Now, look here, Merfyn,' I said. 'I'm going to be honest with you. I do not believe that you had a psychic experience.'

Merfyn was shaking his head vehemently.

I raised my hand as he was about to speak. 'I'm not saying the medium's a phoney. Most likely she acts in good faith. She's extraordinarily adept at picking up signals of agreement or dissent from other people. Tiny things that other people wouldn't notice, OK? So what she's actually giving expression to is what's already on your mind.'

'That's all very well, Cassandra, but you weren't there. If you had been, I know you'd have been convinced. I *know* it's genuine.'

When a discussion reaches that point, there's really nothing more to be said. I was at a loss. I leaned back in my chair and considered the matter. Should I just leave it at that? But what about Merfyn's book? And the future of the department? There was so much at stake. Would Margaret have let it go? Of course not. I didn't need to go to a séance to know that. So what *would* she have done? She would have tackled the situation head-on.

I sat up and looked Merfyn in the eye.

'All right. Next time, I'll come with you.'

'What?' He gawped at me with his mouth open.

'What's the matter, Merfyn? Not really as convinced as all that? Think the process won't stand up to rational scrutiny?'

He rallied. 'Not at all. I'd be delighted for you to come. In fact, I'd planned to go again on Saturday. Do you want to come then?'

'I'll be there.'

Chapter Eight

'Let's begin, shall we?'

Ingrid gestured towards a round mahogany table in the centre of the room.

'Where do you want us to sit?' I asked, for all the world as though this were a dinner-party.

'I'll sit here. If you could be opposite, Cassandra. And – now let me see – if I have Stephen on my left and Merfyn on my right. Does that suit everyone? I think it works best if it goes male, female.'

It *is* just like a dinner-party! I thought. However, there was nothing on the polished table except a small pile of A4 lined paper, a Biro and a couple of pencils. We took our places. Would it be like séances in the movies, where everyone puts their hands on the table? Rather to my surprise it was. We didn't hold hands, but just let our little fingers touch. Ingrid looked round the table, catching the eye of each of us in turn. Then she gave a little nod.

It had begun.

There was a hollow feeling in the pit of my stomach. I don't believe in this, I told myself, I don't believe in it. I pressed my little finger against Stephen's and was reassured by an answering pressure. I hadn't protested much when he had insisted on coming. I needed the support of his sturdy scepticism.

The room grew very still. Outside I could hear the swish of cars going past on Milton Road, could even detect the change in engine noise as they went down a gear to turn a nearby corner. The sound seemed only to accentuate the quietness in the room. I stole a glance at Ingrid. Her face was expressionless, her eyes closed, her lips slightly parted. She wasn't what I'd been expecting. Though, come to think of it, what *had* I been expecting? A fey, New Age figure with long hair and floaty garments? A dotty, dishevelled eccentric like Margaret Rutherford in *Blithe Spirit*? Ingrid was a woman of about fifty, discreetly made-up, wearing deep red nail varnish and what looked like a Jaeger suit. It was easy to imagine her as the mainstay of some consultant at Addenbrooke's Hospital.

I looked surreptitiously around the room. It was crowded with furniture and bric-a-brac. There was a pale deep pile carpet and over-stuffed chintzy sofas and chairs, patterned with big splashy flowers. Family photographs in gilt frames stood to attention on every available surface. The curtains were open. Outside it was bright and sunny and the room was warm. To the left, I could see a shaft of sunlight shimmering with dust motes. Into my mind came a memory from childhood, one I hadn't thought of for years. At about the age of six, half-asleep in my bed one morning, I had been convinced that I had seen a fairy. Now I couldn't remember the actual experience, only my conviction and my mother's polite interest. I know I was being humoured, and I was cross. 'I did see it, Mummy, I did.' 'I'm sure you saw something, darling.' It was years before I realized that my fairy must have been a mote of dust, floating and glimmering in the sunlight.

Stephen cleared his throat. He pressed his foot against mine. The room was getting stuffy. A trickle of sweat was making its way between my breasts. My eyelids were closing. I jerked them up. How long had we been sitting there? I'd lost track of time. It could have been five minutes, it could have been twenty.

The sun clouded over. The room grew darker. There was a draught across the back of my neck. The sounds in the street were fading away. No, not fading away, but taking on a distant rever-berant quality as if I were underwater. Something was happening; the air seemed to be getting thicker, my hands were tingling. I felt queasy. It was as though the air was suddenly alive, electric. A dark pit was opening up in front of me. I grabbed Stephen's hand, but I couldn't help myself. I was falling forward, head-first.

The garden shimmered and rocked in the heat. Sunlight flickered through the trees and threw up dazzling reflections from the pool. I squinted, my eyes watering as I tried to look into the water. This time I had to know what was there. I saw a dark, swollen face. I wanted to scream, but when I opened my mouth, nothing came out. A sour wave of nausea was rising up in my throat. I pressed forward, but my limbs felt heavy as if I was trying to force them through something dense and viscous. I was falling back, losing my footing. Suddenly I was gasping and spluttering as the cold water splashed up around me.

I broke the surface of the water. I was clutching someone's hand.
'Darling, it's all right, I'm here. It's all right, it's all right.'
Stephen's face was looking down at me. I touched my face; it was wet.
'We were splashing your face to try and bring you round.'
Beyond him I could see two pale discs. I tried to bring them into focus. They were faces. One was Merfyn. What was he doing in Margaret's garden? I couldn't quite place the other one. I felt weak and dizzy and sick.
'What happened?'
'You fainted, that's all,' Stephen said.
Merfyn looked shaken. His hair was standing up where he had run his hands through it. Stephen was looking stern, disapproving even. Only Ingrid seemed unperturbed.
'Don't move until you really feel better,' she said. 'I'll go and make some tea in a minute.'

90

'I thought you were going into a trance,' Merfyn said. 'Perhaps you're psychic.'

'Nonsense,' Ingrid said briskly.

'But is she going to be all right?' he asked.

'Right as rain. She just needs to put her feet up a bit more.'

Stephen looked puzzled. 'But, what …'

Now it was Ingrid's turn to look puzzled. She turned to me.

'You don't know?' she said.

But quite suddenly I did know. The lethargy, the dizziness … A series of images and sensations flashed through my mind: Stephen's wet face pressed against mine, clothes discarded on the bedroom floor, a wine glass shattering.

It wasn't delayed shock after all.

I was pregnant.

An hour later I was sitting on the toilet lid in the bathroom at the Old Granary. We had gone straight home with only a detour to a chemist's. I looked again at the diagram in the leaflet. 'If two blue bars appear in the larger window, the test is positive.' It was straightforward enough, but somehow I couldn't get a grip on it. I looked at the white plastic wand again. Yes, there were still two blue bars in the larger of the two perspex windows.

Stephen opened the bathroom door.

'Cass?' he said anxiously.

I nodded and handed him the wand. His gaze moved from my face to the wand and back again. I couldn't read anything in his face except pure astonishment. He looked stunned.

Then he turned on his heels and made for the door. He disappeared through it and I heard his feet on the bare floorboards of the stairs. There was a rumbling sound, like a little avalanche, and a muffled oath. In his hurry he must have dislodged one of the piles of books that lined the treads.

I was only mildly surprised. I went over to the bedroom window to see if Stephen was emerging from the house. Did I really expect to see him get in his car and drive away? I had no idea. I had reached that state of numbness where anything seems possible. Margaret, the least accidental person in the world, had died in an accident; Merfyn believed he was in touch with the spirit world, and now I was pregnant. One thing didn't seem much more surprising than another.

The sun was setting. Shafts of dazzling golden light struck through billowing clouds of pink and orange and dove-grey. The sky had all the splendour of a rococo altarpiece. I was still admiring it when I heard footsteps coming back up the stairs. Stephen appeared with a bottle of Bushmills 5 Years Old Malt and two cut-glass tumblers.

'My best Irish whiskey,' I said. 'Are we celebrating?'

'Well, are we?'

'I don't know. I simply don't know.'

He poured me a drink. I looked at it doubtfully.

'You've been drinking up till now,' he pointed out. 'One more won't make much difference. Anyway you've had a shock. For medicinal purposes …'

'Just a small one.'

I took the glass of whiskey and breathed in its perfume. I took a sip and let the sweet peaty liquor warm my mouth. When I swallowed it, the heat spread through my chest. It seemed to brace me immediately.

We sat down together on the bed. Stephen took my hand.

'How could it have happened?' he said.

'Nothing's a hundred per cent reliable, is it?'

'You didn't forget to take a Pill?'

'I don't think so.'

Of course, I immediately began to wonder if I *had* forgotten. Surely, I would have noticed, wouldn't I? But so much had happened, I'd been so busy. Perhaps after all …

'I suppose you do feel certain?'

'It says on the packet that the test's 98‰ accurate, but

Stephen, that's not all. I've missed a period.'

'Why didn't you say?'

'It's not that unusual for me. I thought it was the shock of Margaret's death ... stress at work.'

'But you'll check with the doctor, yes?'

'First thing on Monday morning.'

The whiskey was leaving a sour taste in my mouth. I handed my glass to Stephen. The shock was wearing off, but so was the bracing effect of the alcohol. I felt the first flutterings of panic.

'What on earth am I going to do?'

'We, what are we going to do?' Stephen corrected me.

'How can I have a baby now? I've just taken over as head of department, I'm fighting to save it from closure; I can't just suddenly disappear for six months or whatever!'

'Look, Cassandra, this isn't any time for beating about the bush. So I'll say right away that I'm very willing to get married, help you look after the child and so on, if that's what you want.'

But was it? At that moment I had no idea what I wanted. I didn't want to have my hand forced like this. It was all happening too fast. I wasn't ready to get married again, perhaps I never would be ready. How much better if Stephen and I could go on indefinitely as we were; leading independent lives, spending the night together at weekends, even going on holiday together occasionally, but always returning to our own separate homes. I liked having Stephen as a visitor, but I didn't want to live with him. So how could we raise a child together?

I could feel Stephen's shoulder trembling against mine. I turned and looked into his face. His mouth was twitching. For a moment I couldn't read his expression. Then I understood. 'You're laughing!'

'What a way to find out! You gave me the shock of my life! I only just managed to catch you in time. You should have seen Merfyn's face. He really thought you were going into a trance!'

'Perhaps he thought I was going to finish his book for him! Oh,

Lord, I didn't get very far with disabusing him, did I? You don't think Ingrid really is psychic?'

'Of course not. A lucky guess. You heard what she said, she works for an obstetrician! I suppose she sees hundreds of pregnant women every week.'

We spent the next day, Sunday, as we often did. We read the papers in bed, had a leisurely lunch and in the late afternoon we went to Evensong at Ely Cathedral. I am never quite sure where I stand on the God question, but I love the beauty and dignity of the 1552 Prayer Book and the Cathedral service has the power to lift me above the mundane. On that occasion it helped to give some order to my tangled thoughts and emotions. Listening to the pure, high voices of the boys in the choir floating up into the octagonal tower, my eyes prickled with tears. Stephen took my hand and squeezed it tightly.

That evening we went round to Malcolm's to return Margaret's rug and painting. While Stephen got them out of the boot of the car, I rang the doorbell. The lantern above the doorway of Malcolm's house sent out a watery, yellow light, illuminating the dark, gnarled shapes of the roses in the central flower-bed. Even in the dimness I could see that they had not been dead-headed. The gravel drive was scored with ruts.

I'd spoken several times to Malcolm on the telephone, but I hadn't seen him since the inquest. He looked much better. His face looked younger, more relaxed, though some of the deeper lines I'd noticed after the funeral were still there.

'Good of you to bring those things round,' he said. 'Come in for a drink, won't you?'

We left the picture and the rug in the hall and followed him into the sitting-room.

As Macolm busied himself with the drinks, I glanced around. The room was clean and tidy enough, though it wasn't as immaculate as it had been in Margaret's day. I noticed a box of Playmobil next to the sofa, and a copy of *Charlie and the Chocolate Factory* on one of the chairs. Malcolm followed the direction of my eyes. He smiled.

'Those are Ellie's. Jane's little girl. I sometimes keep an eye on her when Jane's got an evening surgery. It's the least I can do. Jane's been a tower of strength over the last few months.'

'So you're managing well enough?' I asked.

'Not too badly. I'm beginning to think about some kind of memorial for her. Perhaps some sort of scholarship. I think she would have approved of that. Mineral water, you said?' He handed me a glass. 'And I'd like to put together a volume of her unpublished work ...'

He was too nice to remind me that this was something *I* ought to be taking care of, and this made me feel even more guilty.

'I know I said I'd be literary executor, Malcolm, and I want to do it, it's just ... well, I've been so busy. But let me have the rest of Margaret's papers and I'll see what I can do.'

'Of course, I understand,' Malcolm said. 'It can't be easy having to take over the department.'

For a moment I was tempted to tell him about my pregnancy. I realized that I was beginning to get used to the idea, was even looking forward to seeing people's reactions to the news. Did this mean that I had actually decided to go ahead?

It wasn't until we were in the hall, about to leave, that I suddenly remembered. 'The little lacquer box from Margaret's desk, I forgot to bring it.'

'Don't worry about it. You keep it,' Malcolm saw me hesitate. 'It's not valuable. I bought it for a few dollars in St Petersburg, but it's pretty, isn't it? I'd like you to have something of Margaret's.'

'It's beautifully painted,' I said. 'Do you know what the subject is on the lid?'

'Margaret thought it was the Snow Queen.'

'Of course, I knew it looked familiar. Thank you, Malcolm. I'll keep it on my desk to remind me of her.'

As we drove away, Stephen said, 'Good old Jane.'

'It's funny, you know, that time in the churchyard – the day of Margaret's funeral – I got the impression that she didn't like him very much,' I said.

'I wonder if there's a Mr Jane.'

'Surely, you don't think ...?'

'Oh, probably there's nothing more to it than good neighbourliness. All the same, I wouldn't be at all surprised to hear of Malcolm marrying again.'

'He was devoted to Margaret.'

'Exactly. He liked being married, he's used to it. You mark my words, sooner or later – and it'll probably be sooner – he'll be looking around for someone else. It's the people who haven't enjoyed being married who don't want to try it again.'

I realized that he was probably right, but there was something depressing about the thought. And where does that leave the two of us? I wondered.

'I wonder why they didn't have children, Malcolm and Margaret, I mean?' Stephen said.

'I really don't know. I'd always assumed that it was because she was so taken up with her career.'

But perhaps it wasn't that. I thought of the toys scattered around the sitting-room and the warmth of Malcolm's voice as he'd spoken of Ellie. Stephen was right. Probably he would marry again. Perhaps he might even have children. Before my second divorce that was something I had hoped for, and there had seemed so much time in front of me. And now I was thirty-eight. It might soon be too late. And in any case could I really face having an abortion?

I pulled up outside Stephen's flat and put on the handbrake.

'I'm going to have the baby,' I said.

'Are you sure? If you felt you couldn't ... I mean, I don't suppose it would be too late ...'

'Yes, it would. For me it would. She's here now.'

'She?'

'Oh, all right, maybe he. Of course, it's perhaps not the most convenient time ...'

'We'll manage.' He put an arm round my shoulder and hugged me awkwardly across the gearstick.

'But one thing,' I said, disengaging myself. 'Let's not think about marriage just yet. We don't have to rush into anything. We can go on as we are for now, can't we?'

He nodded. 'Of course.'

'But if you want to come and stay tonight ...'

Chapter Nine

I lay back in bed and listened to Stephen having a shower in the bathroom next door. The sound of the running water was soothing. Through the window I saw clouds drifting across a moonlit sky. How extraordinary it was that in just one weekend everything could have changed so completely. It was a daunting thought, but now that I was getting used to it, a fountain of excitement was welling up inside me. It would be spring when the baby came. A good time with the summer ahead and a good time to have maternity leave, too. Would it perhaps be sensible to consider moving back into Cambridge? I'd heard that there was a good nursery in Barton Road. But no, I couldn't leave the Old Granary, and my mother ... she'd want to meet Stephen now. Oh, Lord. Well, I wouldn't worry about that yet. What a wonderful excuse to buy some more books. At the first opportunity I'd raid the pregnancy and child care section in Waterstone's.

I was almost asleep when the phone rang. I sat up and fumbled on the bedside table. The telephone was balanced on top of a couple of books. It toppled off, taking the books with it, and landed on the floor with a thud and a tinkle. With an effort, I bent down over the side of the bed and made a grab for it.

A tiny sound like the buzz of an angry bee issued from the receiver.

As I put it to my ear, I heard Lawrence saying, 'Cassandra? Cassandra? Are you there?'

'Yes, yes, hello, Lawrence.'

'I tried to get hold of you earlier. You've been out all day,' he stated. 'Bad news, I'm afraid, very bad news. One of your third-year students, Rebecca Westerley, I'm ringing from Addenbrooke's. She's in Intensive Care.'

'Intensive Care? But, what …?'

'She's got a fractured skull. It's too soon apparently to tell if she's going to survive, and even if she does, there may be brain damage.'

'An accident? Her bicycle?'

That was an all too common occurrence in Cambridge, though the results weren't usually as serious as this.

'No. I'm afraid it was a deliberate attack.'

Stephen came whistling out of the bathroom with a towel round his waist. As soon as he saw my face, he stopped in his tracks. I watched the water trickling down his legs and soaking into the rug as though it were the most fascinating thing in the world.

'It must have happened last night, but she wasn't found until this morning,' Lawrence was saying. 'She had hypothermia. It's lucky it wasn't a very cold night.'

'She was attacked? Was she—?'

'Raped? The police aren't saying as yet. Her parents drove down from Newcastle this morning. I went to Addenbrooke's with them, and I've left them there waiting by Rebecca's bedside. I know you will want to speak to them yourself in due course, Cassandra.'

'Of course. You'll let me know the instant there's any more news, won't you?'

'Naturally.'

I was late getting into my office on Monday morning. A visit to the doctor had confirmed that I was about four months pregnant. The

99

first thing I saw as I sat down was my diary lying open on the desk. The appointment with Rebecca was written in for ten o'clock. If it hadn't been for this assault, she might be sitting opposite me now instead of lying unconscious in Addenbrooke's. What might she be telling me at this very moment? The thought nagged at me. I spent almost the whole day in my office so as to be near the phone. I kept remembering Rebecca's anger and misery when I had last seen her, the sulky eyes refusing to meet mine, the noise of the slammed door reverberating down the corridor. The thought popped into my head that the attack had something to do with me, that perhaps it was somehow my fault. Irrational, yes, but once I had entertained the idea even for a moment it wouldn't leave me alone. I found myself going over and over our conversation, trying to remember her words, the nuances of facial expression.

Lawrence rang me around eleven to tell me Rebecca was still profoundly unconscious. She had not been raped but all the same the police weren't discounting a sexual motive to the attack. Stephen rang at twelve to offer to cook dinner. Apart from that, the telephone remained inert on my desk. Around three o'clock I caught myself glancing at it for at least the fiftieth time, willing it to ring with news of Rebecca. I took myself in hand. On the principle that a watched pot never boils, I drove to the university library to continue hunting biographical details for my edition of nineteenth century verse. I forced myself to wait until it was half-past six and time to leave before I rang the hospital. I somehow felt that self-control had earned me good news. My heart sank when the ward sister told me that there was no change.

Stephen's flat is in a block built in the thirties near the river over by Midsummer Common, only a ten minute drive after the rush-hour.

As soon as he saw my face, he said, 'No more news about Rebecca then?'

'Not really.'

100

Walking through the little entrance hall into the sitting-room, I breathed in the smell that I always associated with Stephen's flat; a mixture of the soap he always used, Cussons Imperial Leather, furniture polish and the pleasantly musty smell of old books. There was something cosy and old-fashioned, but also very masculine, about the solid mahogany furniture and the rugs with their warm, faded colours, which he had inherited from the North Devon vicarage where he had grown up.

Stephen took my coat and I sank with a sigh onto the sofa.

'I suppose a large Scotch is out of the question,' he said, 'but there's a shepherd's pie in the oven.'

'Bless you.'

'I can't believe you're four months pregnant,' he said, sitting down beside me.

'It can be quite a long time before it really shows apparently.'

'I keep counting back and wondering when exactly it was.'

'Do you know when I think it was? That day that I burned the letters, when there was the thunderstorm.'

Stephen thought about that for a while. 'That seems appropriate somehow, though I'm not quite sure why.'

Over the meal I told him what I'd found out about the attack on Rebecca.

'She shares a house with some other girls in Cherry Hinton, one of those big Victorian villas. One of her friends found her in the shrubbery, next to where they leave their bikes. I keep wondering if I should say something to the police. Or to Lawrence. About what Rebecca said, I mean.'

'It's hard to see what connection there could be with this attack. I'd be inclined to wait and see what happens. The police may well make an arrest very soon.'

'Lawrence would absolutely not want all this about Margaret and Lucy to come out. You know, Stephen, I think, if he had been the one to find those letters, he would have done just what I did, but not for same reason.'

101

Stephen thought about this. 'He would have wanted to protect the reputation of the college.'

'At all costs.'

'At *all* costs?'

We looked at each other. A nightmare scenario was unfolding before my eyes.

'No,' I said firmly, 'this is sheer paranoia. Burning love letters is one thing, murder is quite another. Lawrence may be unscrupulous, but he's not wicked. Or stupid. He is far too smart to try to cover up one scandal at the risk of causing a bigger one.'

'The college is very important to him, isn't it? He's not married?'

'Divorced. No children. It's true: the college is probably the most important thing in his life.'

'There's no limit to what people will do for love,' he said. 'Or hate, for that matter. That's one thing I've learned in twenty years of being a lawyer.'

'It's one of the lessons of great literature, too. It's usually love of another human being, a spouse, a lover, a child, but it could be – well, almost anything really – a country, a cause, an ideal ...'

'An institution?'

In my mind's eye I saw the desiccated little figure of the Master, dressed in his invariable pinstriped suit of rather old-fashioned cut.

'Stephen, can you really imagine him hiding in the bushes with a blunt instrument and hitting Rebecca over the head? Just to cover up a love affair between a student and a member of staff? It wouldn't have been *that* big a scandal.'

'Oh, I don't know,' he said, as he gathered up the plates. 'Not objectively, perhaps. But just imagine it on the front page of the *News of the World*. "Cambridge College Hotbed of Lesbian Lust".'

'All the same, it's just not his style. A damning critique of one's latest book, yes, but hitting one over the head, no.'

Stephen glanced at his watch.

'It's getting late. Are you going to stay here tonight?'

'I'll have to go home and feed Bill Bailey.'

'Will you be all right on your own? Perhaps I'd better come.'

'Of course I will. I'm not ill, you know, only pregnant.'

I had spoken more sharply than I intended. Stephen was silent.

'Sorry.' I leaned over and kissed him. 'Ring you tomorrow?'

'Fine.'

Stephen's solicitude, my irritation: as I drove home, I wondered if this was going to set a pattern for the future.

It wasn't until I'd parked at the Old Granary and switched off my headlights, that I noticed how very dark the night was. The overcast sky was like a sheet of dark felt. It was hard to tell where the land ended and the sky began. The house was a black featureless mass, its outline broken only by trees and shrubs. Usually I remembered to leave on the light in the little hallway, but this morning I had been too preoccupied. I was suddenly very conscious of how isolated the house was; usually I loved that, but today it did seem very lonely.

I rummaged in the glove compartment for the torch I always kept there. The darkness had never bothered me before, but now I found myself measuring the distance to the front door. I got my keys out of my handbag, put them in my right-hand jacket pocket and opened the car door. The sound of the stream was less of a noise than a kind of intensification of the darkness.

The torch illuminated the crazy paving with a dancing wedge of yellow light. I had my hand on the latch of the garden gate when I heard a slight, but unmistakable, rustling in the bushes. I froze, my heart thudding. I swung the beam of the torch round as though it were a weapon. There was a flash of white near the ground followed by a muffled cry. I lowered the torch to see Bill Bailey gazing benignly up at me. A tail was dangling from his mouth like a strand of spaghetti. He opened his mouth and dropped the mouse on the grass. It lay immobile just long enough for me to decide it must be dead, then it shot back into the bushes. I scooped

Bill Bailey up and carried him, the cat wriggling and protesting bitterly, up the garden path. I clutched him tighter and felt his heart beating rapidly inside the narrow bony cage of his chest. My own seemed to be beating just as fast. Gripping him under my left arm, I groped for my key, opened the door and pushed him in.

I bolted the door. My heart was still racing and I had poured myself a lage Scotch before I remembered that I wasn't really supposed to be drinking. My doctor had said that an occasional drink wouldn't do me or the baby any harm, but I didn't want to take any chances. I poured almost all of it back into the bottle leaving just a film on the bottom of the glass. I filled it up to the top with soda. I restrained my impulse to ring Stephen and promised myself that first thing in the morning I'd arrange to have security lights fitted.

I rang the hospital to see if there was any news of Rebecca. Her condition was unchanged. I fed Bill Bailey and went up to bed with my drink.

For a long time I couldn't sleep. The baby and Rebecca and Stephen and the séance went round and round in my head like an irritating tune that you can't dislodge.

Eventually I put the World Service on so low that I could scarcely distinguish the words. I fell asleep to its background murmur. My last conscious thought was to hope that there would be news of Rebecca the next day. But there wasn't, nor the next day, nor the day after that.

Chapter Ten

The nurse leaned forward and pointed. 'Look, there's her head, can you see?'

Initially I couldn't make sense of the shifting pattern of light and dark, then I saw first the curve of the skull, then a tiny curled hand and two little feet nestling together.

'So it really is a girl,' Stephen said.

The nurse nodded. 'A lovely little girl.'

'Is she all right?' I asked.

'She's fine. You've had the results of your amniocentesis, haven't you? So you can relax and enjoy your pregnancy now. We'll see you in a month.'

'A baby girl,' Stephen said, as we made our way towards the entrance. He was grinning all over his face.

'Daddy's girl already,' I teased.

'You think I'll be a pushover, don't you?'

'Yep.'

'Oh, well, maybe you're right. On the other hand I may turn out to be a rather strict father. I shall practise saying, "And where do you think you're going dressed like that, young lady"?'

I laughed, but he must have caught a flicker of unease on my face.

'What's the matter?'

'Oh, nothing really, it's just that thinking so far ahead makes me feel a bit uncomfortable.'

'Tempting providence?'

'Something like that. After all, we've got months to go before she's even born.'

As the automatic doors opened to let us out of the Rosie Maternity Hospital, a wave of cold air rolled in. Cambridge in November: it wasn't actually raining, but a bitter wind was rushing in from the fens, slapping stinging drops of moisture across our faces.

'Are you going back to college?' Stephen asked.

I glanced at my watch. In spite of the twilight gloom, it was only 3.30.

'No, I need to go to the library, but first I'll go and find out if there's any change with Rebecca and see how her mother's getting on.'

We walked the few hundred yards to Addenbrooke's Hospital, and Stephen left me at the entrance. I got the lift to the fifth floor.

The Ward Sister in charge of the Intensive Care Unit looked so young that she could almost have been playing at being a nurse. She was probably about twenty-three or twenty-four, the same age as my postgraduate students, but she'd already seen more death than any of them would see in a lifetime.

I usually waited outside the ward to see Rebecca's mother, and I was surprised when the nurse asked me if *I* would like to see Rebecca.

'I don't usually ... I'm not a relative ...'

'Oh, I don't think it'll do any harm. Follow me.'

My stomach shrank in apprehension, but I felt that I was being offered a privilege that it would be churlish to refuse. The Ward Sister opened the door of the Intensive Care Unit, and I followed her in. Immediately I was struck by how peaceful it was. I realized that I had been expecting something different. There was no sense of urgency or drama, no exaggerated efforts to be quiet; people

106

were moving calmly about their business with no fuss or wasted effort or unnecessary conversation.

Rebecca was in a special unit for head injuries. The ward was organized in a semi-circle of cells about a central station and she was at one end. I could see Marion sitting by her side. We walked down the ward past white forms and impassive faces from which I tried to avert my eyes.

We reached the foot of Rebecca's bed and stood there unnoticed by Marion. Rebecca lay like a sculpture on a tomb. Under the swathes of white bandage, her face was serene. The petulant set of her mouth had relaxed, and she looked as peaceful and innocent as a young nun. Her hand lay open on the counterpane, palm up, fingers gently curving. I looked at her, feeling awe and respect for the mystery of her unconsciousness. To what distant interior world had she retreated, leaving her body here, the still centre of a network of machinery and purposeful human activity? It was like a legend or a fairy story in a contemporary setting: the court of Sleeping Beauty or Snow White. These days the princess would be on a life support system and would be rescued by a handsome consultant.

The nurse touched Marion on the shoulder. She looked up, smiled, and gestured to a metal and canvas chair next to her. There was a bundle of knitting and a copy of the *Daily Mail* on it. She lifted them off and I sat down.

She said, 'I get so fidgety, sitting here all day. I don't know what to do with my hands. So today, when I went out to stretch my legs, I went into the wool shop on Cherry Hinton Road. I love knitting. I bought the most difficult pattern I could find. And these are Rebecca's favourite colours. Perhaps by the time I've finished it ...'

She gave a resigned little grimace. I looked into the strong, sallow-skinned face. The dark, deep-set eyes had grown more hollowed in the month that she had spent in the hospital. For the first week after the attack, Rebecca's parents had both stayed by her bedside, but there were four younger children to care for and a business to run. Rebecca's father had returned to Newcastle, coming back to Cambridge at weekends to support his wife in her vigil.

We sat watching the tranquil face. Now and again Mrs Westerley squeezed Rebecca's hand or stroked her arm. There was no response of any kind.

After a while I said, 'Shall we go and have a cup of tea?'

She nodded.

We went out through the swing doors into a different, more workaday world. The sound of voices echoed down the corridor. A trolley rattled as it was wheeled past. An orderly dressed in blue was mopping the floor. The sharp smell of disinfectant prickled my nostrils.

As we waited for the lift, Marion said, 'Rebecca's coming off the critical list. They'll be moving her out of Intensive Care in a day or so.'

I could tell from her face and the tone of her voice that this wasn't such good news as it sounded.

'That's because she's breathing without a ventilator,' she explained, 'but she's still deeply unconscious.'

When we were sitting over our cups of tea, I said, 'The Master asked me to remind you that you're very welcome to stay in a college guest room for as long as you want. Why don't you do that? I'm sure you could do with a good night's sleep. You could have an evening meal in college, too.'

'It's very kind of you, but ...'

I knew why she was reluctant. It would be a further indication that she was in for the long haul with no immediate prospect of Rebecca gaining consciousness. The crisis had changed into something less urgent, but in its uncertainty, just as terrible.

I leaned forward and put my hand on her arm. 'Promise me you'll think about it.'

'Yes, I will, I promise I will. Now tell me how *you* are. Have you just come from the maternity hospital?'

I told her the good news about the amniocentesis and the excitement of seeing the ultrasound scan of the baby. A kind of friendship had sprung up between us. She always asked about my pregnancy. It was the only topic from the present day that seemed really to engage her. When I tried to talk about anything else, her eyes grew vague. In return she told me about her own pregnancies and reminisced about Rebecca's childhood. Today, for the first time, it struck me that we were talking about Rebecca as if she were already dead.

I said, 'Any news from the police?'

'They keep coming to the hospital, asking how Rebecca is, how I am. They're very kind, but I don't think they're much further forward. Of course, it would help if they could question Rebecca. But the doctors don't know how much she'll remember or how far she'll be her old self. We'll cross those bridges when we come to them.'

There was nothing I could say. The conversation always ended with the thought that no one wanted to put into words: that Rebecca might never regain consciousness.

I saw Marion to the lift and watched the doors close behind her. By the time I had walked round to the hospital car park, I was chilled to the bone. The car wouldn't start at first, but after a few seconds the engine came grudgingly to life. With the heater on full blast I soon warmed up, but my mood remained bleak as I drove to the university library. It didn't help that a fine drizzle had begun to fall.

It was dark in the car park. Of course, Cambridge isn't actually lit by gaslight these days, but sometimes it feels as though it is. The lanterns on top of the cast-iron posts have long been converted to electricity, but they give off a curiously watery yellow light. The twelve-storey tower of the library loomed up before me, massive, monolithic, portentous. Most of its vertical slits of windows were dark. I stood for a moment looking up at it, feeling dwarfed by its scale. In the long wings on either side, irregular lights showed. It was like the monument of some ancient and mysterious civilization, a ziggurat or a mausoleum big enough to take a king and the whole of his court. This impression vanished as I went up the broad flight of shallow steps and passed through the revolving door into the hall of a busy academic library.

I found a place in the central Reading Room, close to the reference books I needed, and spread out my papers. After a short time, I pushed my chair back and looked around the long narrow room with its high ceiling and long rows of tables lit by desk lamps. As usual during term-time, it was almost full, but the big space soaked up sound. All I could hear was a faint murmur of conversation at the enquiry desk, and the occasional rustle of someone at the next table turning a page. It struck me that the atmosphere was oddly similar to that of the Intensive Care ward.

It had moved me deeply, that room of silent sleepers. I thought again that it was like a legend or a fairy-story. There was something timeless and peaceful about it; there seemed no reason why Rebecca should not lie there for years, as insulated from the world as a child in the womb. There was a tiny snapping noise. I looked down. I had broken the point of my pencil.

I leaned forward and put my head in my hands. It was natural that I should be concerned and disturbed about Rebecca, but was it natural that I should be so very upset? Did I somehow feel that the attack on Rebecca had something to do with the college, and the department for which I was now responsible? Could it really be coincidence that Margaret and Lucy were both dead and Rebecca was lying unconscious in hospital? It could be, I told myself, of course it could. Perhaps it was just an amazing run of bad luck, but what if it wasn't?

I fixed my attention on the page in front of me. Thirty seconds later I realized that I had got to the bottom of it without taking in a single word. My book on Victorian poetry, which I'd laboured on so lovingly for so long, seemed dull and irrelevant. I thought, but what if I was writing a book about *this*, about what's been happening over the last eight months or so? That startling idea seemed to bring things into focus. Well, what would I do? Exactly what I did when I was researching my academic books. I wouldn't take anything for granted, I wouldn't rely on anything anyone told me unless there was evidence to back it up; I'd go right back to the beginning – further probably than anyone else had thought necessary – and work my way forward, casting my net as wide as I could. And all along I'd be weighing the evidence, looking for the connections and patterns, piecing together a picture ...

I went to the periodicals desk and ordered up back copies of *The Times* for April. I soon found what I was looking for. On page four of the edition for 12 April was a small item headed 'Cambridge student dies in fall':

Lucy Hambleton, 28, a postgraduate student from St Etheldreda's College, Cambridge, has died in hospital after an accident in the Derbyshire Dales. Miss Hambleton was found at the bottom of a cliff near Thor's Cave, a site of archaeological interest, by a man out with his dog. She suffered a fractured skull and hypothermia. It is thought that she slipped and fell as she was climbing up to the cave, and that she had lain unconscious in the open all night. Dr Lawrence Osbourne, Warden of St Etheldreda's College, said, 'We are devastated by Lucy's death. She was a very able and popular student, and all our sympathy goes out to her family at this unhappy time. The college hopes to set up a memorial fund in her name.'

I went back into the Reading Room. Just by the enquiry desk there's a bank of telephone directories covering the whole country. I pulled out the one for Derby and District, took it back to my desk, and rifled through the pages until I found the telephone number of The Compleat Angler.

111

Chapter Eleven

'Why are aquariums so strangely fascinating?' Stephen said.

'They really are, aren't they? Perhaps we've got a kind of distant race memory, from before our ancestors left the sea.'

'And of course we start life floating in the womb.'

'Yes: there's a kind of aquarium in here,' I said, placing my hand on the bump under my sweater.

We stopped at a tank where a single fish hung in the water, motionless except for the gentle fluttering movement of its fan-like pectoral fins. The long dorsal fin was streaked with electric blue, and the scales on the upper part of the body were outlined with indigo. Dotted here and there were scales marked like the eye on a peacock's feather.

'What's this?' Stephen said.

I looked at the label below the tank. 'It's a snakehead.'

The broad flat head did look a little snake-like, but the golden eyes seemed to peer out at us in benign enquiry. Stephen put his finger gently on the plate glass of the tank. The fish pressed its mouth against the other side.

'Do you know that Chinese saying?' he asked. 'The fish is the last to know that he lives in water. I wonder what the world looks like from the other side of the glass.'

We strolled on down the dimly lit corridor. We had gone into the aquarium at Matlock Bath to get out of the rain. In here, the only sound was that of the gentle bubbling of air, like the throb of a heartbeat, being fed into the tanks to aerate the water. It was indeed a bit like being back in the womb, I thought.

We passed a tank of red-eared terrapins clambering over one another under a sun-lamp. In the next tank a sad-looking soft-shelled turtle was half-buried in the gravel at the bottom. Outside, the thermal pool, which had once soothed the rheumatic pains of visitors to this little spa town, was full of large carp; black, ivory, gold, coral-coloured; some dappled, some elegantly all of a piece.

The carp moved expectantly towards us. We bought handfuls of pellets from a machine and leaned over the rail, watching the churning water and the flurry of fish as they lunged for the food.

' "Nature red in tooth and claw",' I said, aiming a pellet at one of the less successful fish. He caught it and dashed away, pursued by a bigger fish.

'Yep. The survival of the fittest,' Stephen said. 'Food and sex. That's all they're interested in.'

'And shelter, perhaps,' I said, thinking of the soft-shelled turtle in his gravel. I tossed in the last few pellets.

We went out into the main street. Through the sound of the traffic, I caught the faint roar of the River Derwent as it went tumbling down the valley, turgid with flood water. The rain was now little more than a mist that clung to the sides of the steep valley. The granite cliffs, crowded with trees, and little cable-cars spanning the ravine gave Matlock Bath an alpine air. With its fish and chip shops, ice-cream kiosks and amusement arcades, it was like a faded seaside town picked up and set down in the middle of the Derbyshire Dales. On this cold November day it had a melancholy, raffish out-of-season charm that I'd always enjoyed. I'd been here often with Simon. I hadn't told Stephen that. It was only forty minutes drive from Sheffield and had been one of our favourite places when we'd first met.

'Are you all right?' Stephen asked.

'Just cold.'

113

He took one of my hands in both of his and rubbed it. 'You need a cup of coffee,' he decided.

We went into a café and settled ourselves down by the window.

When the waitress had served us, Stephen said, 'Were there any doubts at the time about Lucy's death being accidental?'

I shook my head. 'I'm sure there weren't.'

Stephen began drawing on the steamed-up window with the end of his coffee spoon.

'What was she like?' he asked.

I shrugged. 'I hardly knew her. The impression I got was that she was lively, sociable, confident. Sporty. She played in the college netball team. So did Rebecca. I looked up her file in the registry yesterday. That must have been how they knew each other.'

'You said she was older than the usual postgraduate.'

'Twenty-eight. She hadn't come straight from her first degree. That's not uncommon these days. It's so difficult to get funding. She'd managed to get a British Academy grant. No mean achievement. She was very bright, very able, no doubt about that.'

'Then one false step and it's all over.' He added a line to the drawing on the window and sat back to consider the effect.

'As it was for Margaret,' I reminded him. I looked at the window. All I could make out was an abstract pattern of straight lines and curves.

'Accidents do happen. So do coincidences.'

'I'd like nothing better than to believe that. I'm hoping that I can find out enough about Lucy's death to put my mind at rest.'

Stephen narrowed his eyes and added a couple of lines to his creation. Was it actually lettering? I couldn't quite make it out.

'I've been thinking, Cass. If the police don't collar someone for this attack soon – the one on Rebecca, I mean – and you'd rather not approach the police formally, you could do worse than have a quiet word with Jim Ferguson. He'd be able to put out some feelers, drop a word in the right ear.'

'Jim—?'

114

Stephen added a couple of dots with the very end of the coffee spoon handle.

'I met him at that conference on crime and the internet – you remember, it was about six months ago – total waste of time. We ended up in the bar and we had a drink together.'

I raised a quizzical eyebrow.

Stephen grinned. 'Well, maybe three or four. Anyway, he's a good bloke. And more to the point, he's a Detective Inspector based at Cambridge nick. I run into him now and then and we keep saying we'll have a drink together.'

'Certainly something to bear in mind,' I said. I tilted my head to see if the writing made better sense from an angle. It didn't.

Stephen stood up and dug in his pocket for some money.

'So what's the plan for this afternoon?'

I got up and put my coat on. 'A visit to Thor's Cave, I think.'

Stephen counted his change out on the table. Then, as if as an afterthought, he leaned over and with his finger drew a heart above the hieroglyphs on the window.

'What *is* that?' I said at last.

He shook his head and smiled mysteriously. With a few sharp strokes he put an arrow through the heart.

As we walked away from the café, I looked back at the window. Now that I was on the other side I could see what Stephen had written in careful yet exuberant Gothic script.

I love Cassandra.

Heading west from Matlock Bath we soon entered a mysterious landscape of narrow lanes and little hidden dales and rivers. We parked at the point where Weag's Bridge crosses the River Manifold, and set off along a metalled path, which had once been the track of the Leek and Manifold Light Railway.

The rain had cleared to leave an intense blue sky. But there was a stiff breeze and, although it was only two o'clock, the sun was low, throwing raking shadows down the hills. The path took us up

115

the valley between the river, which ran gurgling over its stony bed, and a shallow cliff where little trees clung to fissures in the rock. Ivy and moss didn't quite conceal the stratification of the limestone that cut through the cliff in great diagonal lines.

Suddenly a bend in the path brought a huge grey crag into view, disconcertingly close, rising up several hundred feet. Its lower slopes were wooded, but for the last hundred feet or so it was bare limestone, rough-hewn, precipitous. As we rounded the bend a cavernous hole came into view. As far as I knew, I'd never seen it before, but it looked oddly familiar.

We stopped in our tracks.

'My God! Is that Thor's Cave?' Stephen exclaimed. 'Are we really going to climb up to it?'

'That's the idea. I've looked on the Ordnance Survey map. There's a path that goes all the way up.'

Stephen looked doubtful. He let his focus drop to where my bump would have been visible had I not been wearing two jumpers and a fleece. 'It looks awfully steep.'

I said firmly, 'I'll be fine as long as I go slowly. And I'll stop the moment I'm at all tired. Promise.'

Stephen sighed. 'Well, you go first and then if you do slip ...'

'I'll have a soft landing. I'll be very careful. Really. And it's not actually that steep. The path winds about a lot. You can tell that from the map.'

We crossed an old iron bridge over the river and began the ascent. Wet leaves squeaked and squelched underfoot. The feet of earlier walkers had churned the path into thick mud that sucked at our walking boots. We climbed through a grove of hazel trees, graceful and attenuated without their foliage. Close to the path, gnarled and spiky old hawthorn caught at our coats as we passed. My calves began to ache. On and on we toiled. The path got steeper. I planted my hands on my knees as I climbed. Stephen put the palms of his hands in the small of my back to push me up. Several times we stopped so that I could rest.

Near the top, large slabs of rock were set unevenly up the hill to form a rough staircase. As we neared the mouth of the cave, the valley opened out beneath us.

We stood looking down into it, the wind slapping our faces and snatching at our clothes. The river and the path wound round another smaller crag on the other side before disappearing into a fold of the dale. Beyond that I could see the tiny white square of a farmhouse, and beyond that the scattered buildings of a village. The vast airy space seemed to have something tangible about it, as though it had a density greater than normal air. I imagined leaning out and gliding as effortlessly as a bird, high above the valley, borne up by the wind. I felt the first nauseous stirrings of vertigo and pulled my eyes away from the panorama.

We turned to look up at the cave. Once again, I had the feeling that I had seen it – or something very like it – before. Thor's Cave. No doubt the name was a nineteenth century invention, but this did seem a fitting home for the god of thunder and rain. Its mouth was guarded by a sloping outcrop of rock that offered few footholds. Ribbed walls rose up to form the shape of a Gothic arch about twenty feet high. A long fissure in the limestone let in a shaft of slanting light that made the cave look like a primitive cathedral hewn out of rock. After a few yards the passage curved and disappeared into darkness.

'I've got to explore this,' said Stephen.

He felt in the pocket of his fleece and took out a pencil torch.

I looked at the steep, irregular slope of rock. It was shiny and slick with water.

'I'll wait here,' I said.

Stephen clambered up into the cave and disappeared round the bend.

I sat down on a ledge in the rock. Before me was a short, steep, grassy slope, which ended in a cliff after about fifteen feet. I could see the spindly tops of trees that had managed to get a foothold in the shallow soil lower down. Far below, two walkers in bright orange cagoules came into sight. I watched them moving along the path until they reached the point where it disappeared again. My eyes began to water in the wind, and I wiped some tears away with the back of my hand.

I had read in the guidebook that Palaeolithic and Mesolithic hunters had used the cave as a base from which to hunt reindeer, woolly rhinoceros and the mammoth. Archaeological digs had uncovered pottery, whetstones, querns and arrowheads dating back thousands of years, along with the bones of bears, deer, wolves and polecats. I looked out over the dale, thinking about the people who had also sat here all those years ago, scanning the horizon for game. Probably the landscape had not looked very different then: more wooded, perhaps a little wilder, but essentially the same.

Stephen seemed to have been gone a long time. I looked round at the entrance to the cave. And suddenly I knew where I had seen it before; not in real life, but in a painting. That was why I had been confused. It was one of those sinister apocalyptic pictures by John Martin. I'd seen it in the Victoria and Albert, and I'd especially noticed it because the subject was from *Paradise Lost*. A monstrous tunnel carved out of a rock face leading to Hell ... but no, it was worse than that: it was the highway by which Sin and Death came into the world after the Fall.

I shivered. The sun was hidden behind a band of grey cloud. Without its thin warmth, the day was bleaker. My feet were getting numb. I called Stephen's name. There was no reply, but when I called again, I was answered by an indecipherable sound from deep in the cave. A few minutes later, I heard the sound of his boots on the rocky floor of the cave, then a yelp and a thud.

'Stephen! Are you all right?'

'I think so, yes.'

There was a scuffling. He edged gingerly round the bend in the cave.

'I put my foot into a big hole and went down up to my knee.'

He slithered down the rock face and landed with a thump beside me.

118

'It would be easy to have an accident here,' he said. 'The rocks have been worn smooth by people climbing up into the cave, and if they were wet as well, and the light was beginning to go ...'

'And if you hit your head against one of these projecting ledges ...'

I could see it all: the carelessly placed boot, a skid, a cry, arms whirling, the crack of bone on rock, a limp body rolling over and over, turning faster and faster. The thud of impact as it hit the trunk of a tree. Then silence settling again over the valley, and night descending. There was nothing now to fear from bears and wolves, but death was still here in the darkness and the cold.

'I hope she didn't regain consciousness,' I said.

Had the cold and dark been the only things to fear on that night? I wondered. I saw a shadowy figure follow Lucy up the steep path to the cave – a friendly greeting, a conversation, perhaps, then a violent shove.

'But who would want her dead?' I said, thinking aloud.

'How about Malcolm? Or, better still, Margaret?'

'No, oh no.' I stared at him.

'You said yourself that she wouldn't have wanted her affair with Lucy made public. Well, suppose she had tried to break things off and Lucy wasn't having any of it.'

Fragments of Lucy's last letter to Margaret came back to me. *I can't stand this concealment any longer ... it's too painful to go on like this ... I want to sweep all that aside and come out into the open ...*

'What if Margaret drove up to Derbyshire to have it out with Lucy?' Stephen continued. 'Malcolm is away on business. No one knows she's here. Margaret and Lucy go for a walk. They argue. Lucy threatens to expose Margaret. Everything that Margaret holds dear is threatened: her marriage, her job, her reputation. She sees red. One shove and it's over.'

'But how could she be sure that it would be enough to kill her? And, in fact, it *didn't* kill her, or at least, not straightaway. She died later in hospital.'

119

'Margaret doesn't think that far ahead. She just sees that it looks like a long way down. She acts on impulse. Then she panics and drives back to Cambridge. It's a terrible jolt when she learns that Lucy has been found alive, but then she dies and Margaret is in the clear after all. Plausible?'

'Absolute tosh. In all the years I worked with Margaret, I never once saw her lose her temper. She just wasn't an impulsive person.'

'She was impulsive enough to fall in love with Lucy..'

'Well, OK, but that's hardly the same thing. And if she'd murdered Lucy, would she have kept her letters? Surely not.'

'You do have a point there,' Stephen admitted.

In the heat of our discussion we hadn't noticed the time passing. Now I realized that the air had taken on the grainy texture that means it will soon be getting dark. I looked down into the valley. The other walkers had gone. There was no one in sight.

'We'd better go,' I said.

Stephen stood up.

'Where exactly was Lucy found?' he asked.

'I think her fall was broken by some trees, so I suppose it must have been down there.'

He took a step or two further forward for a better view.

And that was when it happened. He put his foot down on a stone hidden by the grass and turned his ankle. He swayed sideways. I was just getting to my feet and I put out my hands instinctively to break his fall. He was teetering, trying to get his balance. He reached out to grab my coat. His eyes met mine. Time seemed to stop for a moment, and in that space it was as if I could see the thoughts going through his mind. The baby! I mustn't ... I wasn't sure if it was my thought or his. I took a step backwards. At the same moment he jerked his hand away. Then he was down, rolling down the slope, scrabbling at the grass as he went, pulling out huge muddy handfuls.

I watched in helpless horror as Stephen went over the cliff.

Chapter Twelve

DEATH CLIFF CLAIMS SECOND VICTIM

I read the headline aloud.

'Reports of my death have been greatly exaggerated,' Stephen said sourly.

'They don't actually say that you're dead,' I pointed out. 'Just that you are a victim. Now where was I? Oh yes. "Cambridge solicitor, Stephen Newley, 41, a partner in the firm of Callow, Newley and Loomis, was lucky to escape with his life when he lost his footing walking in the Derbyshire Dales and fell over the cliff that claimed the life of Cambridge postgraduate, Lucy Hambleton, earlier this year. He suffered multiple injuries—" '

'Multiple injuries!'

'Well, I suppose cuts and bruises, a cracked rib, a sprained ankle and mild concussion could be described as multiple.'

'But it makes me sound as if I'm at death's door!'

'Let's see. How does it go on. . . ? "His heavily pregnant girl-friend, Cassandra James, 40" – bloody cheek! Can't they get anything right? – "scrambled down the mountainside to summon help. Mrs Vickery, landlady of The Compleat Angler, where the couple were staying, said, 'Thor's Cave is very picturesque, but the path up to the cave is very steep, and it's slippery when it's been raining. People don't realize how dangerous it is' . . ." blah, blah, blah.'

I dropped the *Cambridge Evening News* on the bed. It slithered onto the floor, startling Bill Bailey who was curled up at the bottom of the bed.

'How did they get hold of the story anyway?' Stephen wondered.

'Some enterprising stringer hanging around Derby General Hospital, I expect. The article was right about one thing. You *were* lucky. *We* were lucky.'

'I know. It doesn't bear thinking about. Still can't believe I was so stupid.' Stephen closed his eyes.

I watched his face. We hadn't talked much about the accident. It was as though we didn't want to make the horror of what had nearly happened more real by discussing it. Those moments on the hillside after he had vanished over the edge of the cliff had been the most terrible of my life. There had been a crashing and a tearing sound. Then absolute silence had settled over the valley. I was still standing there, frozen to the spot, when I heard Stephen faintly calling. His fall had been broken by a tree. I had made my way slowly down the hillside, willing myself to keep calm for the sake of the baby, going down the steepest parts on my backside so as not to risk falling. Near the bottom I had met two mountain bikers on a rough track. One of them had gone for help, while the other had stayed with me. Stephen had only been in hospital overnight. We had stayed at The Compleat Angler for an extra night to rest, then I had driven the Audi very slowly back to Cambridge on the Monday, with Stephen in the passenger seat, angled as far back as it would go. He was installed in my small spare bedroom on the ground floor of the Old Granary. It was Tuesday evening now.

Stephen opened his eyes and smiled at me. 'One thing,' he said. 'I won't be short of things to read.'

It was true. There wasn't a room in the house that wasn't full of books. Even in here where the bed took up half the space, I had a makeshift bookcase of bricks and planks. This was where the light reading was kept. Stephen had only to stretch out a hand to have a row of classic green Penguin crime novels at his disposal: Nicholas Blake, Josephine Tey, Ngiao Marsh.

'When I'm on my feet again, I'm going to make you some proper bookshelves and I won't take no for an answer.' He gave a yawn that turned into a grimace. 'Do you know, the worst thing isn't the pain – though that's bad enough – but the blasted itching under this dressing on my chest. It's driving me crazy.'

I heard the sound of a car draw up outside. I looked at my watch. 'Seven o'clock. I suppose it's the doctor. He's a bit early.'

The bell rang.

I went over to the window and looked out. The visitor had set off the security lights, but they were standing too near the front door for me to see anything except the back of a cream raincoat.

'It doesn't look like him.'

'Don't take the chain off until you've seen who it is,' Stephen said.

I went into the hall and opened the door a crack.

The person I saw outside, waiting in the rain, was Jane Pennyfeather.

'Cassandra! Are you all right?' Her face was pale in the powerful light.

'Yes, yes, I'm OK.'

'I've come to see Stephen. I'm acting as a locum for Dr Ferris.'

I took the chain off the door. The net of tiny raindrops on her fair hair caught the light as she came in. The chill of the evening came with her, clinging like an aura.

'He's in here,' I said. I opened the spare room door to display Stephen lying on the bed with his blue-and-white pyjama jacket open over his bandaged ribs. There was a bandage round his head from which his hair was sticking up in tufts. His face was scratched where the branches of the tree had caught him. He had a plaster on one cheek, and one of his hands, sore from his efforts to break his fall, was still bandaged.

123

'Jane, this is Stephen. Stephen, this is Jane Pennyfeather.'

'I know I look like something from *The Curse of the Mummy's Tomb*,' he said, 'but it's most cuts and bruises.'

'Thank goodness for that,' she said.

'Take your coat off. Have a cup of tea.'

'Thanks. Yes, I'd like that.'

I helped her off with her coat. Under it she was dressed in a smart red sweater, calf-length navy skirt and matching court shoes. I guessed that she had come straight from evening surgery. When I came back with the tray of tea, she was sitting on the bed beside Stephen, looking into his eyes with a little torch.

'You'll live,' I heard her say. 'But I expect those ribs are still pretty painful, aren't they?'

'I'll say,' Stephen said with feeling. 'It's particularly bad when I'm trying to get to sleep.'

'I'll give you a painkilling injection before I go. That should help.'

I poured out the tea. As soon as I sat down, Bill Bailey jumped off the bed onto my knees, throwing a suspicious glance at Jane. He didn't like strangers coming to the house.

'How's Malcolm?' I asked.

'Not bad, all things considered. He still misses Margaret terribly, of course, but he's coping.'

She sipped her tea in silence. Stephen lay back on the pillows with his eyes closed. I stroked Bill Bailey.

Jane said, 'It's not by chance that I'm here this evening. I *am* acting as a locum for the practice, but not actually for Dr Ferris. When I saw the call listed, I asked to come in his place. I just had to find out what was going on, how you were. Especially you, Cassandra, with your pregnancy.'

'It's sweet of you to be so concerned,' I said slowly.

There was a question in my voice. I waited for her to say more, but nothing came. I looked into her face and saw that she was frowning.

'Jane, what's the matter?'

'It's just brought everything back.'

'Brought what back?' Stephen asked.

'Of course, you don't know, do you? Lucy Hambleton was my cousin.'

'Your cousin?' I stared at her. I had never dreamed of there being any connection between them. How could they be cousins? They seemed to be from different generations. It didn't make sense.

I was about to speak. Jane anticipated my question. 'She was the daughter of my mother's younger sister. I was fifteen when she was born. I've always felt protective towards her. She stayed with me when she first came to Cambridge.'

'Ah,' I said, 'I see.'

So Margaret and Lucy had met socially, not just as head of department and student. That made sense.

Jane looked at me, then at Stephen, and back at me. She reached out to Bill Bailey, who drew his head back.

I waited to see what she would say. The silence between us lengthened.

At last she said, 'What were you doing at Thor's Cave? Was that just a coincidence?'

I didn't know what to say. On the face of it, this seemed a ghoulish thing to do, to go visiting the place where one of your students had died. In the end I didn't say anything. I just shook my head.

'You know, don't you?' Jane said.

'About. . . ?'

'About Margaret and Lucy.'

I nodded.

'I thought you probably did, that day in the churchyard after the funeral.'

'No, I didn't know then.' I thought about what she had said that day. 'What you said about Malcolm, that he might be having an affair: that was a kind of smoke-screen, wasn't it? You didn't believe that, did you?'

'Of course not. But I thought that if I said that, you might let something slip about Margaret.'

Stephen was looking baffled.

'What are you talking about?' he asked.

To me it made perfect sense. I said, 'You wanted to know, didn't you, if there were any rumours floating around the college about Margaret and Lucy? But you didn't want to ask outright, because if there weren't, well, you didn't want to start any. The bit about Malcolm: that was just to float the idea that there was something wrong with their marriage, to see if I'd take the bait.'

She nodded. 'When *did* you find out about it?'

I told her how I had found the letters.

Jane heaved a sigh. 'I was afraid she'd kept those. I was worried that Malcolm might come across them. I even had a surreptitious look through her cupboards when I was helping Malcolm sort out her clothes. What did you do with them? Where are they?'

'I burnt them.'

There was a small shock of recognition between us. Without taking her eyes off mine, she slowly nodded.

'Good. Does anyone else know?'

'Only Stephen.'

Jane said, 'I'm glad you did that. Margaret was desperate to keep it a secret – and to protect Malcolm. I haven't told anyone. I hoped I was the only person who knew. You've got no idea what a relief it is to be able to talk now. I've felt so guilty.'

'You? Why?' I was surprised.

'I should have been there in Derbyshire with Lucy. We used to go for a week's walking every year. But this time Ellie got chickenpox a few days before we were due to leave and I didn't feel I could leave her just with her dad. And it was pretty much about then that it all started to go wrong for Lucy.'

126

I remembered that last letter I had read. 'She forced Margaret into a decision?'

Jane nodded. 'She pushed Margaret too hard. But Lucy was like that: impulsive, uncompromising. She always had to go full out for what she wanted. Margaret rang Lucy in Derbyshire to tell her that she had decided to stay with Malcolm. Lucy must have been beside herself. She tried to ring me, but she got my answering machine. I'd been up with Ellie several nights running, and when she finally fell asleep I just switched on the machine and went to bed.'

Her face creased and tears welled up.

'I didn't hear the message until the next morning. She was crying, she said she was going to try and walk the misery out of her system. That was the last time I heard her voice. She went straight out and had that bloody stupid accident, and I was the one who had to break it to Margaret.'

Jane covered her face with her hands. I got up and put my arm round her shoulder. When she removed her hands, her face was wet with tears. I gave her a tissue from the box on the bedside table.

'How did she take it?' Stephen asked.

'Stunned. Almost catatonic with shock. It was lucky that Malcolm was away on business. But when she recovered a bit, she asked me to help. I had a spare key to Lucy's flat. We retrieved Margaret's letters and burnt them. I gave her some tranquilizers to help her through the worst, and when Malcolm came home, she told him she'd got flu.'

'You weren't angry? You didn't feel that she was to blame for Lucy's death?' I asked.

'No-one was to blame really, and I wouldn't have had the heart when she was blaming herself so much. And she felt so guilty for having got involved with Lucy in the first place. She'd never been unfaithful to Malcolm before. Evening after evening we spent together going over and over it. Then when at last she seemed to have come through it . . .' She shook her head.

127

'It's quite a coincidence, isn't it?' said Stephen. 'Lucy and Margaret both dying within a couple of months of each other?' His voice was strained. I looked at him. His face was pale and drawn. I guessed that his ribs were hurting.

'Coincidences do happen,' Jane said. 'I'm sure it wasn't suicide, if that's what you're thinking. Margaret was genuinely on the road to recovery. There wasn't any question of her not being able to cope.'

'She was having problems at work as well.' I said.

'Well, yes, I know she was worried,' she said firmly, 'but I'm sure there was nothing she couldn't handle. Look: when someone dies in the prime of life, it can be hard to accept that it was just a stupid, tragic accident. I've seen this in my patients, they go over and over it, searching for some hidden meaning. I found myself doing exactly the same thing after Lucy died, and again after Margaret died. But you know, things are usually just as they seem.'

She glanced at her watch. 'Oh, Lord, I really must go. Malcolm was keeping an eye on Ellie, but I ought to get home and put her to bed. And Stephen – what am I thinking of? You'd better have your injection, take the edge off that pain.'

She opened her medical case. She swabbed Stephen's arm with surgical spirit, and took out a syringe and a little bottle. I watched her draw the fluid up into the syringe and check that there wasn't any air in it, just like they do on television or in films. Just for a moment, just for a blink of an eye, I saw the scene as if it were a still from a movie, something by Hitchcock perhaps: the syringe held up to the light, the look of frowning concentration on Jane's face, Stephen on the bed with his arm bared. I felt a momentary impulse to lean over and dash the syringe from Jane's hand. The needle was touching Stephen's arm, he was grimacing and looking away. Then it was over. Jane pressed a piece of cotton wool against his arm. She packed away the syringe and the bottle, and closed the case, clicking the locks shut. I was letting my imagination run wild again. Jane was just what I had first taken her to be: level-headed, sympathetic, and no doubt an excellent GP.

128

As I followed her out of the room, something she'd said earlier came back to me.

'Did Margaret say exactly what it was at work that was worrying her?' I asked.

Jane stopped and looked at me. She narrowed her eyes in an effort of recall. 'Now, what did she say? There *was* something, but just a passing comment. I know she was concerned in a general sort of way about – what is it? – the RE something or other?'

'The Research Assessment Exercise.'

'That's it. She was heading for a showdown with someone, and she wasn't much looking forward to it.'

'Was it a colleague she was talking about, do you think? Or could it have been a student?'

'Oh, a colleague. I think she was talking about a man. Can't quite remember why I got that impression.'

From the spare room window I watched Jane's tail lights diminish to pinpricks and then disappear into the night.

Stephen said, 'Do you think she's on the level?'

'Yes, I think so. It all seems to hang together. And I can't help liking her. She seems so decent and straightforward.'

I wondered who Margaret had been dreading confronting and why. If it was a male member of the English Department, it could only be Aiden or Merfyn, unless she had been thinking about Lawrence. That was the most likely thing.

Stephen said, 'Are you quite sure you're doing the right thing?'

I looked at him and saw that he was frowning.

'What do you mean?' I asked, puzzled.

'Keeping Malcolm in the dark about this, covering up Margaret's affair.'

I felt a surge of irritation. 'Why are you bringing this up again? I thought we'd finished with all that.'

'It didn't seem so bad when it was just between the two of us and we thought no-one else knew.'

'But what's the point of causing him unnecessary pain?'

'So we smooth everything over, conspire to protect him? Aren't we treating him like a child? It just sticks in my gullet,' he went on, 'the thought of the poor guy mourning for his perfect marriage, when we know otherwise.'

I remembered the flash of complicity between Jane and me. All the same, I was nettled by Stephen's accusation.

'Well, OK, so it wasn't perfect. But what relationship is? They had a lot of good years together and don't forget, Margaret had decided to stay with him. She *did* love him. She didn't want to hurt him by telling him about what happened with Lucy. Why sour his memory of her now when it's not absolutely necessary?'

'What might you see fit to conceal from me for my own good?'

'So that's what this is all about!'

I glared at him. He glared back. The telephone rang.

Fuming, I walked into the kitchen and snatched up the receiver.

'Hello,' I snapped.

'Cassandra, this is Lawrence. I hope you are feeling better?'

I made an effort to compose myself. 'Yes, I am, thank you very much, Lawrence. I'll be back in college in the morning.'

'And Stephen, improving I trust?'

'Very much so.'

'Splendid,' he said urbanely. 'Good news all round then. I'm ringing to let you know that Rebecca is showing signs of regaining consciousness.'

130

Chapter Thirteen

'Good news, isn't it, Dr James? About Rebecca?' John was beaming all over his face.

I realized that I was, too. I had the feeling of wellbeing that one has on a sunny day. It was only since Lawrence's phonecall the evening before that I had understood how much I had been steeling myself against the possibility that Rebecca might never recover. Perhaps, I thought, she might soon be able to throw light on who had attacked her and why. Things were starting to move at last.

'And Mr Newley? Is he on the mend?'

I smiled. The porters always know everything.

'He's fine. I know he's feeling better because he got his secretary to bring him some work.'

'And you yourself, are you well? My eldest is expecting her third in January.' John said, too polite to refer directly to my pregnancy.

'Grand, thanks. And all the better for this news,' I said.

Even the most voluminous jumper could not disguise my swelling figure. What's that old saying: love and a cold cannot be hid? Well, pregnancy is a by-product of love, I suppose. No point in imagining it was not public knowledge. I was growing used to acquaintances, and even perfect strangers, making detailed enquires about the state of my health, handing out advice – and occasionally even wanting to pat my belly! Older men were avun-cular, older women indulgent. Childless women of my own age looked thoughtful.

'How is your daughter?' I asked.

'Oh, doing nicely, thank you,' replied John.

Still smiling, I headed for the staff pigeonholes to collect my post. Turning round the corner into the Senior Common Room, I bumped straight into Aiden who was coming the other way. As he grabbed my arms to steady me, the sheaf of papers he had been carrying flew up into the air and fluttered down around us.

'Oh, Lord. I'm so sorry, Aiden. I wasn't looking where I was going,' I said.

'Are you all right?' His hands were still on my arms, and he was looking into my eyes. One of his pupils was an irregular shape, spilling over into the green of the iris. I hadn't been this close to him since the debacle amongst the books in Smith's. I wondered if he was thinking of that, too. The moment stretched out. Then he blinked and released me.

'We can't go on meeting like this, Cassandra,' he murmured. 'People will start talking. No, no, don't worry,' – as I started to bend down – 'I'll do that.'

He squatted down and began gathering the papers up.

'I was thinking about Rebecca,' I said. 'You've heard the news?'

'Yes, thank God for that.'

I leant against the table by the pigeonholes and watched him. I remembered that he still hadn't given me any details of what he was working on, and in all the worry over Rebecca I hadn't got round to chasing him up.

'I still don't have your research plan, Aiden.'

He paused. His back was towards me so I couldn't see his face, but he smoothed back his thinning hair.

'Ah, yes, sorry. I'll make that a priority.'

'What *are* you working on at the moment?'

'Oh, it's still Romanticism. I'm at the ideas stage.'

132

'Perhaps we can have a chat about it sometime?'

'Sure. Not now though, I'm seeing a student.'

With one fluid movement he stood up without touching his hands on the ground. I was envious: I hadn't been able to do that even when I wasn't pregnant.

It wasn't until he was halfway down the corridor that I saw he had missed one of his papers. I stooped awkwardly and picked it up.

'Aiden!'

When he turned, I waved the paper at him in explanation. As he walked back towards me, I glanced down at it. My eye was caught by a name scrawled in a bold hand – Annabelle Fairchild. The name rang a bell.

Aiden stretched out his hand, looking at the paper as he did so. I was surprised to see him blush right up to his hairline. I hadn't the slightest idea what was the matter, but embarrassment is infectious and I felt my own face grow hot. He snatched the sheet of paper from my hand, turned on his heels, and went striding off.

Rebecca had been moved out of Intensive Care into a small side room off one of the medical wards. Marion was sitting by her bed. She looked up when the ward sister showed me in. The shadows under her eyes like bruises were still there, but the air of weary stoicism had gone and her face was alight with hope.

She got up and came towards me. Clutching the flowers I had brought in one arm, I put the other around her. She hugged me.

'Oh Cassandra,' was all she could say.

The smiling ward sister took the flowers and said, 'Perhaps you could take Marion down to the café and persuade her to have some lunch. She hasn't had a break for hours.'

'I didn't want to miss anything,' she explained as we went down in the lift. 'She actually spoke to me earlier on.'

We settled ourselves in the café.

'It started yesterday afternoon,' Marion said. 'I was sitting doing

133

some knitting when I thought I saw a movement out of the corner of my eye. I was beginning to think I'd imagined it when I saw it again. Her hand was actually twitching! I was so excited. I went running for the nurse and she got the doctor. He said not to get my hopes up. It might be just a reflex. But it was more than that. He was there standing by the bed with me when she opened her eyes, looked straight at me and said "Mum".'

There was a shrill, ear-splitting sound. The fire alarm had gone off. The other people in the café were looking around, some were covering their ears. The noise was so loud and strident that it was impossible to talk, impossible almost to think. Uncertainly we got to our feet. The catering staff were emerging from behind the counter, customers were beginning to move towards the exit. Still the alarm continued, intense, vibrating, almost palpable.

I felt my baby jerk. I put a protective hand on my belly, and with the other hand snatched up my coat and bag.

'Come on,' I yelled to Marion.

She followed me like an automaton. We joined the throng heading towards the main exit. We had almost reached it when, as suddenly as it had begun, the noise ceased. The aftershock was still ringing in my ears when the alarm began again. Still, the brief interruption was enough to break Marion's trance. She clutched my arm, her face distorted with anxiety.

'Rebecca!' she said and turned back into the hospital.

Her path was blocked by a bulky security man in a navy sweater.

'I'm afraid you can't go back in, madam.'

'But my daughter, she's in there!'

'I'm sorry, madam.'

She tried to brush past him, but he stretched out his arm to bar the way.

I grabbed her hand and held it tight.

'Of course he can't let you back in, Marion. The nurses will look after Rebecca. They'll know what to do. You'd just be in their way.'

'That's right, madam. Now you go with this lady,' he said to

Marion. 'Ten to one it's a false alarm and you'll be able to come back again in a bit.'

Her hand relaxed in mine and I led her onto the forecourt. The throng of people pressing out of the entrance pushed us into the car park. When we reached a part that was less crowded, we turned and looked back at the hospital. Only then did I release Marion's hand.

I scanned the façade of the hospital for fire or smoke. I could see nothing. There was a distant undulating noise that grew more insistent. Two fire engines swept up. Around us, little knots of people were talking animatedly or lighting up cigarettes. I glanced at my watch. It was only three o'clock, but already dusk was in the air. The sky was as grey as stone and a mean little drizzle was falling. A dull ache was spreading across my lower back. Marion shivered.

'You're not wearing a coat,' I said. 'I think I've got an old one in the car. Come on, we might as well get in it. We'll be warmer and I need to sit down. We'll be able to see when people start going back in.'

I settled her in the passenger seat and draped the coat around her shoulders. All the fight had been knocked out of her. She sat and stared at the entrance to the hospital, like a dog waiting for its master. I sat in silence, too. I told myself that fire alarms went off all the time: at least they did in St Etheldreda's, where we found ourselves assembling on the lawn at least once a month. This was probably a false alarm, as the security guard had said, and if not, well, the hospital was a huge place. Rebecca was probably a long way from the fire, and no doubt there were procedures for moving the patients with the minimum of fuss. On and on went the sensible voice in my head, but all the time anxiety was spreading through me like a dark, viscous fluid.

After about an hour, there was a stirring near the entrance. The crowd flowed towards the door like iron filings pulled by a magnet. We joined it.

When we got out of the lift on the fifth floor, everything looked

135

as it had earlier in the day. Marion headed towards the ward. It seemed to me that there *was* something different after all. I stopped and sniffed the air, but it was just the familiar smell of disinfectant. Then I caught it again, the faintest whiff of something unpleasantly acrid.

Marion had almost reached the swing doors into the ward. As she reached to push them open, they opened outwards and the ward sister came out. She placed her hand on Marion's arm. The look of compassion on her face sent a chill through me. Marion turned away abruptly, shaking her head and raising her hands in denial. As I moved towards her I saw the blood drain from her face. Her eyes rolled up, her knees buckled. The sister caught her deftly under the arms and lowered her gently to the floor.

Stephen was propped up on the bed wearing his reading glasses. His eyes remained on the document he was reading.

He said absently, 'Before I forget, your mother rang. She wanted to know how you are. We had quite a chat.'

All the misery I felt over Rebecca – and perhaps some left over from Margaret, too – came welling up. I just stood there in the doorway with hot tears rolling down my cheeks.

'Rebecca,' I managed to say.

Stephen looked up. He took his glasses off. 'Oh, no. She's not . . .'

I nodded. I was too choked up to speak.

'Oh, darling. Come here.' He patted the bed.

I sat down beside him and he held my hand tightly. Still the tears came. My shoulders started shaking. I caught my breath in gulps. I pulled a sheaf of paper tissues out of the box by the bed. When the worst was over I turned towards Stephen and rested my cheek on his, breathing in his familiar, reassuring smell, He rubbed his face against mine.

'I feel useless,' he said. 'I wish I could give you a great big hug.'

At last I managed to say, 'Somehow it's even worse than with

Margaret. Rebecca was so young, and just when she seemed to be turning the corner.'

I thought of her saying 'Hello, Mum', and another wave of emotion engulfed me.

Stephen said, 'How about a drink?'

I scrubbed my face with tissues. 'But what about the baby? And your painkillers?'

'One glass won't hurt either of us. Where's the key to the wine cellar?'

'Right here.'

I took a copy of *The Lost Weekend* off the top shelf of the makeshift bookcase and opened it. It was hollow. I tipped a key out onto my hand.

'Interesting sense of humour the previous owner had. Give me a hand,' said Stephen.

I put my shoulder under his arm and helped him to manoeuvre his way into the kitchen. He lowered himself carefully into a chair at the kitchen table.

The wine cellar was actually just a large cavity in the kitchen wall where once there had been a chimney. It was blocked off by a shallow cupboard that could be swung back like a door and screwed in place by a key. It did actually contain some bottles of wine – half a dozen that Stephen had given me as a 'not altogether disinterested' present – but I had regarded it as an amusing piece of whimsy, until I had thought of a more important use to which it could be put.

'What else do you keep in there?' Stephen said.

'Apart from wine? Oh, anything that's worth stealing. You hear horror stories about burglars taking not only the computer but the disks as well, so I've got into the habit of keeping backup disks in there, too. And things like my building society passbook. When I'm away my laptop goes in there, as well.'

I opened a bottle and poured out two glasses.

'We'd better have something to eat with it,' he said.

'I don't think I could. I'll cook you something, though.'

'You haven't had anything since lunch, have you? You must have something. Why don't you make some scrambled eggs?'

As I whisked eggs into a bowl I told him what had happened at the hospital.

'The nurses were only away from her for fifteen minutes while they were moving another patient. When they came to move her, she was dead.'

'And there really *was* a fire?'

I nodded. 'I don't think it could have been a very serious one, or we wouldn't have been allowed back in so soon.'

'You know, it was always on the cards that she wouldn't recover. Head injuries are very unpredictable things.'

'Two pieces of toast?'

'Yes, thanks.'

'Look Stephen, suppose someone took advantage of the fire alarm, or perhaps they set if off themselves as a distraction and then . . .'

'And then what? What could they have done?'

'I don't know, injected her with something?' I reached up and took a pan off a hook on the wall.

'With what? Would *you* know what to do, and how to get hold of a syringe?'

'No, of course not. I bet I could bloody well find out, though!'

'It would take some nerve, and why did they wait until now? It's been over a month since the accident.'

'Yes, but until yesterday she was in Intensive Care. Don't you see? No-one could have got to her in there. She was under obser-vation all the time *and* she was all wired up. No: yesterday would have been the first real opportunity. And the other thing – she was beginning to show signs of recovery. Perhaps she would have been able to tell the police about the attack.'

'Well, there's bound to be a post-mortem. Because whichever way you slice it, this'll be a murder inquiry. Even if she wasn't murdered today, it'll still be murder if she died as a result of the original attack. If they want to charge someone with that in due course, they'll need evidence of the cause of death. And if her doctors thought she'd turned the corner and they weren't expecting her to die, they'll want to know what happened, too.'

'So maybe they'll find something – apart from the head injury, I mean. But in any case, I think I'm going to have to talk to the Master.'

'Why not go straight to the police?'

'Lawrence first, I think. After all, if there's a chance of all this about Lucy and Margaret coming out, forewarned is forearmed. It'll be much worse if he hears it from someone else.'

I put two plates of scrambled eggs on the table and sat down opposite Stephen. I was ravenous. Stephen picked up his fork carefully.

I said, 'I'd better cut that up for you.'

'Oh, good, toast soldiers. Haven't had those since I was about five. Remind me exactly what Rebecca said to you when she lost her temper.'

As I dealt with the toast, I cast my mind back. 'She said that Lucy would still be alive if she hadn't come to St Etheldreda's.'

'You know, Cass, I do think what happened to Lucy was an accident.' He made a gesture to indicate his injuries, and winced at the effort.

'So do I, really.' I turned my attention to my own plate. 'But this with Rebecca . . . Someone *did* attack her in the first place. No doubt about that.'

'I'll tell you who would be able to find their way into Addenbrooke's carrying a syringe,' Stephen said suddenly. 'Who better than a doctor? What about Jane?'

'Jane!' I stared at him, a forkful of scrambled egg halfway to my mouth. I thought of Jane as she had been the evening before, holding up the syringe, her thoughtful expression as she injected Stephen.

'Has she been here today?' I asked.

'No. The district nurse came this time.'

I came to my senses. 'No, it's ridiculous. For one thing, she'd be afraid of being recognized.'

'Not necessarily. I don't suppose GPs actually meet consultants and nurses all that often. When they refer patients, they do it via a letter, don't they? And she'd know what to inject into Rebecca and how to get hold of it.'

'No, stop! Stop!' I buried my face in my hands. 'What possible reason could she have for doing that? You can't really think that!'

'As a matter of fact, I don't. But without evidence of any kind, one theory is as good as another. I think you're right. It's best to go to the police. Probably they'll find that most of your department, including the students, will have been in lectures or tutorials, or whatever, won't they? That'll put your mind at rest.'

'Well, actually, there isn't any teaching on Wednesday afternoons. That's to allow students to play sport. I suppose some of them do, but I bet a lot of them go shopping or have sex or simply lie on their beds listening to the Manic Street Preachers.'

'All the more reason for letting the police look into their alibis.'

'They don't always get their man, or woman, do they?'

'Oh, I don't know. The clear-up rate for murder is pretty good. The original police theory is still the most likely. Rebecca is in the wrong place at the wrong time, falls in the way of some warped bastard and then dies of her injuries a few weeks later. But if there is a chance that it isn't that, they need to know everything that you know.'

Chapter Fourteen

'I know about Margaret's relationship with Lucy Hambleton. Margaret had the good sense to come and see me shortly before Lucy Hambleton's death. She had decided to end the relationship and was fearful of Lucy's response. She wanted me to have prior warning.'

After all my agonizing about whether to tell Lawrence, I couldn't believe that he had known all along. Margaret must have been expecting a very rough ride with Lucy if she'd been driven to confide in Lawrence.

'Lucy's death appeared to have put an end to the matter,' he continued. 'And now you tell me that Margaret had kept her letters. Sheer folly quite beyond belief! However, from what you say, it's most unlikely that anyone else knows of them. I can rely on you to be discreet, I know that, Cassandra.'

Lawrence's face was pinched, his skin lined and colourless. In the window behind him the leafless branches formed an irregular tracery through which a dull unemphatic light seeped into the room.

'But the police. . . ?'

Lawrence's eyes met mine and slid away. He picked up his silver propelling pencil and tapped it softly on the desk.

'I don't see any necessity to inform the police. The fewer people who know about this, the better. One can't rely on anyone's discretion these days. Just one phonecall to the tabloid press, that's all it would take. In any case, what possible connection can there be with Rebecca's death?'

'Wouldn't it be better to let the police decide that?'

Lawrence got up and pushed back his chair. He stepped back and leant against the windowsill.

'I don't think you quite appreciate the complexity of the situation, Cassandra. I have to consider the welfare of the college as a whole. The next year or so will be crucial to our long-term future. We simply can't afford this kind of unwelcome publicity. Applications to your own department in particular are likely to be affected if that relationship becomes common knowledge.'

'Are you threatening me, Lawrence?'

'Far from it,' he said calmly. 'Simply pointing out that with the future of yourself and your colleagues hanging in the balance, you would be ill-advised to rock the boat – if I may mix my metaphors. Of course, I would be the first to go to the police if I felt there was any substance to your concerns, but Rebecca died of injuries sustained outside the college and its grounds, and I really can't believe that there is any connection with the unfortunate business of Margaret and Lucy Hambleton. I don't suppose we'll be able to keep the police out of college altogether, but I don't want to give them any reasons to linger. Is that understood?'

'I understand.'

Lawrence ignored the edge of irony in my voice. He returned to his seat. I almost expected that if I looked behind the big mahogany desk, I would see that his small feet in their well-polished shoes didn't quite touch the floor. It struck me that he was out of scale, diminished by these grand surroundings.

He put his elbows on the table and made a steeple with his hands. 'I know how much Rebecca's death must have upset you, Cassandra.' His voice had softened in a way I hadn't heard before. 'Losing a student is always very hard. And in your condition it's natural that you should overreact a little.'

142

'I can't believe I'm hearing this! A student is *dead*, Lawrence! And I'm pregnant, not feeble-minded.'

'We'll do everything that's proper,' he went on. 'A memorial service certainly and some form of commemoration: a tree-planting, perhaps. But it is time for other matters to claim our attention. Life must go on: a cliché, but true for all that, like so many clichés.'

Oh, you pompous bastard, I thought.

'I don't need to remind you that your RAE submissions must be sorted out before you go on maternity leave. I hope that is well in hand.'

It wasn't, of course. Over the last few weeks, worry about Rebecca had pushed it to the back of my mind.

I thought the interview was at an end, but Lawrence had one more shot in his magazine. As I got to my feet, he said, 'As you know, the college is getting more and more strapped for cash. Belts will have to be tightened all round. I can't guarantee that I would, after all, be able to redeploy Cathy in the event of our having to close your department.'

'You told me she'd be all right! I promised her!'

He shrugged. 'I'm afraid you had no authority to make any such promise.'

I walked back to my office along corridors that were almost deserted. The combination of fluorescent lighting and a dying winter's day created an inexpressibly dreary atmosphere.

Bastard, bastard, bastard, I thought. As I slumped in the chair at my desk, a hairgrip slipped down inside my shirt. A loop of hair uncoiled itself and slithered down my back. Cursing, I retrieved the hairgrip and skewered it back into place. My face ached with the effort of holding back the tears of mortification and anger that were pushing to the surface. I felt tired and heavy and defeated.

I knew I should be fighting back, but it was all too much: Rebecca's death, the struggle to keep the department open, Stephen's accident, my pregnancy. There was Merfyn, too: I was still waiting for him to come up with the next chapters of his book. I just wanted to run away or barricade myself behind a pile of books and read, read, read. I looked around for something to distract me. My eye was caught by the Russian box on my desk. The delicately painted face of the Snow Queen looked up at me.

She reminded me of someone. I looked more closely. How beautiful she was with her white-blonde hair and her serpentine figure swathed in pale fur. I tried to remember the story. I had a copy of *Hans Christian Andersen's Fairy Tales* somewhere. I got up and searched the bookshelves. Yes, there it was: a cheap paperback reprint that I'd picked up in a remainder shop. I turned the pages and began to read. The story began with a diabolical mirror in which the good appears bad and the bad appears good. It breaks and a splinter of silvered glass pierces little Kay's heart and turns it into ice. I read on. The Snow Queen appeared:

> The snow flake grew and grew, and at last it turned into a complete woman, clad in the finest white gauze, which seemed to be made up of millions of starlike white flakes. She as so beautiful and grand, but of ice – dazzling, gleaming ice – and yet she was alive.

I had just reached the part where she kidnaps Kay and takes him to her palace where everything is made of snow and ice, when the telephone rang. I was so absorbed that it took me a second to come to myself. I reached awkwardly across my desk to answer it and knocked a pile of essays over. With the received in one hand, I grabbed at the essays with the other. I caught a couple, but the rest slithered over the edge and fanned out over the carpet.

Sighing, I put the receiver to my ear, just catching the end of what the person on the other end was saying.

'—Annabelle?' said a light, female voice.

'I'm sorry. There's no Annabelle here. You must have a wrong number.'

144

There was a little gasp followed by a short silence. Then she said, 'No, no. *I'm* Annabelle.'

I heaved a sigh of exasperation. She was talking 'upspeak': the voice goes up at the end of every line and the speaker sounds like someone in an Australian soap opera. My students did it all the time and I hated it.

'OK,' I said. 'We've established that you're Annabelle. Who is it you want to speak to?'

'Umm, Beth.'

'Beth who?'

'You know, I really think I must have a wrong number. So sorry to have bothered you.'

With a bit of clattering the receiver was put down at the other end.

I hung up and sat looking at the telephone. Something about this exchange puzzled me. The name Annabelle sounded familiar, but no face came to mind. Young, certainly, to have picked up that irritating way of speaking, and there had also been a slight drawl that led me to think of one of the more expensive girls' schools from which we occasionally interviewed. It wasn't one of the students in our department, but from elsewhere in the college perhaps?

There was a knock on the door. Cathy put her head round.

'Do you know anyone called Annabelle?' I asked. 'In the college?'

She shook her head. 'Doesn't ring a bell. I'll look through the list, shall I?'

'It's not important.'

'Alison left this for you while you were with the Master.'

She handed me a yellow cardboard folder. I wondered if I should tell her that Lawrence was intending to go back on his word and that she might find herself out of a job. Before I could decide, she had gone back to her own office.

Inside the folder was a sheaf of typewritten pages. The top one read: 'The Heavenly Cloud Now Breaking: Jane Lead's Apocalyptic Writings' by Alison Stirling. I read the first page of the article and skimmed through the rest, reading a paragraph here and there. Jane Lead, it seemed, was an East Anglian poet and mystic, a kind of seventeenth century Julian of Norwich. This wasn't my period and I hadn't heard of Jane Lead, but I was impressed by the elegance and succinctness of the article. If the scholarship was as impeccable as the style, Alison wouldn't have any difficulty in getting this published.

The sight of that article put new life into me. It was the first hopeful thing to happen for weeks.

I thought of what Lawrence had said. The message was clear and I knew he wasn't bluffing. If I went to the police, it would be another nail in the department's coffin. He would be only too glad of another excuse. The thought of doing nothing at all was seductive. After all, there was a possibility, perhaps a strong one, that I was quite wrong in thinking that Rebecca's death had something to do with the college. Didn't I have enough to concentrate on with my own work and the department and my pregnancy? And wasn't it arrogant to think that the police wouldn't be able to sort it out without my help?

But what if they *didn't* sort it out? What if I let this go and Rebecca's killer was never found? How would I feel then? My eye fell on *Hans Christian Andersen's Fairy Tales* lying open on the desk in front of me. It occurred to me that there were times when a splinter of ice in the heart would be a useful thing to have. Deep inside me, something similar was forming: a hard, cold compact ball of sheer bloody-mindedness.

Was I going to allow myself to be bullied by Lawrence? *Was I hell!* Of course, there's more than one way to skin a cat. Or as the New Testament more subtly puts it, *Be as wise as serpents, as innocent as doves.* I've always like that injunction.

I reached for the telephone.

*

It was the evening of the following day when I arrived home to find Jim Ferguson drinking tea with Stephen in the kitchen. He stood up as I came in.

He had very short fair hair and a squarish face with blunt, open features. The deeply incised crow's feet suggested a man who laughed a lot. When Stephen introduced us, Jim held out his hand and looked into my eyes. It was like stepping into a force field. His whole attention was focused on me. I felt an impulse to step back, but was tethered by the warm, dry hand that gripped mine firmly. This was a formidable, intelligent man, and there was something else about him . . .

We sat down and Jim said, 'Stephen's given me an outline, but I'd like to hear it all from you. And I mean all of it.'

'There may be nothing to it,' I said.

'That's right,' he agreed, 'but don't let it worry you. Let me put it this way. When Mrs Smith's neighbour calls us because she hasn't seen Mrs Smith for a while and she doesn't like Mr Smith's explanation of her absence, ninety-nine times out of a hundred Mr Smith was too embarrassed to admit that Mrs Smith had packed her bags and gone home to mother. But there's always the hundredth time. That's when we find Mrs Smith at the bottom of Rutland Water with weights tied to her arms and legs.

'And it's worth hearing the ninety-nine stories for the hundredth one. OK, just let me put my thoughts in order.'

Jim and Stephen heard me out without interrupting.

When I had finished, Jim said thoughtfully, 'I see what you mean. Nothing much you can put your finger on, is there? But it's suggestive all the same. How many people would you say there are in your department, staff and students included?'

'Including postgraduates? Forty-five? Fifty? It's a small department.'

'And in the space of – what? – eight months, one woman dies after she falls off a cliff and hits her head, another woman drowns and her body is found to have suffered a blow to the head, and a third is assaulted and left with a fractured skull? Mmm . . . For a nursing home it might be par for the course, but for a Cambridge college, and none of the women over forty? It seems a little excessive.'

'So you really think. . . ?'

'Well, it's hard to say. There can be connections between things without there necessarily being anything sinister. You know the kind of thing: Lucy dies, Margaret is upset, she's careless, falls in the pool. Or it could all be just coincidence. They happen too, surprisingly often in fact. But even so I do think certain aspects of these cases deserve a closer look.'

'And Rebecca. . . ?' I asked.

'Her case is still very much active, of course, more so than ever now she's dead. I'm not giving anything away if I tell you that forensics weren't able to come up with anything much at the scene of the crime. The ground was wet and it had been thoroughly churned up by her friends and then by the paramedics. And we haven't found the weapon. Or her bag. A search of the neighbouring gardens didn't turn anything up.'

We sat in thoughtful silence.

Stephen said, 'So where do we go from here?'

'I'll pass on what you told me. It'll suggest a closer look at the college and new lines of questioning. Now, have you told me everything?'

I nodded, 'I think so.'

'Anything else out of the ordinary? People acting strangely in any way at all?'

'Well . . .' I hesitated and glanced at Stephen.

'You'd better tell him about Merfyn,' he said.

When I'd finished, Jim sat back and roared with laughter. I thought then that he really was an extremely attractive man.

'I can quite understand that your boss wouldn't want *that* to come out!' he said.

'I haven't told him,' I had to admit. 'It would make him even more determined to ditch Merfyn. And talking of things that Lawrence doesn't know, I'd really much rather he didn't get to hear of this conversation.'

'If it all does turn out to have anything to do with Rebecca's death, there won't be any possibility of keeping quiet about it,' Jim said.

'Of course, I know that, but if there isn't a connection?'

'I'll do my best. I'll have a quiet word with the bloke who's in charge of the case. No doubt he'll want to stir things up a bit at the college, but I'll ask him to be discreet when he interviews your boss. It's a good job you did speak to me. Lucy's death was dealt with by Derbyshire police, so there's no reason why anyone would have connected it with the two Cambridge deaths.' He glanced at his watch. 'My God, is that the time? I promised my wife that I'd be home before nine for once.'

He looked at me and I knew then what it was that had struck me earlier on. He was very highly sexed. He had it firmly under control, but there was an intensity that was quite different from Aiden's flirtatious manner. I guessed he couldn't look at a woman without wondering what she would be like in bed, and as soon as you realize that about a man, you can't help wondering yourself . . . I pulled myself up short. Was this any way for a pregnant woman to be behaving?

'One last thing, Cassandra,' Jim said. 'This house. It's great, but it's a bit isolated, isn't it? I don't want to make you nervous, but until we've looked into this, it would be better perhaps if you weren't alone here too much.'

I saw him out and came back shivering in the current of cold air that came in when I opened the door.

'I told you he's a good bloke,' Stephen said.

I nodded. 'I'm glad I told him. It's a weight off my mind.'

But it was disturbing, too. Up until now, I had been able to tell myself that I was letting my imagination run away with me.

149

Thoughts that had been only in my own head and in Stephen's had now been let loose into the wider world. They might shape the future in ways I had not foreseen. Perhaps I had set in motion something that I would regret?

'You look a bit pale. Are you OK?' Stephen asked me.

'Yes, I think so. I hope all these shocks and upsets aren't bothering the baby too much.'

'I expect pregnant women have always . . .' Stephen began.

'Oh!' I cried.

I could see my own surprise reflected on Stephen's face.

'What's the matter?'

'She kicked me! She really kicked me! It was as if she was answering my question.'

'You've felt her move before, haven't you?'

'Not like that, it was a definite thump.'

I walked round to where he was sitting and took his hand. I placed it on my belly. 'Here. Feel this.'

I watched his face. As the baby kicked again, I saw his frown of concentration give way to a smile. He glanced up at me and shook his head, lost for words.

'I suppose we'd better eat,' I said. 'It'll have to be something out of the freezer.'

I got out some chicken breasts.

'I'll be glad when you're up to cooking again,' I said.

Stephen didn't seem to hear me. 'Cass?'

'Mmm?'

'I think it would be best if I stayed on here. I don't feel I can let you live alone while all this is going on.'

The chicken breasts landed on the work surface with a little thud. 'Can't *let* me?'

'Don't jump down my throat. As Jim pointed out, it's very isolated here.'

I looked at him suspiciously. 'What did you say to him before I got here? Did you put him up to warning me?'

'It wasn't like that! But if it had been, could you really blame me? If you're right about Rebecca's death, then there's someone out there who is prepared to walk into a busy hospital and murder someone in their bed.'

I leaned over the table and took hold of his hand.

'OK, sorry I snapped, but surely you don't want to drive in and out of Cambridge during the rush hour every day?'

'All right: why don't you move in with me, then?'

'Oh, sweetie, I can't do that. I need my study and all my books. And what about Bill Bailey? He'd be miserable in your flat. We mustn't feel stampeded into a decision we might regret.'

'I really would feel happier if I was out here with you, Cass. It needn't be permanent, if you don't want it to be.'

He had a point. I thought of the long dark evenings, and the night when I had been so startled by Bill Bailey – and that had been before Rebecca's death. True, there were new security lights on the house and by the gate. I'd had to take out a bank loan to buy them. But how much protection did they really give? The Old Granary was half a mile away from the nearest farm, and there was the baby to consider now. I was slower, more vulnerable. I was carrying a heavy cargo and sailing lower in the water.

Stephen squeezed my hand. I looked into his face. The bandage around his head had gone, but there were still scratches on his cheek and a bruise on his forehead. I thought of that moment on the side of the cliff when Stephen had snatched his hand away from mine so as not to imperil our unborn child.

'OK,' I said. 'Let's give it a try. At least until Rebecca's murderer has been found.'

151

Chapter Fifteen

That was Friday evening. When I arrived in college on Monday morning, the police were already there. I was impressed and rather taken aback by the speed of this reaction. The college was buzzing with activity. I had instigated all this disruption. It was as thought I had poked an ants' nest with a stick.

By the porter's lodge, students were hanging about in little groups speaking *sotto voce*. I looked at their serious young faces and felt sorry that this shadow had fallen upon them. For all their bravado and adoption of streetwise manners, they weren't much more than children who were upset by Rebecca's death and disturbed by this disruption of the everyday. I didn't really think that they had much to fear from the police enquiries. Their defiance of the law wasn't likely to go much further than breaking the speed limit or smoking the occasional joint, but I could understand their unease. I had that familiar feeling that the presence of authority always arouses in me, that somehow without knowing it, or perhaps without remembering it, I had transgressed, and now I was going to be found out.

At the lodge, John was busy with the switchboard and his usual place by the counter had been taken over by a police constable who was ticking off names on a list and arranging interviews. It was as if the college had been taken over by an alien occupying force.

The constable knew immediately who I was. 'Oh, yes, Dr James, you're the girl's tutor, aren't you? Chief Inspector Hutchinson would like to see you as soon as possible. I wonder if you could go along to the interview room right away?'

When I was ushered in, I saw two men sitting at the big central table. One was a burly man, probably in his forties and completely bald, the other was dark and cadaverous and much younger.,

The burly man got heavily to his feet and extended a hand. He had the yellow fingers of a heavy smoker.

'Dr James?' he said. 'I'm Chief Inspector Hutchinson.'

He introduced his sergeant and waved me to a seat opposite the two of them.

The interview room was actually the teaching room where I held my seminars on Victorian poetry. Usually I was the one asking the questions in here. Today there were butterflies in my stomach and my mouth was dry. I could smell the stale cigarette smoke coming off Inspector Hutchinson's clothes even from the other side of the table. There was a packet of Silk Cut lying in front of him like a mascot.

'A bad business this,' he said. 'Let me begin by thanking you for coming forward. Inspector Ferguson has passed on what you told him. Now let me see . . .' He turned over one of the papers on the table. 'I've got a summary of it here.'

He read it out. I was impressed by its concision. My opinion of Jim rose even higher.

'Anything to add to that?' he said.

I shook my head. 'Not really.'

'Right then. So, we need to know where you were yourself on the evening of Saturday 14 October, and also last Wednesday afternoon.'

'On 14 October I was with my boyfriend. We spent the night together.'

He glanced down at his summary. 'That would be Mr Stephen Newley?'

I nodded. 'And last week I was actually at the hospital.'

'That's right. We've got a statement from Rebecca's mother saying that she was with you from the moment you arrived in the ward until you both returned to the hospital after the fire alarm. And the security guard gave us a good description of you.' He smiled. 'Everyone remembers a pregnant woman.'

Emboldened by this pleasantry – though also resenting it some-what – I asked him if there really had been a fire.

'A small one. In the staff toilets on the fifth floor, in a wastebin. Could have been caused by someone having a sneaky fag and being careless. It's strictly no smoking everywhere in the hospital. It's going the same way everywhere. Even down at the station,' he added sourly.

'And Rebecca? Do you know what it was? What happened at the post-mortem?'

He picked up the packet of cigarettes, examined it, and put it back on the table. For a moment I thought he wasn't going to reply. Then he raised his head. Two shrewd, rather bloodshot brown eyes met mine.

'Not as yet.'

I wasn't sure that I believed him.

'I don't think we need detain you any longer, Dr James.'

As I closed the door behind me, I heard him say to his sergeant, 'For pity's sake, find me an ashtray, would you?'

The Senior Common Room was crowded and buzzing with conversation. Over by one of the big sash windows, Aiden, Alison, Merfyn and Cathy were sitting on two sofas on either side of a low coffee table. As I threaded my way through the little groups of people and shabby overstuffed sofas, Aiden saw me coming and moved over to make room for me. I sank down onto the sofa beside him. It was a tight squeeze.

Merfyn was looking gloomy.

'It's a bloody nuisance to have to postpone my seminar on

154

"Literature and Imperialism",' he was saying. 'I don't know if I'll be able to find another slot for it so near the end of term. If you ask me, the police are being over-zealous. They can't seriously think anyone here is responsible for the attack on Rebecca. They're clutching at straws.'

For once Aiden seemed to agree with him. 'Trying to deflect attention from their complete lack of progress,' he said, nodding.

'Perhaps they know something that we don't,' Cathy said.

Silence followed this remark.

Alison said, 'You've already had your interview, haven't you, Cass? What did they ask you?'

I hesitated, although Inspector Hutchinson hadn't actually asked me *not* to say anything. I looked at the four people whose faces were turned expectantly towards me. They looked just as they always did. Merfyn, sitting opposite, was wearing a tweed suit complete with waistcoat, watch chain and red silk handkerchief overflowing from his breast pocket. He was leaning forward with his clasped hands dangling between his knees. Aiden, lounging beside me, was wearing a black leather jacket, a black T-shirt, black jeans and Doc Martens. Beyond him was Cathy in her favourite red sweater with a cup of coffee in her hand: as usual her reading glasses were on top of her head, nestling in dark hair that was as springy as heather. Alison was sitting next to Merfyn, the review section of the *Guardian* open on the lap of her blue woollen dress. It seemed ludicrous to imagine that one of them might be a cold-blooded killer. 'A cold-blooded killer'! With what readiness that cliché of tabloid journalism had sprung into my mind! What was happening to me? I was letting my imagination run away with me, that was what.

I said, 'They wanted to know what I was doing on the day that Rebecca was attacked, and between two o'clock and five o'clock on the afternoon that she died.'

Cathy and Aiden both spoke at once.

'Last Wednesday?'

155

'But surely—?'

Cathy gestured to Aiden to continue. 'Surely,' he said, 'that can't be important.' Understanding dawned. 'Unless . . .'

The same thought appeared to be registering on the faces of the others. No-one wanted to complete the sentence.

Merfyn said, 'They're going to be asking us all where we were last Wednesday afternoon?'

'I'm sure it's just routine,' I said.

'It's a bit awkward all the same.'

'Why, where were you?' Aiden asked.

Merfyn said nothing, but he gave me a glance that was clearly intended to be full of significance; I had no idea what it meant.

Aiden laughed. 'Man of mystery.'

'I suppose you can account for your own whereabouts?' Merfyn said coldly.

'I spent the afternoon in the university library.'

'See anyone you know?'

'Oh, stop it, you two,' Alison snapped. 'You're like rutting stags, always trying to score points off each other.'

Merfyn looked indignant. Aiden grinned. He sat back and crossed his legs. He was wearing his sardonic Jack Nicholson look, but he wasn't as relaxed as he pretended to be. He was tapping his foot rapidly on the floor. Where his leg was touching mine on the sofa I could feel the vibration.

'Anyway,' Alison went on, 'I don't suppose for a moment that you'll be the only ones who'll find it difficult to account for their whereabouts.'

Aiden and Merfyn needling each other, just as they always did, and Alison mildly irritated by them, just as she always was. There had been dozens of mornings like this. Except that Margaret wasn't there and a student was dead; two students, in fact, I reminded myself.

'Two students and the head of department in – what? – six months, nine months?' Aiden said. It was as though he had read my mind. 'You can't blame the police for wanting to poke about a bit.'

There was silence around the table.

He looked at his watch. 'Must go. I want to get over to the library.'

He stood up.

As we followed him to the door, Cathy fell into step beside me.

'By the way,' she said, 'I checked the list of college undergraduates for an Annabelle, but we haven't got a student of that name. Why did you want to know?'

'Oh, it was just a rather strange wrong number,' I said.

Aiden must have paused momentarily because Cathy trod on his heel and bumped into him. He turned and darted a sharp glance at me.

It was that glance that reminded me. Annabelle was the name on the piece of paper that Aiden had snatched from my hand. Annabelle Fairchild. But I didn't have time to think what that might mean because Merfyn was touching me on the arm.

'Can I come and see you, Cass? This afternoon?'

'It's very awkward,' Merfyn said.

I was sitting behind my desk and he was sitting beside it on the upright chair that I usually reserve for students.

'Last Wednesday,' he went on. 'You see, I was with Ingrid. At least for the first part of the afternoon. It's embarrassing, having to tell the police that I was at a séance.'

Don't worry, I nearly said, *they already know*, but I stopped myself in time.

Instead I said, 'All the same, I really think you should.'

'I thought I'd better have a word with you first. You did say that you didn't want it to get around.'

'Just as a matter of interest, what were you doing the rest of the afternoon?'

'Oh,' Merfyn raised his eyebrows and shrugged, 'just wandering around, thinking things through.'

He stood up to leave.

'Wait a moment,' I said firmly. 'Sit down, Merfyn.'

He seated himself reluctantly.

'How is it going now, the book?'

'Oh, much better, in many ways. I'm plugging on with it and I'm getting encouraging responses from Conan Doyle.'

I sighed. It went against the grain to act as though I accepted this, but if Merfyn really was making progress. . . .

'In what ways *isn't* it going well?'

'What?'

'You said, in *most* ways it's going well. That suggests that there are ways in which it isn't.'

'Ah.'

Our eyes met and Merfyn looked away quickly. I picked up a pencil and began to tap it softly on my desk. I realized that I was behaving exactly like Lawrence and put it down again immediately.

The silence stretched out between us.

Merfyn pulled the red silk handkerchief out of his top pocket and blew his nose with a loud trumpeting sound. This seemed to give him confidence. He stuffed the handkerchief away in his trouser pocket with an air of decision.

'There are problems with the publishers,' he said.

'Don't they like it?'

'No, no, they think what they've seen is first-rate.'

'Well, then?' I sat back and spread out my hands. 'Where's the problem?'

'Well, about a week ago, a message came through from Conan Doyle. He wants the book to be translated.' He hesitated.

'Translated? You mean German? French? What?' I found that I was fiddling with my pencil again.

'He says he wants the message of spiritualism to reach the

widest possible audience. He wants my book to be published in Esperanto.'

I dropped my pencil. It rolled off the desk onto the wooden floor.

'The thing is,' Merfyn went on, 'Esperanto was all the rage when he died in 1930. He's sure it must have become a universal language by now. He won't take any notice when I try to explain that no one uses it. He says that St Etheldreda's was founded to further internationalism and that we ought to lead the way. I don't know what I'm going to do.'

He looked as if he was on the verge of tears.

My mouth was hanging open. I closed it. For a while I didn't feel anything, nothing at all. Then I did feel something, but I didn't know what it was. It hit me like a shot of neat vodka. It was anger: pure, white-hot, liberating anger.

Merfyn seemed to sense what was coming. His eyes opened wide. He pressed himself against the back of his chair.

'You don't know what to do?' I said. 'I'll tell you what you are going to do, Merfyn. Are you listening?'

He nodded.

'Really listening?'

'Yes,' he said hoarsely.

'Good.' I found I was enjoying this. 'First let me make my own position quite clear. I do not believe that Conan Doyle has contacted you from beyond the grave. I do not believe that he is dictating your book to you or that he wants it published in Esperanto.'

Merfyn opened his mouth to speak. I lifted up my hand. He closed it.

'I can't prove it. I don't know for certain what happens to us when we die. But this I do know.' My voice was rising. 'I know that the problem of finishing this book is *your* problem, not Conan Doyle's. And you *are* going to finish it, make no mistake about it. It is all that stands between you and redundancy. In fact, it's all that

159

stands between all of us and redundancy. So I don't want to hear a single word more about séances or writer's block. I've had enough, Merfyn. I've reached the end of my rope.'

I leaned as far forward as I could; given the fact that I was almost six months pregnant, it wasn't all that far.

'You'll get off your backside,' I said. 'You will go away and you will write this book. You will finish it and get it published. *In English!*'

I thumped my fist on the table. Merfyn flinched.

'IS THAT CLEAR?' I roared.

He nodded. We regarded each other, our eyes locked, for a few seconds. Merfyn was the first to look away. He got up and left the room, closing the door very softly behind him.

I felt intoxicated. Would losing my temper with Merfyn have done any good? Who knew? who cared? A sense of wellbeing and relaxation was permeating my entire body. It was like the relief that comes from a storm breaking. It didn't last long. Intoxication never does. It soon ebbed away, leaving me wondering if I had been too histrionic. Reasoning with Merfyn hadn't worked, so perhaps this would.

My eye fell on a pile of student essays on the corner of my desk. I had tutorials with these students the next day. I sighed, and glanced at my watch. Five o'clock. It was time to collect Stephen from his first day back at work. I'd have to take the essays home with me.

Already there was a touch of frost in the air and the glow from the porter's lodge struck sparks of light from the pavement. I paused on the threshold to pull my hat down over my ears, and fumbled in my coat pockets for my gloves.

The car park is tucked round the side of the college and is reached by a narrow path that runs along one of the residential wings. I'd been late that morning, so the car, Stephen's Audi, was parked near the far end. This was a favourite spot in the summer because it was sheltered by a group of mature trees, but today, with my bulging briefcase pulling my shoulder down, the extra distance was irksome. The car park was pock-marked with shallow potholes in which delicate feathery films of ice were forming.

I opened the car door and put my briefcase on the passenger seat. As I fastened my seat belt, my thoughts ran ahead to the Old Granary, a warm welcome from Bill Bailey, a pot of lapsang souchong tea. There were some crumpets left, too. If I got a move on, I could get through the essays in an hour and a half, a couple of hours at the most. Then dinner with Stephen, and an early night with an undemanding book, perhaps *not* a crime novel. There was a copy of the latest Anne Tylor novel that I hadn't started yet.

It took me a moment to realize that, although I had turned the key in the ignition, nothing had happened. I tried again. Still nothing.

The battery was completely dead.

The perfect end to a perfect day.

I folded my arms on the steering wheel and laid my head down.

Soon I'd go back to the porter's lodge, sort the situation out, be my normal competent self. But just for a second I needed to surrender to the awfulness of everything and the cussedness of inanimate objects.

I buried my head deeper into the cradle of my arms.

That was why I didn't hear the footsteps approaching the car and why I jumped as if I'd been electrocuted when I heard the tap on the window.

161

Chapter Sixteen

Alison's anxious face was looking in at me. I put my finger on the button for the electric window, forgetting that it wouldn't work. With a sigh I opened the door.

'You OK there?' she asked.

'Yes, yes. I was just allowing myself to feel miserable for a bit. The car won't start. I think it's the battery.'

I dragged my briefcase over the passenger seat, cursing as I caught it on the hand-brake, and struggled out of the car.

'What are you going to do?'

'I'll go back into college and ring Stephen, ask him to get a taxi and come over to pick me up as well. No point in ringing the garage until first thing in the morning. They'll have gone home by now.'

'I was wanting to have a word with you anyway, Cass. I'll walk back with you. Here, let me take that.'

She reached for my briefcase. I surrendered it to her.

'What on earth have you got in there? Bricks? Gold bullion?'

'If only. Let me see.' I counted them off on my fingers. 'Laptop, batch of student essays, proofs of an article – overdue – two books that should have been back at the university library last week, and a kind of compost of unanswered correspondence. My briefcase is a mobile pending tray.'

'You won't have had a chance to look at my article yet, then?'

'I'm afraid that's in there too, Ali. But I have skimmed through it, and read the beginning. I thought it looked terrific.'

'I've got some good news. I sent a copy to the editor of *Literary Women* and he rang me this afternoon to say that he's got an unexpected gap in the Spring edition. He wants to use it.'

I was impressed. It was quite a prestigious journal. 'It'll be a great boost to our research profile. And wonderful ammunition against Lawrence. He's been on my back about the RAE submission.'

'Well, you've had other things on your mind, haven't you?'

We walked in silence, thinking about those other things.

Alison said, 'Any news yet about Rebecca's funeral?'

'No. I suppose the family will have to wait for the police to release the body. I don't know when that's likely to be.'

'Poor Rebecca,' Alison said. 'And even if she had survived, what kind of life would she have had? Perhaps she would have been dependent on other people for everything.'

Her voice was troubled. I looked at her. We were just passing under a light. It caught the single lock of white in her hair and emphasized the pallor of her face.

'Death isn't always the worst thing that can happen, is it?'

She's not really talking about Rebecca, I thought.

'Paul's worse, isn't he?' I said.

She nodded.

We reached the porter's lodge. I said, 'When I've rung Stephen, let's go and have a cup of tea and you can tell me all about it.'

Tea was being cleared away from the Senior Common Room, but we were just in time to grab a cup. The large room was deserted except for a solitary lecturer from the Spanish department reading the *Daily Telegraph* in the far corner.

When we had settled ourselves, Alison said, 'It's his eyes at the moment. He's having trouble focusing. He can still cook, just about, but he can't read without getting a terrible headache.'

I felt a pang of sympathy. I couldn't imagine anything worse than not being able to read. What was it that Logan Pearsall Smith wrote? 'People say life is the thing, but I prefer reading.' I often think that should be my motto.

'He's been like this before, hasn't he?' I said.

'Yes. It may well improve, so I mustn't make too much of it. I'm probably just tired. We've had a few bad nights lately, and I've been working hard, too.'

I nodded. She was about to say something more. Her lips parted, her eyes met mine. Then she seemed to think better of it.

'What is it?' I said.

She pushed back her hair.

'Well, I was wondering – the thing is, it's a bit ghoulish – about the RAE – will we be able to count Margaret's work? If there was stuff that was just about finished, but hadn't been published, well, could we get it published and use it for the RAE? Or is that too macabre?'

I turned it over in my mind.

'Do you know?' I replied slowly. 'I think you've got something there. Malcolm did ask me if I would see about getting her unpublished work into print, but that's another thing I haven't had time to do. There *is* a lot of stuff, mostly on disk fortunately. He let me have it months ago and I haven't looked at it since. I'll have to ask Lawrence about the policy for posthumous publication. There might be things that are almost ready. Or joint publication could be a possibility.'

The lecturer from the Spanish department folded up his newspaper. He switched off the standard lamp by his chair and left the room, nodding to us as he passed. We listened to his footsteps retreating down the corridor. The college was very quiet now and it was warm in the Senior Common Room. The only light came from the table lamp next to us. I stifled a yawn and slumped deeper into the sofa.

'You won't overdo things, will you?' Alison said. 'You should be taking things easy. With the baby coming, I mean. I'd be happy to help if I can.'

I was touched by her concern. 'You are kind, but it needs a nineteenth century specialist. I'll get round to it sooner or later. After the end of term.'

We sat in silence for a while.

Alison asked, 'What are you going to do when the baby's born? About Stephen, I mean.'

'He'd like to get married,' I admitted.

'But you're still not sure?'

'Oh, we're good companions, yes, but . . . Oh, I just feel there's something missing. I'm not sure what it is – passion? romance? But then, do I really want those, considering where they've got me in the past?'

'Well, marriage is about the long haul, you know. Romance isn't everything,' Alison said with mock solemnity. 'As my mother used to say, there's more to marriage than—'

'Four bare legs in a bed!' we concluded together.

'It's a bloody good start, though,' I said.

'Looks to me as if you've already made a start!'

We were still giggling like two schoolgirls sharing a dirty joke when Stephen appeared round the common room door.

I struggled to my feet, feeling guilty. 'You should have asked the porter or the cab driver to look for me,' I said.

'It's better if I move around, I don't get so stiff.'

The three of us walked slowly together towards the porter's lodge. Just as we reached the seminar room that the police were using for their interviews, the door opened and Aiden came out. He tried to smile at us, but he was obviously rattled. Without a word he brushed past us and walked off rapidly down the corridor.

'So much for Mr Cool!' said Alison.

'I wonder what's wrong.'

'Perhaps he didn't spend last Wednesday in the library after all.'

I said, 'There probably isn't any way of knowing for sure, if he didn't see anyone he knew.'

'Isn't there?' said Alison. There was a sardonic inflection in her voice.

165

I looked at her curiously. 'What do you mean?'

'The library is doing a survey of reader use. They're keeping a record of who uses the library, and the times they go in and out.'

'But the information's supposed to be confidential, isn't it?'

'How long do you think that will last in a murder inquiry?'

'But surely you don't think that Aiden's involved? I mean, what possible reason could he have?'

'No, no, I very much doubt that it's got anything to do with the college at all, but he's so bloody cocky. I'd just like to see him sweat a bit.'

Stephen hadn't uttered a word during this exchange. I looked at him for a response. He was leaning heavily on his aluminium crutch and was peering in the direction in which Aiden had gone.

'That was Aiden, was it?' he said. 'I'm sure I've seen him somewhere before.'

'The college Christmas party?' I suggested.

'More recently than that.' Stephen shook his head. 'It's maddening when that happens. I just can't think where it was.'

You little bugger!' I shouted.

I ran down the stairs to the sitting-room. Bill Bailey bounded ahead of me, sliding along on the wooden boards. He tore across the sitting-room floor, ears flat against his head, swerving like a racing driver to avoid the furniture. His tail disappeared round the corner of the stairs to the kitchen. He was in a skittish mood and anxious to prolong the morning game of hide-and-seek for as long as possible.

I followed him over to the kitchen. With difficulty I got down on my knees and pulled the squirming bundle of fur out of the tangle of plastic bags in the space between the cooker and the fridge. I up-ended him and cradled him like a baby in my arms.

'You rascal,' I said.

He purred and narrowed his eyes benignly, accepting that the game was over. I tucked him under one arm and stepped outside.

Stephen was waiting by the gate, glancing impatiently at his watch. I pulled the door shut with my free hand and tipped the cat onto the ground. He sauntered down the path in the weak wintry sunshine, immediately absorbed in the sounds and smells of the garden.

The low rays of the winter sun flashed off the water in the dyke and dazzled me as I drove along the track to the road. I drove as slowly as I could, but even so Stephen winced with every bump. I felt heavy and listless. I wanted to go back to sleep and couldn't stop yawning. I hadn't finished my marking until eleven o'clock the night before and then I had passed a restless night. I couldn't remember exactly what I had dreamt, but it had left me feeling uneasy.

On the way to my office, I looked in on Cathy. She was sitting at her desk with her head in her hands, kneading her scalp. When she looked up I saw that there were shadows under her eyes.

'A migraine?' I asked.

'I'm hoping it won't develop into that. I might just be tired. Hannah didn't get in until one o'clock last night.'

I tut-tutted in sympathy.

'Selfish little cow,' she said.

I must have looked started because she added hastily, 'Oh, I don't mean that really. She's only fourteen. I can't expect her to understand just how much I worry.'

'Can I get you anything? A cup of tea? Some paracetamol?'

'No thanks, I've taken one of my special pills.'

I was on my way out when she said, 'Oh sorry, Cass, I almost forgot to tell you. Merfyn's wife rang in. He's ill and won't be able to see his students today. I've put a note for them on his door.'

When I reached my office, I sank into my chair with a groan and clasped my head. Yesterday's euphoria seemed incomprehensible. How could I have kidded myself that losing my temper with Merfyn would do any good? I should have realized that retreat would be his instinctive response. Now I would probably never get another written word out of him. Perhaps I wouldn't get any teaching from him either.

The morning didn't get any better. Half my students didn't turn up. They were being interviewed by the police, or were waiting to be interviewed, or were using the situation as an excuse to bunk off. Those that did come were vague and distracted. Under the circumstances it was hard to expect them to work up much interest in the later work of Henry James. I didn't feel very interested myself. I smiled to myself as I remembered how Margaret used to classify the novels of Henry James: James I, James II, and the Old Pretender. I made a note not to include *The Wings of the Dove* or *The Golden Bowl* on next year's syllabus.

By midday my head was throbbing. The office was stuffy. The ancient radiators, lumpy with many generations of peeling cream-coloured paint, were always too hot to touch; either that or they were stone cold. I opened the window and let a current of cool air refresh me. I was just deciding to buy a sandwich and an apple from the buttery when the telephone rang.

'Car OK?' Stephen asked.

'The garage man's coming out this afternoon.'

'Oh, good. I won't come home with you this evening. I've got to work late and Rod's going over to Ely, so he'll give me a lift back later. And listen, I suddenly remembered where I saw Aiden. I was dictating a letter to a client as a follow-up to a meeting we had in the Garden House Hotel the Wednesday before last. That's where he was – quite unmistakable, dressed all in black like an undertaker. And he was with a very attractive woman. They were walking through the reception together. Actually I noticed *her* first, because she was wearing a really beautiful camel coat, and the point is, I overheard him say: 'Same time next week then.' I remember that because, well, I thought all right for some.'

'You thought . . .'

'Yes, love in the afternoon. He was looking, well, elated is the only word.'

168

'And it sounded as if they were going to meet again the next week? It's bloody expensive there.'

'Perhaps she was paying?' Stephen suggested.

'Annabelle,' I said.

'Annabelle?'

I told him about the piece of paper that Aiden had snatched out of my hand, and about the mysterious phonecall.

'What did she look like?' I asked.

There was a short silence. Then, 'You know what, I'm not sure. I don't think I really saw her face.'

'So how do you know she was attractive?'

'Only an attractive woman would wear a coat like that.'

I knew what he meant.

'And also . . .' He fumbled for words. 'Something about the way she carried herself. Her confidence. I think she was blonde, and another thing, she wasn't young. I'm certain of that.'

Instantly an image appeared in my mind's eye. A woman of a certain age, understated and sure of herself, a curtain of fair hair expertly cut and tinted, clothes by Nicole Farhi or Katherine Hamnett. Married to a wealthy farmer – there are still plenty of those in East Anglia – or a commuting stockbroker. Could I imagine Aiden with a woman like that? Is the Pope a Roman Catholic?

Only one thing didn't quite fit.

'She sounded young on the telephone,' I objected.

'It's easy to be deceived about that when you can't see the speaker.'

'Mmm.' I wasn't quite convinced. Something about that voice had been wrong for the Annabelle of the Garden House Hotel. The way the voice had gone up at the end of each sentence: that was a young person's habit, and the speaker had so easily been thrown off balance by her mistake.

I was still pondering this as I went to buy my lunch. Turning the corner into the corridor that leads past the police interview room, I was struck by a sense of *déjà vu*: Aiden was again emerging and

169

closing the door behind him. I stopped and stared. It wasn't quite the same today, though. Aiden was smiling and there was a spring in his step. As soon as he saw me, he too did a double take. At the same moment, as though we were taking part in a dance, we moved forward to meet each other.

I looked at him enquiringly.

Aiden cleared his throat. 'There was something I remembered that I hadn't told the police. Nothing important.'

'Annabelle.'

The word was out of my mouth before I knew it. Whatever had possessed me to blurt that out? I couldn't believe I'd said it. The blood rushed to my face. My cheeks grew hot.

Aiden looked equally amazed.

'How on earth did you find out?' he said.

'Stephen saw you with her at the Garden House Hotel.'

He stared at me as though he didn't know what I was talking about.

Then his face cleared. 'Ah.' It came out as a long sigh of enlightenment.

For a moment I thought that he wasn't going to say any more. Then he laid a confiding hand on my arm.

'I hope this needn't go any further. For various reasons it really wouldn't do for my connection with Annabelle to become public knowledge.'

I stepped back, letting his hand fall away.

'It's nobody's business, but yours,' I said stiffly. 'As long as it's not one of our students, that is.'

'Oh, I can promise you that she most certainly isn't.'

Was there a touch of irony in his voice? I felt myself blushing again.

'Well,' he continued, rocking back on his heels, at ease now. 'Must be getting on. Lots to do. Places to go, people to see.'

'Of course.'

He went off down the corridor. I walked slowly on, thinking that my sense of disorientation most likely came from feeling that I'd made a fool of myself.

I looked back just in time to catch Aiden doing exactly the same thing. I turned quickly away, but not before I got the distinct impression that he was laughing.

The afternoon wore on. When neither of my last two students arrived for their four o'clock tutorial, I decided to go home.

It was dark when I drove up to the Old Granary. As I pulled up by the gate the security lights came on immediately, triggered by the movement of the car. They had cost me a fortune, but it was worth it. I got out of the car expecting Bill Bailey to tear out of the bushes and wind himself around my legs, but there was only stillness. Beyond the semicircle of dazzling white light that spilled down the wall and across the garden, the darkness seemed solid.

I quickly let myself into the house. In the kitchen I filled the kettle and draped my coat over a chair. Struggling up the stairs to my study, I decided that it was time to stop carrying half the contents of my office around. I opened my briefcase and tipped the contents onto the desk. Oh, God, the library books. If I hung on to them much longer, I'd have to take out a bank loan to pay off the fine. Promising myself that I'd take them back tomorrow, I sifted idly through a sheaf of old letters and memos. It was all too much. I swept the whole lot off the table. Some went straight into the bin, others landed on the floor.

I heard the click of the kettle switching itself off in the kitchen. As if that had been a signal, the telephone began to ring.

It was in the second of silence after the first shrill peal, that I heard a soft, muffled thud overhead.

There was someone upstairs in my bedroom.

Chapter Seventeen

The telephone went on ringing. My outstretched hand froze in mid-air.

There was a pattering sound and Bill Bailey appeared at the top of the stairs, stretching and yawning. He bounded down, his fluffy tail held high, greeting me with a stream of affectionate little noises.

I collapsed onto a chair by my desk, breathing heavily. My heart seemed to have come loose from its moorings and was banging about in my breast. Bill Bailey sprang onto my knees.

I reached for the telephone.

'Cass?'

'Stephen!'

'What's the matter?'

'I've just had the shock of my life. I thought there was someone in the house.'

'What?'

'It's OK. It was only Bill Bailey. He must have got shut in.'

'Oh, the cat? No, but you—'

Even as he spoke, the same thought occurred to me. Bill Bailey had left the house with us that morning. How had he got back in? It was the middle of winter: all the windows were shut. Anyway, none of them was accessible to a cat. He *must* have come in through the front door. That meant someone had let him in. What if the thud hadn't been Bill Bailey? Perhaps even now someone was waiting in my silent house, breathing very quietly, listening as I spoke to Stephen. As these thoughts flashed through my mind I jumped to my feet. Bill Bailey rolled off my knee and landed on the floor with a thump and a yelp.

The receiver was still at my ear. I heard Stephen say, 'Get out of the house! Lock yourself in your car and ring me from your mobile.'

What I did next is a blur in my memory. I don't remember scrabbling on the table for my car keys and phone or running down the stairs. But I must have done, because seconds later I was sitting in my locked car, panting for breath.

I kept my eyes on the house. I'd left the door open and light was spilling out onto the path. Bill Bailey appeared on the doorstep. He sat down, stuck one leg up in the air and began some energetic bottom-washing. It seemed very unlikely that there was anyone still in the house. I thought about what must have happened. Bill Bailey would have been waiting in the laurel bush. As soon as the front door was opened, he would have streaked in and hidden behind the plastic carrier bags in the space by the cooker. The intruder hadn't been able to find him when they wanted to leave. He was a timid cat. He would have stayed in hiding until the stranger had left. All the same, when my mobile phone rang, I jumped in fright.

'Cass, what the hell's going on?' It was Stephen.

'I'm fine. I am in the car, but I think whoever's been in the house is almost certainly long gone.'

'All the same, stay where you are. Look, I'll ring for a taxi and come straight home.'

'But your appointment?'

'Sod that.'

It seemed a long time before I saw the headlights of the taxi appear from the main road and come jerkily along the uneven track.

Together, Stephen and I searched the house, not believing that we would find anyone, but looking for signs that things had been disturbed or that something was missing. Everything seemed just as we had left it that morning.

'I'd better check the wine cellar,' I said.

I got the key and shone a torch into the gloom. It illuminated a row of bottles and the cardboard box in which I keep my computer disks. I flicked through them. The sight of Margaret's backup disks reminded me that I really had to get down to trawling through them for publishable material. I mustn't let all this business about Rebecca distract me from the RAE. I heaved a sigh.

'I don't think there's anything missing.'

'God, I could do with a drink,' said Stephen.

We sat down at the kitchen table. I poured half a glass of sherry for myself and a full one for Stephen.

'Do you think we've overreacted?' he said. 'I panicked when I realized that you were alone in the house. Could Bill Bailey have doubled back and slipped in while we weren't looking?'

I thought back. 'I pulled the door shut before I let him go. I think.'

'How many sets of keys are there?'

'Yours and mine and there's a spare set.'

'Where are they?'

'Oh.' I stared at him. 'They're in college. I keep the spare set in a drawer in my office. In case I lock myself out.'

'And who has a key to your office?'

'There's one at the porter's lodge. Cathy has one, too. But it wouldn't be difficult for someone to take the keys from my office drawer. I often leave my door unlocked for a few minutes if I'm just popping out to the loo.'

Stephen looked grim. 'We'd better have the locks changed.'

'I'll ring a locksmith first thing in the morning. Meanwhile I'd better make supper.'

'I'd better ring that client. Make my apologies.' He went up to the sitting-room to use the phone on my desk.

174

As I assembled the ingredients of a meal I could hear the low murmur of conversation over my head. Then it stopped and a few moments later Stephen called down the stairs. 'Cass? Where's that piece of china I bought you?'

'I put it on that shelf in the bookcase with the others. By my desk.'

'It's not there now.'

I went upstairs. Stephen was right: the bowl with the print of the mother and child playing at horses was gone. It wasn't immediately obvious because the remaining pieces had been rearranged so that there wasn't a gap.

'You didn't decide to put it somewhere else?' Stephen enquired.

'No. I like to keep them where I can look up and see them when I'm working. Is it on the carpet somewhere? Perhaps Bill Bailey climbed up and knocked it off.'

We looked at each other.

'I think I can get down there more easily than you can,' I said.

I got down on my hands and knees and searched around, moving piles of books to look behind them.

'If it was a bit tidier around here . . .' Stephen remarked.

'Not there,' I said. I got awkwardly to my feet.

'You know, even if it was Bill Bailey, he's hardly likely to have moved everything to close up the gap, is he?' Stephen pointed out.

I had a vision of two white paws gently patting the cups and saucers and plates into place. I snorted with laughter. Stephen looked at me anxiously. There was an edge of hysteria to my mirth, I thought.

'Apart from us, who's been in the house over the last few weeks?' he asked.

I had to think about this. 'There were the men who came to install the security lights. They had to come in to use a power point. There was the man who came to read the meter a couple of weeks ago, and there was Jane, of course, but she didn't come up here, did she?'

175

'When was the last time you remember seeing the bowl?'

'I simply can't remember.'

'I really don't like this. I'm going to speak to Jim. I'll phone him now.'

He wasn't at home. Stephen left a message for him and we went down to the kitchen. Stephen sat down at the table and watched me lining up three plates on the work surface next to the gas hob and pouring olive oil into a frying-pan. I took a fillet of cod from the first plate, wiped it through the lemon juice on the second plate, then through the flour on the third. It went into the pan with a hissing and spitting of hot fat.

Stephen said, 'Term ends tomorrow, doesn't it? Normally you'd be working at home after that, wouldn't you? Why don't you stay with your mother for a while?'

'What about Bill Bailey?'

'Take him with you. He's been before, hasn't he?'

'Only for a day or two at a time. And then there's my work. I really need the university library.'

'Won't the British Library do?'

'Well, maybe.' I added another fillet to the pan.

'Think it over. I really don't like the thought of you here on your own, while I'm at work.'

'My mother's out at work all day, too.'

'Yes, but her house isn't as isolated, is it? We don't have to tell anyone where you've gone. I can tell people that you needed to get away and have a complete rest – which is nothing but the truth.'

I shook a packet of pre-washed salad into a bowl. The thought of my mother's thoroughly urban little house in Kew, centrally heated and snugly situated in the middle of a mews terrace, certainly had its attractions. But all the same . . .

'Oh, I don't really think so.'

'I can't make it out about you and your mother. Don't you get on?'

'Oh yes . . .' I said vaguely.

'Well, when am I going to meet her?'

I didn't want to be having this conversation now.

'All in good time,' I said, putting a plate of fried fish in front of him.

By the time Jim rang back, we were in bed. Anne Tyler had been abandoned; I was reading E. Nesbit's *The Enchanted Castle*. I always turn to my old childhood favourites when the going gets tough. Stephen was reading Redmond O'Hanlon's *Into the Heart of Borneo*, which was just as escapist in a more masculine fashion.

Stephen answered the phone. I heard him outlining the situation and watched him listening to the response. The conversation seemed to be developing in unexpected ways. There was an exchange of goodbyes, and Stephen hung up.

He turned to me. 'The results of the post-mortem have come through.'

I sat up. 'And?'

'It didn't establish the cause of death. They don't know why Rebecca died just when she did, but so far there's no evidence of foul play, other than the original attack, of course.'

'And the fire?'

'No proof that it was arson.'

I tried to take this in. I had been so sure that I had been used as a decoy, that the fire alarm had been contrived. Had it all been a coincidence after all?

'Is Jim satisfied? And Chief Inspector Hutchinson?'

'No, they're not. The very uncertainty about what killed Rebecca is odd in itself. To all intents and purposes she seemed to be recovering, and it's not difficult to set a fire and leave no traces. On the other hand the police have to follow the evidence in targeting their resources, as Jim put it. So they're concentrating on finding out who hit Rebecca over the head.'

'What did he think about what's just happened here?'

177

'Not enough to justify sending out a crime scene officer. I didn't think there would be, because there's no sign of forcible entry, the cat *could* have sneaked in behind our backs, and a visitor to the house *could* have taken the bowl on an earlier occasion. But he certainly thought it was a good idea to change the locks.'

'Oh, great.'

He stretched out his arm. I settled myself with my head on his shoulder, taking care not to lean against his chest.

'I've got a bad feeling about all this,' I told him. 'I think there's something we're not seeing. Do you remember when we went to the Monet gallery in Paris and stood in front of the pictures of water-lilies?'

He nodded. 'Up close all you could see were patches of colour.'

'You had to stand well back for the painting to make sense. It's like that now, I feel I'm too close to everything. I can't see what it means because I'm standing in the wrong place. Or perhaps it's more like being on the wrong side of a tapestry, lots of dangling threads.'

Long after Stephen had gone to sleep I lay awake beside him in the dark, listening to the tiny noises that are part of the life of any old house: the creak of contracting floorboards, the gurgle of water in the pipes. I knew the house was securely locked and bolted, but in my mind's eye I saw a shadowy figure flitting from room to room, touching my possessions, perhaps even sitting at my desk, rifling through the drawers.

Was this the first time he or she had been here? Or just the first time they had been found out?

At last I fell into a heavy, uneasy sleep. I dreamt I was running down the corridor of the hospital, pursued by someone in a white coat and surgical mask. My belly was huge. I was about to go into labour and I had to find a safe place. I turned a corner and found myself outside the Intensive Care Unit. I pushed through the swing doors and ran down the ward, past beds with occupants swathed like mummies. At the very end was Rebecca. I wasn't at all surprised to see her sit up and gesture urgently to me, inviting me to hide under her bed. The fire alarm went off, screeching and clanging in my head. I froze in terror. I knew what this meant: *the killing was about to start.* I woke up, shaking, unspeakably relieved to find that I was in my own bed. After a while I fell asleep again.

I woke up in the morning, feeling drugged and clogged with sleep, the menace of the dream still somewhere in the back of my mind.

The weather reflected my mood. A thick grey layer of cloud blotted out the light. As we drove across the fens, I felt as though the sky was bearing down on us, pressing us to the ground.

I arrived at college to discover that Merfyn had disappeared.

The first indication was a note on my desk.

I didn't read it until I'd looked in the drawer for my spare house keys. They were in a tangled heap at the back mixed up with rubber bands and old salary slips. I left them there. After today they wouldn't be any use to anyone. I looked through the Yellow Pages and rang a locksmith who agreed to go out to the Old Granary that day.

I then turned my attention to the note. Cathy's handwriting informed me that Merfyn's wife had rung to say that he wouldn't be coming in to college again before Christmas. She had put a sick note in the post.

That was all I needed. I opened the door into Cathy's office. She was tapping away at her computer keyboard. It couldn't have been a migraine yesterday after all; she was back to her usual, energetic self.

'Did Celia say what was wrong with Merfyn?' I asked her.

She paused with her hands suspended over the keyboard. 'No, but she left a number in case you wanted to speak to her.'

I tried the number only to be told by her assistant at the Home Office that she was in a meeting with a minister.

179

I didn't manage to get through to her until after lunch.

'Ah, Cassandra,' she said briskly. Her accent was slightly clipped, emphatically upper-class. The girl from Roedean and the boy from the Valleys. Thirty years ago, she and Merfyn must have seemed an unlikely couple.

'Merfyn thought it was only fair to let you know that you are unlikely to see him again before the middle of next term,' she said.

'The middle of next term?' I was incredulous.

'He has the first four weeks off as study leave, so you wouldn't be expecting him in college then, would you?'

'No, but you mean he won't be coming in *at all* before that?'

'I'm afraid not.'

'Well, what's wrong with him?'

'Stress.'

'Is he too ill to talk to me himself?'

Celia hesitated. 'Not that precisely.'

'What then?'

'He won't have easy access to a telephone at the moment.'

What could this mean? That Merfyn was in hospital? In a mental institution? I felt myself growing hot and cold.

'For God's sake, Celia, stop talking like a civil servant and tell me what's going on.'

'Oh, very well. He came to the station with me this morning and caught a train to Stansted Airport. He is probably airborne even as we speak.'

'He's gone abroad?'

'That was his intention.'

'But where?'

'I really couldn't say.'

I was dumbfounded. Then it struck me that there was more than one way of interpreting this statement.

'Do you *know* where he's gone, Celia?'

'As it happens, I don't. But if I were to hazard a guess, I would say Spain, or possibly Crete or Malta.'

180

Ideas of extradition floated crazily in my mind.

'But what about the police?' I blurted out.

'What about them?' Celia sounded surprised. 'Oh, you mean the investigation into the death of that student. Merfyn's given a statement to the police. There's really no reason for him to stay around.'

'But aren't you worried not knowing where he is?'

'Not really, no. It's happened once or twice before. Things just get on top of him and he has to get away for a while. He's been building up to it for weeks. He'll buy the cheapest ticket available to somewhere warm and book into a hotel. I expect he'll give me a ring in a few days. And now, Cassandra, I must go: I have someone waiting to see me. Bye.'

I was left goggling at the telephone. I remembered what Stephen had said about the mystery of other people's marriages. Could Celia really be as unconcerned as she sounded? What was really going on? Was his departure merely a safety valve as she had implied, or was it something more sinister? Had the preoccupation with séances been a sign that Merfyn was going off the rails?

I was still brooding when there was a knock on the door.

Cathy popped her head round and said, 'I've collected some stuff from your pigeon-hole for you. I didn't want you to forget your cake.'

She gave me several envelopes and a small silver gift box decorated with gold stars.

'I wasn't sure that you'd have time for it this year.'

She smiled, 'Actually I think it's turned out to be one of my best ever. And you haven't forgotten about the sherry party, have you?'

All workplaces have their Christmas rituals. Cathy's cake distributed through the staff pigeon-holes on the last day of term was one of ours. So was the sherry party. There were over three weeks to go until Christmas, but it's a festival that's celebrated early in Cambridge colleges. The undergraduates go home in the first week of December, and after that it's difficult to get both full-time and part-time staff together.

'I suppose I'd better show my face. I'll join you when I've looked at my post.'

It included several Christmas cards from students and colleagues, a second stern reminder from the university library about the two overdue books, and a letter from an editor asking for the proofs of an article to be returned as a matter of urgency. In the anxiety of chasing up other people, I was in danger of forgetting my own contribution to the RAE. There were some bibliographical details I needed to check. I resolved to go straight to the library after the party.

In fact it was a subdued affair, scarcely a party at all. The Christmas tree in the Senior Common Room had been bought before Rebecca's death, but no-one had the heart to put up more decorations. And they weren't the only things that were missing.

'Where's the rest of our department?' I asked Cathy.

'Alison went home early. Paul had a very bad night apparently.'

'And Aiden?'

Cathy grinned and pointed to the far end of the room. Craning my head round, I spotted him in animated conversation with a very chic postgrad from the French department.

'You look tired,' she told me. 'Why don't you sit down? I'll get you a drink. Orange juice?'

I nodded gratefully and sank down into a sofa whose springs had long gone. She came back with drinks and a plate of cheese straws.

'Can't say I feel in a very Christmassy mood,' I said. 'I haven't bought so much as a card yet.'

'It's been a grim old term. Still, you've got the baby to look forward to. Next Christmas'll be lovely. Makes it all seem worthwhile. She won't understand about the presents, but she'll love the wrapping paper.'

'What does Hannah want for Christmas?'

'Would you believe, a tongue stud! Until she's sixteen she can't have it done without my permission.'

'And you won't give it?'

'Not on your life! She thinks it would be such a wild and rebellious thing to do, but actually she just wants to be exactly like her best friend, Eleanor, who is exactly like half the other fourteen-year-olds in her class. "How sad is that?" as Hannah would say. Eleanor's mother was weak-minded enough to agree to the tongue stud and gave Eleanor a letter of permission. And do you know what Hannah did? Took some of my headed notepaper and copied Eleanor's letter. She came unstuck when the body-piercing place rang me up to check. After that, I wouldn't even let her have her ears pierced. There was a lot of door banging, and weeping on her bed, but I stuck it out.'

I thought about this as I drove to the library. Up until now I had seen my little girl as a cooing baby or as a charming toddler lurching about unsteadily. I hadn't imagined her as a sulky teenager festooned with ironmongery. Oh well, time enough to worry about that, I thought, as I pulled into the car park.

I'd intended to work through until six o'clock, but by half past four I was ravenous. I had a cup of tea in the tearoom and ate Cathy's Christmas cake. I felt hungry all the time these days. Could I really be eating only for two? What if I was expecting twins? I was expanding so rapidly now that I could almost believe it, despite the evidence of the scans. I was so tired, as well. I could have put my head on the table and slept, right there and then. One more reference to check and then I could go home with an easy conscience.

An elderly creaking lift carried me up to the sixth floor of the north front of the library where the nineteenth century biography is housed. It's always dark up there. The lights between the rows of grey metal stacks are controlled by time switches, black plastic dials that you twist to the right and allow to jerk stiffly back to nought. I dumped my folder and bag on one of the small wooden

183

tables in the narrow corridor between the stacks and the high oblong windows. I switched on the fluorescent light.

It struck me that no one in the world knew exactly where I was at that moment. It's a thought I always enjoy. I looked out of the window. Immediately below was Clare College, and beyond it I could see King's College Chapel, bone-white in its floodlights. As I admired the view over Cambridge, I forgot the pettiness and backbiting of academic life and the bureaucratic irritations. There was nowhere else I would rather have been than this library in this city. In fact, I'd like to *live* in the library. I'd often wondered if that would be possible. Of course you'd have to hide at closing time. There was actually a bed in the library: in a little sickroom off the corridor that led to Rare Books. The door was always ajar and I'd often glanced in wistfully at the narrow, neatly made-up bed and the little washbasin. And why leave it at just living in the library, I thought? It would also make a wonderful mausoleum. I could lie in state in the central reading room. Then it could be bricked up with me inside. Perhaps I'd at last get round to reading *Ulysses*! What else would I need apart from books to see me through eternity? Bill Bailey. Perhaps he could be mummified. I saw him swaddled in bandages, with his little black and white face poking out of the top. Too unkind . . .

I came to my senses with a sudden awareness of how quiet the library was. My desk was a little island of light in the darkness. It had a melamine surface of indigo-blue with a criss-crossing of little whitish lines. And the green carpet tiles: I hadn't noticed before that they were flecked with yellow. What an extraordinary texture they had; they were wiry and hairy, like a very rough tweed. Or was it more like something alive, moss perhaps, or the pelt of an animal? The richness of colour and texture seemed too extravagant; I closed my eyes to shut it out.

Across the inside of my eyelids, like a film being projected in a cinema, a series of pictures was flickering past. I was entranced. The film flowed so fast that I could scarcely register all the images.

I saw myself in the Senior Common Room listening to Cathy talking about Hannah. Now I was looking at the little lacquer box decorated with the Snow Queen – she was actually smiling at me. Next came my interview with Rebecca. This time, though, I was on her side of the desk, looking at my own face. How comically stern I looked! I started to giggle. Then I saw Margaret's garden, and her body floating in the pool. Why had I been afraid to look? I leaned forward for a better view and found myself falling into a black hole. I jerked my eyes open.

Ahead of me the parallel lines of book stacks and the wall converged on what I'd thought was a blank white wall, but now I saw that there was a door in it. As I watched, the doorknob slowly, very slowly, began to turn. Something dreadful was behind that door. I had to get away. My eye was caught by something red. Close to the top of one of the stacks a few yards away was a red light. It had a shade upon which the word 'Stairs' was picked out in transparent glass. As I moved towards it I saw the door at the end of the stacks opening wide. I did not want to see, *must not see*, what was emerging. I plunged down the stairs, swinging myself round corners as the staircase twisted from floor to floor. My hair had come loose. A loop of it whipped across my face. The metal walls boomed as I crashed against them, ricocheting between wall and banister like a ball on a bagatelle board.

My baby, I mustn't hurt my baby. I forced myself to slow down. From a window I caught a quick, photographic glimpse of two elderly dons deep in conversation as they walked down the library steps. As I stumbled down the last flight of stairs, I shouted for help. I emerged into the broad corridor that runs from the tearoom to the issue desk. I saw heads turning, expressions of surprise.

And that was when I started to laugh. How silly it was to be frightened! There was nothing to fear in the library. The books and manuscripts, all the knowledge and all the power that knowledge brings, they belonged to me. They were all inside my head.

I had *become* the library and now that I knew everything, that had to mean I knew who had killed Rebecca, and that was what I was trying to explain to the anxious faces rocking and swaying around me. But the words wouldn't come, and a dark wave was breaking over me, sweeping away faces, library, knowledge, everything.

Chapter Eighteen

A brilliance was seeping under my eyelids: it must mean that there had been a fall of snow overnight. I would open my eyes to a world transformed, but not just yet, not until this feeling of convalescent weakness had passed. I must have had a fever, or perhaps a bad dream, but it was all right; Mummy was somewhere nearby. Soon I'd be able to get up and play in the snow, but there was no hurry. I was perfectly content to lie there, comfortably suspended between sleep and wakefulness. There was a delicious smell, something faint but very familiar – what was it? – and nearby someone was talking very quietly. I couldn't quite hear what they were saying, but it didn't matter. The sound was soothing, like having the radio on low.

I wanted to sink back into sleep, but there was something uncomfortable caught on my hand. I tried to move, but my arm appeared to be tethered to the bed. My other hand was free and was lying outside the bedclothes, but they were strange, too. My hand slid over a cool cotton sheet. What had happened to my duvet? The pleasant drowsiness was ebbing away.

With an effort I opened my eyes.

I was not at home in my own bed with the radio playing and snow falling outside. I was in a white room, lying in a hospital bed attached to a drip. I was wearing a hospital gown.

187

I turned my head to locate the source of the murmuring sound. Stephen was standing by the window talking to himself, or perhaps to someone invisible. I didn't find this surprising, merely interesting.

He turned towards me and smiled. The lower part of his face was dark with stubble. On his cheeks were the lines of scratches that had almost healed.

He said, 'She's waking up. Yes, thanks for phoning.'

He folded the mobile phone into his hand and sat down beside me.

'How are you feeling, sweetie?'

How was I feeling? I would have to think about that.

'Head aches,' I decided.

Stephen's hand was warm in mine. I couldn't float very far away while he was holding on to me, so perhaps I would go back to sleep. I was unable to do that just yet though, because something was nagging at me, something very, very important. When I knew what it was, my heart turned over.

'The baby?'

'She's fine, absolutely fine. Look, this is monitoring her heartbeat. See? She's OK.'

There were wires snaking out from under the sheet. I turned my head to follow them. I squinted at the screen. A series of regular green blips was moving across it.

I turned my attention back to Stephen. He put my free hand to his lips. I smiled at him. Now something else was puzzling me, refusing to allow me to sink back into sleep.

'The phone?'

'Lawrence asking after you.'

My mouth felt dry. There was a jug of water on the bedside table. Stephen intercepted my glance. He put a pillow behind my head and held a glass to my lips.

'What time is it?' I asked.

'Nine o'clock.'

'Nine o'clock. So it must be . . .' I couldn't quite work it out.

'It's Friday. Do you remember being brought in on Wednesday night? They gave you a sedative. You slept most of yesterday.'

'What happened?'

'You collapsed in the library. They called for an ambulance. One of the library staff knew who you were and rang the college. Lawrence rang me.'

Fragments of the bad dream were coming back to me. The terror of being trapped in the library, the wonderful exhilaration of realizing that all the books were in my own head, a voice shouting – was it my own voice? I couldn't be sure – hands holding me down, a struggle, a pulsing blue light, a siren wailing. There was a gap and later, Stephen's face looking down at me, strangely distorted, like a face reflected in a spoon.

'How do you feel now?'

I considered this. My limbs felt heavy and limp, but I was growing clearer-headed by the moment.

'Not too bad. Did I really sleep all yesterday? And have you been here all the time?'

'You don't think I'd leave you here on your own, do you?' He squeezed my hand tightly. He looked exhausted: hair tousled, bags under his eyes. 'I stayed with you on Wednesday night. Yesterday I rang your mother. She came up and sat with you last night. I went home and got some sleep.'

So that accounted for what I could smell. *Diorissimo*, my mother's favourite scent. I looked vaguely around me as if she were there in person and I had somehow overlooked her.

'I sent her off to my flat to get a few hours' rest. I don't know what I would have done without her. I've told her everything, she's been a tower of strength.'

I stole a glance at him. He had met my mother and that was all he had to say about her?

The door opened and a tall man in a white coat came in.

'This is Dr Nathan,' Stephen said. 'He was on duty when you came in.'

189

He was about fifty with thinning grey hair and a tired, much-lined face. He unhooked a clipboard off the end of the bed and looked at it.

'And how are you today?' he asked me.

'OK I think.'

'Fine, fine,' he said absently. He sat down on the edge of my bed and took hold of my wrist, referring to his watch. After a while he nodded and put my hand gently back on the bed.

'Your pulse is back to normal. Your partner here has told you that the baby seems just fine?'

'Thank God for that. But what happened to me?'

'Just a moment; I need to ask you a few questions.'

He picked up the clipboard.

'Your full name, please?'

'Cassandra James.'

He ticked something off.

'What year is it?'

I told him.

Another tick.

'How old are you?'

'Thirty-eight.'

Tick.

'Who is the Prime Minister?'

Disraeli.'

The pen had already begun to descend. It halted abruptly and his head shot up.

'Sorry,' I said. 'It's Tony Blair, of course. I sometimes wish it *was* Disraeli, or rather, Gladstone. I don't suppose I'd have voted Tory even in the nineteenth century.'

He tossed the clipboard onto the bed.

'I don't think there's much wrong with *your* mental processes,' he said dryly. 'Now, your partner and your mother tell me that, as far as you know, nothing like this has ever happened to you before. Is that the case?'

190

I nodded.

'You were in a pretty bad way when you got here. You were having hallucinations, thought someone was trying to murder you. At first we were afraid you might have something called eclampsia. It's pretty rare in this country, because high blood pressure is an early symptom and that's checked at the antenatal clinic, but if it is not detected, it results in fits and can be very serious. No, it's all right,' he said, catching the anxiety on my face. 'We don't think you have it. Now I need to ask you some more questions. I gather from your partner that you're not a drug user?'

I shook my head.

'Alcohol?'

'Virtually none since I've been pregnant. Just a glass of wine now and again. That couldn't have—?'

'No, no. Any psychotic episodes? Hallucinations? No? Any history of mental illness at all?'

'Mild depression a few years ago after my marriage broke up. I had anti-depressants for a few months, that's all.'

'Ever had an epileptic fit?'

A cold pit opened up in my stomach.

'No. Do you think that's what it could have been?'

'It's hard to tell without an EEG – an electroencephalogram, that is. We'll do that later today. It's about 95 per cent accurate at detecting epilepsy. Try not to worry. Even if it was, it could just be a one-off thing, possibly related to your pregnancy. That's not uncommon.'

More and more was coming back to me. I remembered rushing headlong down the library steps, stumbling, bouncing off the walls.

'You're really sure about the baby? That I couldn't have hurt her by throwing myself around?'

'This is your first, isn't it?' he said kindly. 'Well, babies are tougher than you might think. We monitored her heartbeat when you were brought in, and she was a teeny bit distressed. But it's quite normal now—'

Off to my left a door was opened and the doctor saw the newcomer before I did. He stopped in mid-sentence. His eyes widened and he forgot to close his mouth. His face registered a mixture of surprise, enquiry and, yes, even a touch of reverence. All of a sudden he looked years younger.

I sighed and turned my head to look at the figure on the threshold of the room. She was dressed in a chunky sweater in a neutral colour, cut short to reveal a glimpse of a white T-shirt and a plaited leather belt on a pair of well-cut blue denim jeans. Her long legs ended in soft brown suede ankle boots. She wore her ash-blonde hair shoulder length with a feathery fringe. She looked like a woman from a magazine article about models who were famous in the sixties. They tell the interviewer how they have at last found true happiness with six children in a croft in the Orkneys, or running an animal sanctuary in the West Country. In the photographs they are more stunning than ever in a casual effortless way.

'Hello, Mother,' I said.

The results of the EEG came back that afternoon. They were normal.

'I want to go home,' I told Dr Nathan.

He was leaning against the rail at the end of the bed, looking at me over the top of half-rimmed glasses. Stephen and my mother were sitting on either side of my bed, and Stephen was holding my hand. I was sitting up against the pillows. My mother had brushed and plaited my hair for me and brought in a proper nightdress. Now that I was out of the hospital gown I felt more like my old self and was ready to put up a fight.

'That wouldn't be wise,' Dr Nathan said. 'I've agreed with your obstetrician that the best thing would be to transfer you to the Rosie and keep you under observation for at least a few more days. Possibly longer.'

'But the neurologist couldn't find anything wrong. No-one can find anything wrong. You said so yourself.'

'Grounds for cautious optimism,' he admitted. 'But I wouldn't feel justified in allowing you home yet. You need complete rest. Stress may well have played a part in this.'

After what had happened to Rebecca, this was the last place I was likely to feel relaxed. I remembered my dream of being chased through the hospital. It was still as vivid as if it had really happened. In fact, it was more vivid in the way that dreams sometimes can be. I felt sick just thinking about it. I couldn't stay here. But what would the doctor think of my mental state if I told him that I thought one of my students had been murdered in the hospital? I looked at Stephen. He was frowning. I guessed that he was probably thinking the same thing.

I'd already opened my mouth to speak when my mother cleared her throat. I looked at her. She caught my eye, winked slightly and gave a barely detectable nod. I didn't know what was coming, but I knew it was going to be good. I relaxed against my pillows. She stood up and *Diorissimo* wafted across the room. She put her hand on the rail next to Dr Nathan's, lifted her face and looked straight into his eyes. I'd seen that look before. It was guaranteed to stun a man at a hundred paces. I knew that from experience; it had bowled over every single one of my boyfriends – except, it seemed, for Stephen. In classical times that expression could have launched a thousand ships and burned the topless towers of Ilium. The doctor swayed like a tree in the breeze.

'I'm afraid it really is impossible for my daughter to stay in hospital a moment longer than is strictly necessary,' she said gently. 'You see, she suffers from hospital phobia.'

If that hadn't been true before, it certainly was now. The most convincing lies are always composed largely of the truth. I was desperate to get out of the place. Out of the corner of my eye I saw Stephen registering faint surprise. I glared at him. He gave an almost imperceptible shrug of his shoulders.

For a moment I thought Dr Nathan had swallowed this whole. Then he rallied.

'There's nothing about it in her notes,' he said, 'and, if this is the case, why didn't she request a home delivery?'

Why indeed? I knew I was about to find out.

'That was my doing, Doctor. Perhaps it was selfish of me. I had such a hard time with my own babies, I couldn't let Cassandra take any risks.' A brave little smile played around her lips.

Was this too much? I examined Dr Nathan's face. He caught my eye. I hastily arranged my face into a simper.

'But surely you must have noticed,' my mother went on, 'that we haven't left her alone for a single instant. She'd panic immediately if one of us wasn't with her.'

Bravo, Mother, you are a genius, I thought.

'Well . . .' said Dr Nathan.

My mother pressed home her advantage. 'If there are any problems at all we'll bring her straight back, won't we, Stephen?'

'Oh, yes, of course.'

'I'll have to consult my colleague,' Dr Nathan warned her.

'Naturally.' She beamed up at him. 'Thank you so much, Doctor.'

He paused at the door.

'But it must be clearly understood that complete rest means just that. There is no question at all of Dr James going back to work.'

'Oh, surely . . .' I began.

'We'll see that she follows your instructions to the letter,' Stephen said hastily.

He looked at me sternly. 'Is that a promise?'

I nodded. He left the room.

'Well, Laura,' Stephen said. 'You're wasted as an accountant. You should have been an actress.'

She checked her already immaculate make-up. There was an air of triumph in the way that she snapped shut her Mary Quant powder compact.

'Or possibly a master criminal,' I said.

'Of course, he couldn't have forced Cass to stay,' Stephen went

194

on. 'If the worst had come to the worst, she could have discharged herself.'

'Of course she could, darling, but Cass is too law-abiding to feel happy doing that.'

I recognized this picture of myself and winced.

'And quite right, too, with the baby coming,' she added hastily. 'He could make things very difficult for her.'

I wound down the window on the passenger side.

'I can't help feeling a bit defeated,' I said. 'There's still so much to take care of at the college.'

Stephen put his hand over mine on the edge of the car window.

'They'll have to manage without you. Nothing's more important than your health and the baby's. And it'll be a relief to me to know that you're safe in London.'

I closed my fingers around his. My mother tactfully busied herself with Bill Bailey, who was complaining bitterly from his cat carrier on the back seat of her BMW.

'Forget about the college for a while,' he said. 'Ring me as soon as you arrive, OK?'

To my chagrin I felt tears welling up. I squeezed my lips together and nodded. His ribs were still too bruised for him to bend down and kiss me. He gently unpeeled my fingers, raised the palm of my hand to his mouth.

'I'll come down next week,' he said.

He released me and stood back. I pressed the button for the electric window. The glass barrier rose up between us.

Mother started up the car. Bill Bailey immediately began a rhythmical wailing that I knew he would keep up indefinitely. He'd be hoarse by the time we got to London.

As we drove down the street, I watched Stephen's reflection grow smaller in the wing mirror. When we pulled out onto the road by the river, I saw him give a final wave before he turned to go into his flat.

195

It felt as though something was ending, and in a way it was. I didn't know it at the time, but the play was nearly over. What kind of play was it? A tragedy, in which the spring was wound tight and was almost ready to be released.

But it was to be several weeks before the last act would begin.

Chapter Nineteen

It was on a Saturday towards the end of January that the call came.

I was lying on the sofa in the first floor sitting-room of my mother's little mews house, where once hay and tack had been kept. Downstairs, where the horses had lived, were two small bedrooms, a bathroom and a kitchen. Over the weeks a routine had been established. I spent my days resting or working quietly on my book, occasionally catching the Tube to the library or having a walk in Kew Gardens. Stephen came down at weekends. Bill Bailey had at last settled in. Today he was stretched out full-length on the window seat in a pool of winter sunshine. Stephen was in an armchair next to him, reading the *Independent*. My mother was out shopping. I was reading one of my favourite Trollope novels, *The Small House at Allington*, in a little blue World's Classics edition.

When the phone rang, Stephen got up to answer it.

'For you,' he said, putting the phone down on the table beside me.

It took me a few seconds to extract myself from my book, where the most serious thing that could happen was that Adolphus Crosbie might jilt Lily Dale.

'I hope I'm doing the right thing ringing you,' Cathy sounded close to tears. 'The Master expressly told me not to bother you, but I thought you ought to know.'

My heart sank. I closed my book. 'What's up?'

Stephen was sitting again with his newspaper, but I could tell he wasn't really reading it.

'Everything's going wrong, Cass. We're weeks behind with preparing the RAE submission.'

'But I thought you were dividing that between you!'

'Alison made a start, but I've hardly seen her for the past fortnight. Paul hasn't been well. I think it might be really serious this time.'

'Oh, no, poor Alison – and poor Paul.'

'I know, I know. I feel awful worrying about the department at a time like this. Aiden's doing what he can, but of course Merfyn's away on study leave and we can't manage everything, just the two of us. And that's not all! Oh, Cassandra . . .'

Now she was really crying. I'd never known her to do this before. 'What is it?'

'I don't know if I should tell you.'

'Oh, come on, you've got to now.'

'Well, I came into college this morning to try and catch up with things a bit and I found Tim from Estates in my office. He was measuring it up!'

'What?'

Stephen had given up all pretence of not listening. His eyes were fixed on my face. Bill Bailey was affected by the change in atmosphere, too. He sat up as if he'd suddenly remembered an urgent appointment and began to wash one of his back legs assiduously.

'I asked him what the hell he was doing and do you know what he said? At first he just muttered something about rationalization of office space, but when I pressed him, he got annoyed. He said I must be the only person in the college not to realize that the department was going down the tubes and that we'd soon be out on our ears. He said . . . He said that . . .' She didn't seem able to spit the words out.

198

'*What* did he say?' I insisted.

I saw the door open and my mother came in. Stephen caught her eye, looked in my direction and grimaced. She went over and sat down next to Bill Bailey on the window seat.

'He said no-one thought you were up to the job and that when you failed it would give Lawrence the excuse he needed. The Master had been wanting to get rid of the department for years and that was why he had appointed you as head, and when you had to take sick leave, it was money from home!'

'He thought that, did he? I'll be in college first thing Monday morning!'

Stephen was frowning and shaking his head vehemently. I glared at him and clamped the receiver closer to my ear.

'Are you sure you're well enough?' Cathy was saying.

'I'm much, much better. Now listen, try not to worry. I'll sort all this out, OK? See you soon.'

I hung up.

'That bastard.' I was seething.

'Calm down,' Stephen said. 'This isn't good for you.'

'OK, OK, yes, I will calm down. What is it people say: "Don't get mad, get even"? That is exactly what I intend to do.'

My mother and Stephen exchanged glances.

'I've got to go home soon in any case,' I said. 'If I don't, I'll end up having the baby here.'

There wasn't much Stephen could say to that. The two of us had taken over my mother's bedroom, leaving her to shoehorn herself into the tiny spare-room. The house was splitting at the seams already.

'And we need to start getting things ready,' I added. 'We haven't even bought a cot yet.'

'But do you have to go back to work?' Stephen asked,

'Do you think I would be able to relax at home knowing what's going on? That Lawrence is scheming to sack us all?'

'If only the police had found Rebecca's attacker. . . .'

199

'I know, I know, but I've got to go sometime. Cathy ringing up like this has just tipped the balance, that's all. I've been feeling . . . oh, I don't know, but I really want to get back. There's so much to do.' I paused, not knowing how to describe the strange restlessness that I'd been feeling in recent days, and the deep pull of home.

'It's the nest-building instinct,' said my mother unexpectedly. 'It may be nearly forty years ago, but I remember feeling just the same before you were born. Are you sure the baby isn't due until the middle of March?'

A series of images and sensations flashed through my mind: the heat of a June night, the crack of a thunderclap, a rumpled bed, the sound of breaking glass. I looked up and caught Stephen's eye.

'Pretty sure,' I said.

My mother intercepted the glance and laughed. 'I suppose you should know.'

Stephen put the cat carrier on the lawn and opened its door. Bill Bailey edged out suspiciously. When he saw where he was, he leapt into the air and raced round and round the garden. He wasn't the only one glad to be home. I was smiling as I unlocked the door. I had to push it a bit against the pile of letters, free newspapers and junk mail that was backed up behind it. Stephen dumped my bag in the hall and went back to the car to bring in the box of books that had accumulated at my mother's over the weeks.

I went upstairs with the post. The sitting-room seemed uncared for, even though Stephen had made a point of spending an occasional night in the house. The heating had been left on low to stop the pipes from freezing, but it was still chilly and there was damp in the air. A couple of old newspapers were strewn over the sofa. A half-drunk cup of tea, lumpy with curdled milk, stood on my desk. I went over to the window and stood watching diamonds of

200

reflected light flashing off the stream below. I gave a great sigh of contentment. Home at last. I turned and ran a finger along a shelf of books. How I'd missed these old friends!

I was collecting up the newspapers when the telephone rang. My thoughts flew back to that evening when I had thought there was an intruder in the house. Stephen is here, I reminded myself, and the locks have been changed. All the same I let it ring half a dozen times before I picked it up.

'Cassandra? This is Jim Ferguson.'

'Jim.' I lowered myself onto the sofa.

'We've got someone for the attack on Rebecca. I thought you'd want to know straight away.'

My heart turned over.

'It's no-one you know, and it's pure chance, I'm afraid, that led us to him. We were called to a house in Cherry Hinton last night to deal with an intruder, a man in his twenties thieving to feed a drug habit. When we questioned him, he broke down and confessed to attacking a girl last autumn.'

Stephen came in with the book box. He looked at me in enquiry and I motioned him to the sofa beside me.

Jim went on, 'He followed her and grabbed her bag. He had a spanner in his pocket all ready for a spot of breaking and entering. When she started screaming, he hit her with it, then he panicked and ran off.'

I tried to get to grips with this. 'So Rebecca dying when she did, with the fire alarm going off, that was just a coincidence?'

'I know,' he said sympathetically. 'I don't like them either, but they do happen.'

A thought struck me. 'A confession on its own won't be enough, will it?'

'No, it'll have to be backed up with forensic evidence, but we're hopeful of getting that. There was blood on the spanner and on his coat. He hid them both in someone's garden. Until we've retrieved them, I'd like you to keep this to yourself, by the way.'

201

'Of course, yes. I thought there'd already been a house to house search for the murder weapon?'

'Probably didn't extend far enough. We're trying again.'

'I feel a bit of a fool,' I said ruefully.

'Well, don't. You had good reasons for being suspicious.'

He then chatted to Stephen while I pottered about, unpacking books and putting them back in their places.

'Great news!' Stephen said, when he at last hung up the telephone.

'Mmm, I suppose so.'

'I thought you'd be so relieved!'

'You would think so, wouldn't you?' I admitted. 'But I don't really feel anything much. A bit depressed, if anything.'

'Come and sit next to me.'

I slumped down beside him on the sofa.

'Anyone would think that you were disappointed to discover that there isn't a killer lurking in the college,' he said. 'It's a weight off my mind, I can tell you. I'm going to see a client in Bury St Edmunds tomorrow. I won't have to fret myself into a lather about getting home before you do.'

I leant against him and put my head on his shoulder.

'Somehow I can't really get excited about it,' I said. 'And I do feel such an idiot for letting my imagination run away with me, when in the end it turns out to be something so stupid and senseless and accidental. In a strange sort of way it's a bit of an anticlimax.'

'Well, things did look suspicious. I thought so, too, remember.'

I sighed. 'You known, it's irrational, but deep down I must have felt that finding Rebecca's killer would somehow make everything all right again. But she's still dead, and Margaret, too, come to that. *And* I've still got a fight with Lawrence on my hands.'

I had never before seen a maze made out of books, and what beautiful books: bound in dark blues, and greens, and reds, and

202

tooled in gilt. The walls were as high as my head. My task was to find the centre. There was something there that I needed. I didn't know what it was, but I knew that it would solve all my problems. I stepped in the dim passageway between the walls of books. I had read somewhere that in a maze you should keep turning left, but when I did that I soon reached a dead end and had to double back. I found myself back near the entrance. I decided to turn right and this seemed to get me further into the labyrinth. I saw that the books here were all numbered. I reached up and took one off the top of the wall. I opened it to find that it had my name on it, not written on the flyleaf, but actually printed on the title page. I turned over the pages. Everything that I had ever done, every thought that I had ever had was recorded here. It was the story of my life. I looked at the number printed on the outside: 6.9.1965. That date had been my first day at school. I was about to pluck down another book when I noticed that I was not alone in the maze. I could hear footsteps. Someone was coming up behind me, someone I didn't want to see. It was more vital than ever to get to the centre: I knew I would be safe there. I walked faster, the footsteps walked faster; I stopped, they stopped. When I walked on, they matched their pace to mine. I began to run and the footsteps pattered behind me, growing louder and louder until I realized that they weren't footsteps anymore, but rain, big drops of rain bouncing and splashing off the books! A wind was getting up, the walls began to sway. A book slid off and hit the floor with a thud. It was followed by another and another. Then the walls were crashing down behind me as I ran, closing the way back. I was running faster and faster, nearing the centre, one more turn and—

I woke up covered in sweat, my hair sticking to my face and shoulders. I felt a pang of loss. If only I'd been able to get to the centre of the maze; everything would be all right then. Perhaps I could still go back into the dream? I was so evenly balanced between sleeping and waking, that it did seem possible. But then the things around me began to assert their reality: I felt the

203

warmth of Stephen's body by my side, there was a grey square in the blackness that I knew was the bedroom window. The dream world was slipping away rapidly like mist in the morning sun.

It didn't all disappear, however. It was one of those dreams that stay in your head like a hangover. I was still thinking about it as I walked into college later that morning. At the porter's lodge John glanced my way and did a double-take.

'Dr James! We weren't expecting to see you yet. How are you?' He made a valiant effort not to stare at my belly. I couldn't blame him for wanting to. It seemed to me that everyone's attention must be focused on it. I felt enormous.

'Fine, thanks. The baby isn't due for another seven weeks. And your daughter. . . ?'

'A fortnight ago. A little boy. Our first grandson. They're both very well.' He was beaming all over his face.

I beamed back. 'Congratulations! And lucky her. To have it over with, I mean.'

I was about to move on when he said, 'I've got a couple of packages here. I was going to bring them down to your pigeon-hole. Do you want to take them?'

He handed over two padded envelopes. I recognized the return address on the smaller one and knew that it would contain the proofs of an article. The other, larger one hadn't been through the post. My name, care of St Etheldreda's, was written on it in neat black felt-tip pen. I didn't recognize the handwriting.

'Did this come through the inter-college post?' I asked.

'No, it must have been left by hand. I didn't see who delivered it; it was here when I came on duty.'

The Christmas cards that I had opened two months ago were still on the desk with their torn envelopes. Cathy had opened anything that looked official: those letters would be in her office. The rest, no doubt Christmas cards for the most part, were in a tidy pile next to the computer. I struggled out of my coat and edged gingerly round my desk. I was forever bumping into doors and catching myself on the edges of tables nowadays. I couldn't get used to taking up so much more space in the world. I had to push my chair well back before I could sit down.

Where to start? The serene face of the Snow Queen regarded me from the Russian lacquer box on the desk. I remembered the hallucination that I'd had in the library, her lips turning up in an enigmatic little smile as if she knew something that I didn't. I sighed. Maybe she *did* know something. After all, there were plenty of loose ends. I still didn't know if Merfyn might be having a nervous breakdown. Would I ever see him in college again? And what about Aiden and the mysterious Annabelle? I hadn't got to the bottom of that – and probably never would.

There was no point in sitting around brooding. I opened the door to Cathy's office. She looked up from her work. Her face lit up with a smile of relief and welcome.

'It's lovely to see you,' she said.

Impulsively she got up and kissed me. Then she held me at arm's length and looked into my face.

'You're sure you're OK?'

'Fine. Now let's get cracking,' I said. 'If you could start getting the RAE material together, I'll begin on the report.'

A shadow crossed her face.

'I thought you'd want the RAE stuff, but it isn't all here. The box file with photocopies of all the articles is missing. Alison must have taken it home. I've been trying to get in touch with her all weekend.'

'Me, too. I wanted to know how Paul was, but it's always the answering machine. I'll try again.'

I went back into my office and punched in the numbers that I knew by heart. This time the answering machine didn't click on. The ringing tone continued; I counted twenty rings. Then I hung up and sat back to consider. On the whole I thought it was a good sign that the answering machine had been switched off. At least it meant that someone had been there since the last time I'd rung.

But why hadn't Alison got back to me then, if she'd received my messages?

Absent-mindedly I picked up the paper knife and opened the smaller padded envelope. More proofs, more queries. Back to the library that afternoon. Could I ring Alison's daughter to find out what was going on? But I didn't know her number or her married name. Perhaps I should just go round there right away and check up? I paused with the paper knife in my hand. I didn't want to intrude. However, it wasn't merely a sense of delicacy that was holding me back: I saw myself standing in the sunshine outside Margaret's house, listening to the doorbell ringing inside, walking carelessly round the side of the house, the swishing sound of the water-sprinkler. Silly thoughts, really, because what could have happened to them? I decided to wait a bit longer. If I hadn't managed to contact Alison by tea-time, I'd drive round before I went home.

I slit open the larger of the packages that John had given me. A sheaf of white A4 paper about two inches thick and bound by a rubber band slithered out and flopped onto the table. The first page was headed 'Chapter One: The Legacy of the 1890s', and it was typed in double-spacing. I pulled off the rubber band and rifled through the pages, pausing when my eye was caught by a familiar name: 'M.R. James had many imitators, but few peers': 'Elizabeth Bowen's "The Demon Lover" and "Pink May" are among the most important ghost stories to come out of the Second World War'. Here and there I read a paragraph right through, my excitement mounting. The text had the unmistakable authority of someone totally in control of their material.

How had this got here? I shook the envelope again. A single sheet fluttered out. It was a letter addressed from a hotel in Malaga. *Dear Cassandra*, I read, *There's all of my book here, except for the last chapter. I'll e-mail it to Celia, who will print it out and deliver it to college for me. The publishers promise to have it out by the end of the year if I get everything to them by Easter. I'll be back in a fortnight with the rest of it. Hope everything is well with you and the baby. Love, Merfyn. P.S. Thanks.*

The whoop I gave brought an anxious Cathy out of her office next door. I handed her the letter and rang Lawrence's office.

His secretary answered. Lawrence was in a meeting, could she take a message?

'It's Cassandra. Tell him I'm back – and this time it's personal.'

'Oh, Cassandra, good. Yes, what was that last bit again?'

'Never mind: just tell him that I have the RAE report in hand and that Merfyn's book will be out by the end of the year.'

Magically, my mood had lifted. I felt like a new person: someone efficient, cool-headed and determined. I leaned back in my chair. A hairgrip fell to the floor and a coil of my hair flopped down onto my shoulder. I twisted a lock of it thoughtfully around my finger.

Now that I *felt* like a new person, perhaps it was time to *become* a new person.

As soon as I walked out of the hairdresser's, an icy blast stung the back of my bare neck. I turned up the collar of my coat. As I walked along, I moved my head from side to side, trying to familiarize myself with the change. My head felt so much lighter. It *was* lighter. It was only now that the two-feet long plait of hair lay coiled up like a snake in the bottom of my briefcase that I could fully appreciate how much it had weighed. The hairdresser had told me that she could sell it for me, but I had decided to take it home.

I walked through the courtyard of Clare College, the cold pressing against my face, squeezing the tips of my fingers in my gloves. I stopped to rest for a moment on the bridge over the Cam, and leaned my bump against the railings. The fretted outline of King's College Chapel was blurred not by the damp, raw, grey fog so usual for Cambridge, but by a mist that was luminous, suffused with sunlight. Everything around me – buildings, trees, people – seemed to glow as if lit from within. I walked on to the library through an enchanted world.

I stood for a while in the cloakroom, admiring my new self. I looked stronger, sharper, yet at the same time more feminine. The cap of dark hair gleaming with auburn highlights revealed the shape of my head, and my eyes seemed enormous. Fronds of hair, released from the weight that had previously held them straight, curled around my face.

I went into the reading room and settled myself at a table. As I looked around, getting my bearings, I spotted Aiden sitting about twenty feet away. He was tapping away on his laptop, totally absorbed. Now and again he looked up and stared straight ahead as if searching for the right word. Then his hand would shoot up to smooth back his hair, and the dark head would bend again to his task. He had no idea that I was watching him. I sat back and surrendered to the pleasure of observing while remaining unobserved. I examined his features one by one: the thinning hair, the rather pointed nose, the slightly blemished skin. In repose he wasn't a good-looking man. It was the power of his self-belief and his easy manner that made him attractive to women.

Again I wondered about Annabelle Fairchild. I had thought of it as an upper-class name, but was there a touch of the Highlands about it, a whiff of Celtic twilight? I could see a cloud of auburn hair, a snub nose, freckles on a milky skin. It could almost be the name of one of those fey *fin de siècle* figures like Jessie MacDonald or Fiona Macleod, whose poetry I had included in my anthology. Fiona Macleod? It was as if a light had been switched on in my head. An extraordinary thought occurred to me. I looked thoughtfully at Aiden. He had rolled up his sleeves. A muscular arm covered in fine black hair rested on the table. It couldn't be, or could it?

I went out to the bank of computers in the catalogue room and called up the post-1977 catalogue. Cambridge University Library

208

is a copyright library, so it receives a copy of every book that is published in Britain. When the answer to my query came up, it was like the moment when one fills in the last line of a crossword.

I went back to the reading room and sat next to Aiden. I scribbled a line in my notebook while I waited for him to look round. When at last he raised his head, his eyes widened and he pursed his lips in a soundless whistle of appreciation. It took a while for me to realize that he was admiring my new haircut. I smiled. I tore out the page and pushed it over. He took it and read it. He raised his eyebrows and turned back towards me. Our eyes met and he gave a little nod of rueful capitulation.

Chapter Twenty

'How did you guess?' Aiden asked.

We were in the tearoom. On the table between us lay a fat paperback. The cover showed the distant figure of a woman standing on a headland looking out to sea. The colours were restricted to tones of misty blue and grey. Gold capitals discreetly announced the title and the author: *Many a Summer* by Annabelle Fairchild.

I said, 'Have you heard of Fiona Macleod?'

Aiden shook his head.

'Of course in the nineteenth century it was usually women who wrote under male pseudonyms: George Eliot, George Sand—'

'The Brontës – I've always thought that Currer Bell was a magnificently masculine pseudonym.'

'I agree. Now and then men went in for a bit of gender-bending, too. Fiona Macleod was the pseudonym – well, actually more the alter ego – of William Sharp. No-one realized that she didn't really exist until after his death. He even wrote a bogus entry for her in *Who's Who*. Annabelle Fairchild – well, I suddenly thought that she sounded almost too good to be true. Then I realized: Aiden Frazer. The initials were the same. Everything fell into place.'

I turned the book over so that I could read the blurb. 'In a field hospital in war-torn Europe, a surgeon falls in love with the woman whose life he has saved, only to find that they are separated . . .' Much of the rest of the cover was taken up by endorsements from newspapers and women's magazines: 'Move over, *Captain Corelli's Mandolin*'; 'Heart-rending, unputdownable: I cried my eyes out'; 'Perhaps once in a generation a book comes along that for sheer scope and emotional power rivals *Gone With the Wind* and *Doctor Zhivago*. This is one such book.'

'Blimey!'

'It's selling very well,' Aiden admitted modestly. 'And I've been short-listed for the Betty Trask Award.'

'Excellent! Congratulations . . . Annabelle.'

Aiden's mouth twitched.

I said, 'You know who I thought she was, don't you?'

'The beautiful and mysterious Annabelle? How I wish I really did have a mistress like that! The expression on your face was so deliciously disapproving, Cassandra! I was tempted to own up on the spot.'

'So who *was* that at the Garden House Hotel?'

'My agent. We'd been meeting a film producer who's optioned *Many a Summer*. And that wrong number you got? That was the new assistant in the publisher's office. She got my pseudonym and me muddled up, then tried to cover it up by pretending that *she* was Annabelle!'

'You know, even then I thought that the name sounded familiar. That day in Smith's: that's where I saw it. You weren't standing by the . . .'

'Soft porn? No! I'm afraid I was admiring my own book on display.'

'The W.H. Smith Romance of the Month, no less.'

'Oh God!'

His face creased and laughter lines sprang up around his eyes. The full, rich comedy of it burst on me, too. I began to giggle.

211

Aiden's shoulders were shaking. I was laughing aloud now. I tried to get a grip on myself, but then I remembered the expression of surprise on Aiden's face as he lay on the floor with a cascade of blue-and-white paperbacks tumbling down on his chest. Laughter lifted me up like a huge wave. I gasped for breath, my ribs were aching.

The people at neighbouring tables turned towards us, startled, and then tactfully looked away.

I realized that Aiden was trying to say something.

'Cassandra,' he managed to get out at last. 'Don't you think . . . you should . . .'

'What?' I shrieked.

'Stop! You might – you might go into – labour!'

This struck me as the funniest thing I had ever heard. What could be more appropriate than to give birth to my baby in the library? It would guarantee her a good supply of reading matter right from the start. Aiden's face was grotesque with laughter. I roared. Tears poured down my cheeks. All of a sudden I wanted to stop. My eyes met Aiden's. Sanity was returning to his face and he looked worried. He leaned over, took my hand and gripped it hard. I hung on to it, bit my lip and pressed my other hand flat on the table. I closed my eyes and mouth and breathed in deeply through my nose. A few convulsive hiccups and splutters and I was myself again. I opened my eyes. Aiden smiled at me and released my hand. I fished in my handbag for a handkerchief and dabbed my face.

'I haven't laughed like that for ages,' Aiden said.

'There hasn't been much to laugh at,' I admitted.

'Almost as good as sex.'

'No, please,' I lifted a warning hand. 'Don't start me laughing again. Tell me how you came to write a romantic novel.'

'Oh, well, I've always enjoyed what's disparagingly called "women's fiction". Used to read my older sister's Georgette Heyer novels under the covers when I was a teenager.'

'No doubt imagining yourself as a sardonic Regency buck in skin-tight breeches?'

He grinned. 'That kind of thing. Then two or three years ago I was visiting my sister and I picked up the novel she was reading. It was pretty feeble and I thought I could do better. She challenged me to have a go and I found I was rather good at it. Annabelle Fairchild was my sister's idea.'

'But Aiden, why did you let me make such a fool of myself? Couldn't you have told me?'

He was silent for a few moments.

Then he said, 'I did think of it, of course, especially after Stephen spotted me in the Garden House, but I didn't know how you'd take it. You see, Margaret was absolutely livid.'

I stared at him. 'You told Margaret?'

'She'd noticed that I wasn't spending much time on my academic writing, and wanted to know why.'

'When was that?'

'Oh, not long before she died. The week before maybe? She wasn't amused. I don't think she would have minded so much if I'd been writing something obscure and highbrow – but popular fiction, that just put me beyond the pale. She told me that I should be devoting all my time to boosting the department's academic record. That was what I had been appointed for and anything less than a hundred per cent commitment just wasn't good enough. I could see her point of view. If you're going to be a successful academic these days, you have to be at it more or less non-stop.'

I couldn't deny that.

'So what does the future hold, Aiden?'

'Well, I don't want to quit academic life altogether – not yet anyway – but I wondered about going part-time. And I also thought . . . well, how would if be if I set up a creative writing course? They're very popular at the moment.'

'Does this mean that you're going to come clean?'

'Oh, I think my cover's blown now, don't you? You're not the

213

only one who knows. I had to tell the police: they thought it was hilarious. You can just imagine! I don't think it's going to stay a secret for long. What about my idea for the course?'

I sat back and considered. How would Lawrence react to this? What if it got into the newspapers? It would be the quirky story of the week: the romantic female novelist who's really a male academic. Oh, God . . . But then I saw the flip side of it. How would it look if everyone in the department that had nurtured a best-selling new talent was made redundant? What would Lawrence think about having *that* all over the papers? I couldn't wait to see his face when I pointed this out to him. As for the RAE, if Aiden went part-time we could still use his academic books and articles, *and* we could appoint another part-timer whose research could also be used. Aiden wasn't a liability, he was a trump card. And he was quite right about the popularity of creative writing courses: students would flock in.

I was still smiling to myself when I got out of the lift on the top floor of the library. It was a few moments before it occurred to me that I hadn't been up here since the day of my collapse. As I made my way through the dark stacks to the front of the building, I was glad to see that there were other people working up there today. There was even someone at the table where I'd been sitting. The tables and the carpet tiles had assumed their mundane identities and nothing could have looked more ordinary or familiar. I sat down at the table nearest to the one I had sat at before. It was chilly up here. When I put my hand on the radiator, it was luke-warm. I looked down the corridor into which the tables were squeezed between the windows and the stacks. I could see an occasional head bent over a book.

In the blink of an eye everything changed. It was dark, the heads had disappeared; in the white wall at the end of the corridor a door was opening. For a moment I felt a nightmare terror of danger and entrapment, and with it an absolute conviction that I was on the brink of a momentous discovery. I gasped and blinked

214

again. The wintry sunshine, the other scholars, the ordinary day had returned. My pulse was racing and my mouth had gone dry. I put both hands palm down on the table. The floor felt reassuringly solid beneath my feet. The flashback had lasted for only a split second, like a flash of lightning across a dark landscape.

Cautiously I closed my eyes and opened them again. Nothing happened. I got up and looked out of the window. Down below, the mist had grown thicker. I could see the outlines of Clare College and, beyond, King's College, floating in mid-air like ghosts. If the weather got worse I might not be able to get home. I wondered if I should ring Stephen and go back with him, but I remembered that he was seeing a client in Bury St Edmunds this afternoon. Was I fit to drive? I tried to assess the situation objectively. The momentary sensation had been more like a vivid memory than a hallucination. I was completely fine now. But it was difficult to weigh up the pros and cons in a rational way, because all of a sudden I longed more than anything to be at home. The Old Granary drew me to it like a beacon. The central heating had been on for twenty-four hours, the fridge was full of food and Bill Bailey would be waiting for me. I decided to drive very slowly and pull over and use my mobile phone if I felt at all odd. I absolutely couldn't wait a moment longer.

As I hurried down the stairs to collect my coat and bag, I decided not to go round and see Alison. I'd ring her again from home. If there was still no reply, I would get in touch with Jane and ask her to check up on them. She lived only ten minutes' walk away from them. The folder of articles could always be collected tomorrow.

I didn't have to make a conscious effort to drive slowly. On the A14 the fog rolled towards me in milky waves. By the time I turned off onto the single-track lane that leads to the Old Granary, I could scarcely see more than two or three feet to either side of me. The drainage channel that runs to the left of the track was completely invisible. It would be all too easy to veer off into it. I changed down to second gear and slowed to a crawl. The windscreen looked greasy with moisture. The fog hung in front of me like a thick curtain of cobwebs. My eyes began to ache from peering into it. I had to resist the notion that if I opened the car windows I would be able to see better.

When the track turned away from the channel, visibility improved a little. Behind me, a large low sulphurous sun was releasing a dingy yellow light into the fog. Monstrous forms moved steadily towards me, assuming their identities as trees or pieces of farm equipment only when they were almost upon me.

I hit a denser patch. Here I could see less than a metre ahead, and the side of the track had disappeared. I pulled up. Should I leave the car and walk the rest of the way? It would be easier to be sure that I was still on the track if I was on foot.

I rang Stephen on my mobile phone. When he answered, I could tell from his voice that he wasn't alone.

'You're still with your client?' I asked.

'Yes, where are you?'

'I'm about a quarter of a mile from home – about halfway up the track. It's dense fog. I'm going to leave the car and walk the rest of the way.'

'Oh, God. Are you all right?' His voice was fading.

'Yes, fine.'

'I'll leave right away.'

'Stephen, be careful. It's very foggy on the A14 and I think it's getting worse.'

'I will. Bye.' His voice was very faint as if it was coming from a great distance.

I heard a click from the phone. The brief contact had been comforting while it lasted, but now I felt more alone than ever.

I decided to move my car off the track so that Stephen wouldn't run into it. When I opened the car door it was as if a cold, damp flannel had been pressed to my face. Gripping the door, I struggled awkwardly to my feet. Even after a few feet the outline of the car grew blurred. As I thought, I was on the edge of a field. I got back into the car and eased it gently onto the verge. I took the torch out of the glove compartment and put it in my coat pocket. My mobile phone went in the other one. My briefcase is the kind with a shoulder strap, so I put my handbag in it and slung it across my body so as to keep my hands free. Now that the moment had come, I was reluctant to leave the warm, enclosed space of the car, but it was time to go. I locked the car and turned towards home.

In moments my coat was covered in hundreds of tiny globules of water, and the damp had penetrated to my scalp. I reached as if to lift my hair so that I could put my collar up. I was disconcerted when I felt only my bare neck. Of course: I had short hair now. I stepped forward, careful to plant each foot firmly, looking every time to check that I was still on the track. It was like trying to find your way around a house in the dark. It required all my concentration, but at the same time it was monotonous. There was nothing to see except the rutted track. The sound of my footsteps was muffled, and they echoed dully in the fog. More than once I stopped abruptly, thinking for a moment that someone was following me. But always when I stopped, the echo did too. I plodded on.

The sun had almost disappeared. It was no more than a faint intensification of light behind me. The rhythm of my footsteps and the lack of stimulation had a lulling effect; I felt dreamy and detached. The fog seemed to be getting into my head. Thoughts and memories drifted through my mind in a lazy, inconsequential way. I saw again the stream of images that had appeared on the inside of my eyelids with cinematic vividness – my conversation with Cathy at the party, the little face of the Snow Queen looking up from her lacquered box, my interview with Rebecca. It was as if the visit to the top floor of the library had shaken things loose in my mind. I saw them again, but now they were mingled with more recent memories: Jim telling me that the police had made an arrest, the moment when I knew who Annabelle Fairchild was, the pages of Merfyn's book tumbling out of the envelope. So much had happened that I didn't seem to have absorbed it all. The images went round and round in my head like figures on a carousel. Every time I tried to focus on one, it vanished and another took its place.

The rhythm of a tune began to form itself in my head. De de de de de diddly-de, de dum diddly-de . . Words attached themselves to it, fragments of a song perhaps: 'the stress of the storm, the post of the foe'. No, not a song, but a poem, something stirring, heroic, portentous. How did it begin? 'Fear death?': the words rang out in my head like the notes of a trumpet. Yes, that was it. 'Fear death? To feel the fog in my throat, the mist in my face.' It was by Browning, but I couldn't remember any more. Those few lines played themselves out again and again in my head, and I noticed that I was walking in step to their rhythm.

The fog was tinged with blue. I looked back and saw that the sun had disappeared. My toes and fingers were numb. It was getting colder and I wasn't moving fast enough to keep warm. I felt that I had been doing this for a long, long time. It was hard to visualize a world of warmth and light and distant horizons. Surely I ought to be home by now? I raised my arm to look at my watch. There was a burst of light, as though I had commanded the sun to rise in front of me and it had miraculously obeyed. I was rooted to the spot, dazzled and confused. Then I realized that I had triggered off the security light.

Once inside with the door bolted behind me, I went round the house putting on all the lights. Bill Bailey followed at my heels. When I sank gratefully into an armchair in my study, he sprang up and landed neatly on my knees. Still the half-remembered poem jangled infuriatingly in my head. After a bit I pushed Bill Bailey off my lap and heaved myself to my feet. I took my collected Browning off the shelf and looked up 'Fear death?' in the index of first lines. I turned to page 656 and read:

Fear death? To feel the fog in my throat,
    The mist in my face,
When the snows begin, and the blasts denote
    I am nearing the place,
The power of the night, the press of the storm,
    The post of the foe;
Where he stands, the Arch Fear in a visible form
    Yet the strong man must go.

The strong woman, too, I thought. I had just read those extraordinary lines for the second time when I noticed that the little red light on the answering machine was blinking. I reached over and pressed playback. The whirr of the tape rewinding was followed by Jim's voice, terse and apologetic: 'Cassandra, I'm sorry, but the business with the drug addict is a complete non-starter. He's remembered all of it, the dozy bugger: the attack wasn't in Cambridge, turns out it was Welwyn Garden City. He was too high to see that the girl was more frightened than hurt. That's why we didn't make the connection. Look, take care of yourself. I'll speak to you again soon.'

At the very moment that the machine clicked off, my stomach lurched. Low down in the small of my back, I felt a gripping pain at once strangely familiar and entirely new. In that instant my life seemed to fly apart and fall into a new shape like the pattern in a kaleidoscope. Everything that had gone before seemed now to have been only a preparation for this moment.

I was alone in a fog-bound house in the middle of the fens and I had gone into labour.

Chapter Twenty-One

My first instinct was to consult a book. Perhaps these might be the notorious false pains that I had read about. Probably the baby wouldn't come for days, I told myself, this is just a trial run, a limbering up for the main event. Even if it is the real thing, first deliveries are usually very slow. I've probably got hours and hours. I pushed to the back of my mind stories of peasant women giving birth in the fields in a break from digging up turnips.

I opened my handbook for expectant mothers and flicked hastily past rather graphic images of foetuses and uteruses to find the section about the onset of labour. At first I couldn't take it in. I forced myself to focus on the page. False labour pains were common in the few weeks before delivery, I read, but they could be easily recognized because they were irregular and would diminish in a few hours; true ones came at regular intervals and would gradually increase in intensity. I knew that if it was true labour, ten-minute intervals were the signal that I ought to get to hospital. I looked at my watch. A few minutes past five.

I put the book down open on my desk and looked out of the window. The fog was dingier and greyer. Night was falling. I sat for a while, trying to relax and wondering when the next contraction would come.

The telephone rang.

'Cass? Oh good, you've got home safely,' Stephen said. 'I've decided not to come home along the A14. You know what lunatics people can be in this sort of weather. I don't want to be involved in a pile-up so I'm coming along the back roads.'

'Where are you now?'

'Just outside Mildenhall. The fog's so thick that it's like driving into a loaf of bread. I've already passed a couple of minor accidents.'

I told him about the pains and about Jim's message.

'Oh, my goodness! Are you OK? How do you feel?'

'I'm fine. It's probably not – oh, ouch!' I said, more in surprise than pain.

'What's that? What is it?'

'Just a twinge.' I lied. 'And even if it's the real thing, nothing's going to happen for ages, perhaps even days.'

'Look, if it gets any worse, ring for an ambulance. I'll be there as soon as I can.'

He hung up. That was all very well, I thought, but how is an ambulance going to get here through this fog? I looked at my watch. Twenty-five minutes since the last contraction. I looked again at the book: 'The contractions of true labour initially last about thirty seconds and occur at regular intervals of about fifteen to twenty minutes.'

I rang my doctor's surgery. The line was engaged. On impulse I flicked through the phone book and tried another number.

'Hello, Dr Pennyfeather speaking.'

'Jane, hello. It's Cassandra.'

'Cassandra! How are you?' she said warmly.

Just the sound of her voice was reassuring.

'Well, actually, I think I may be going into labour. And I'm stuck here at home on my own and it's incredibly foggy. Stephen's on his way, but I don't know how long it will take him.'

'OK. The first thing is to relax. Now, when did you get the first contraction? And how long between that and the next one?'

I told her.

'You're right. If the baby's not due for another six weeks, it's most likely a false alarm, and even if it isn't, you've probably got hours. But Cassandra, you must stay put. Don't try to get to a neighbour's. If things suddenly speed up, you need to be where it's warm and light.'

Peasant women in fields. I saw myself lying panting in a ditch like someone in a Thomas Hardy novel. I thought of something that had horrified me when I read it as a student: Tolstoy's terrible description of Princess Lisa dying in childbirth. During my pregnancy I'd managed to put it in the recesses of my mind, but now it all came back to me: the shrieks and helpless animal moans, and at the end of it, the doctor rushing distracted from the room . . .

'Cassandra? Cassandra? Are you still there?'

'Oh, God, what am I going to do? I don't want to be alone.'

'You won't be. Who's your GP?'

'I'm registered with Dr Devlin in Ely.'

'I'm acting as locum in Histon – you've come through to me here on my mobile – so I'm probably as near as anyone. I'll leave now. If the pains get worse or the time between contractions drops down to ten minutes, let me know. Oh, and Cassandra, one last thing: keep yourself occupied. Do some work, bake a cake or read a book.'

After we had stopped speaking, I stood by the window looking out. I couldn't even see the ground. I seemed to be floating in a void. It struck me that being in the womb might be like this. I turned to look into the room: the lamps shed pools of soft light, but the corners of the room were dim. I became aware of a gentle rumbling: it was Bill Bailey snuffling. He was coiled up in a tight ball on the chair, his white nose buried in a tail nearly as thick and bushy as a fox's brush.

I switched on the radio and heard the end of the news and then the weather forecast. 'There is thick fog over parts of East Anglia. Visibility is extremely poor and driving conditions hazardous. Motorists are advised not to travel unless their journey is essential.'

I heard Big Ben striking six. As if on cue there was another contraction and the phone rang.

'I'm at Fordham now,' Stephen said, 'but I can only go at a snail's pace. How are you?'

'It might be the real thing.'

'Oh no!'

'It's all right,' I said with an assurance that I didn't feel. 'There's a long time to go yet, and I rang Jane Pennyfeather. She's coming over from Histon.'

'OK. Keep your chin up, sweetie. See you soon.'

In my mind I saw a map of the area and on it two cars crawling towards me from opposite directions, their drivers peering through windscreens, inching forwards into the fog. I went back to the window and gazed out. I thought of one day telling my daughter about how we'd been here alone together in the fog and the night as I waited for her to arrive. Something flickered on the extreme edge of my field of vision. I turned my head. The fog had parted momentarily, and just for an instant I thought I saw a dark shape standing there. The fog closed in again and it was gone. I stared and stared, straining my eyes against the opaque resistance of the fog. I saw nothing. A shrub or a tree, I told myself, that's what it must have been. The fog was disorientating and I couldn't quite think what was at that side of the garden.

I found myself gritting my teeth against the next pang. Remembering the few antenatal classes that I'd managed to get to, I inhaled slowly and relaxed on the out breath. This time the pain ran through my whole body in a spasm that left me aching all over. I glanced at my watch: six fifteen. Jane's advice to keep busy was good – and God knows, I had enough to do – but like a lot of good advice, it was very hard to follow. At this rate, I would be finishing the RAE report in the maternity ward. I wished that I had managed to get hold of the missing box file.

I got up and paced slowly up and down. As with my walk through the fog, the soothing rhythm seemed to summon up a

223

train of thoughts and impressions. Images drifted into my mind: Cathy shaking her head as she talked about Hannah forging her signature, Aiden standing by the rack of books, Merfyn bracing himself for the impact of my anger, Alison and Paul in the back room of their house in Newnham. I concentrated on that picture. I could see Alison's hand on Paul's shoulder, and his smile as he looked up at her. I reached the windowsill and leaned against it, staring out into the fog. It was hard to imagine now that it had ever been the height of summer. I remembered the smell of Paul's cigarette, my head swimming with the scent of the hot summer garden. There was a kind of seismic shift in my mind: one moment I was standing too close to the picture, all I could see were unconnected patches of colour; the next I had taken a step back and the picture had come into focus.

That's it, I thought. I knew now that Margaret's death had not been an accident; I knew who had searched my house and what they had been looking for; I knew why I had collapsed in the library: everything clicked into place. There was a second of sheer intellectual delight at the rightness of it, followed instantly by horrified disbelief. Could it really be true?

If so, the key to the mystery had been at hand ever since the day I had found Margaret's love letters. Clinging to the handrail, I made my way carefully down the stairs to the kitchen. I took the key to the wine cellar out of the hollow book, and got out Margaret's disks. I clambered back up to the study and spread them out on the desk. Most had the names of completed books and articles written on them in Margaret's precise hand. I picked out a disk marked 'Miscellaneous' and switched on my computer. It gave its usual plangent buzz. Bill Bailey's ears twitched. He sat up and yawned. I slotted the disk into the computer. Many of the folders on it were identified only by a date. I called one up at random and read, 'Darling, darling M'. I scrolled down to the signature, 'Your Lucy'. I might have guessed: this had been a truly modern love affair conducted via the latest technology as well as by old-fashioned paper correspondence. There were scores of e-mails – they must have contacted each other every day for months – and Margaret had preserved them as lovingly as if they were letters tied up with red ribbon. I closed the document and ran the cursor down the screen until I found titles like 'Draft' and 'Chapter One'. I called up 'Chapter One'. It was Lucy's PhD thesis. She had shared everything with her lover.

Before I was halfway down the page, I knew beyond a shadow of a doubt what lay behind Margaret's death.

I scarcely noticed the next contraction.

My train of thought was broken by a piecing yowl. Bill Bailey was sitting by my chair regarding me with a pleading expression. Automatically I got up and made my way downstairs, Bill Bailey racing ahead of me. I was halfway down when I saw the security light go on. As I reached the hall, the doorbell began to peal urgently and continuously as though someone were leaning on it.

Jane at last, thank God, I thought.

Bill Bailey was winding himself around my legs in a frenzy of anticipation as I pulled back the bolt and opened the door.

Alison was standing outside.

I froze with my hand on the doorknob. She was staring at me as if she had expected to see someone quite different.

'Your hair,' she said hoarsely.

Then, as smoothly as if we had rehearsed it, Bill Bailey shot out, Alison took a step back, and I slammed the door shut. I rammed the bolt home and stood with my back against it.

I could see down the hall into the kitchen. My briefcase was still where I had left it on the table. I forced myself to leave the door, go into the kitchen and turn the case upside down onto the table. A book and a folder fell out, followed by the rope of plaited hair. It hit the table with a slap like an eel being tipped out of a basket. My mobile phone slid out, too. I seized it. Behind me, Alison was knocking gently on the door. My fingers were trembling so much that I couldn't key in Stephen's number. It took me a moment to remember that it was in the phone's memory. I called it up. There was a rapid bleeping followed immediately by the click of the phone being answered at the other end.

I said, 'Stephen, listen to me. Alison killed Margaret and Rebecca, and she's here now, outside. I want you to ring the police. Do you understand?'

He replied, 'Yes, I understand. What's going on? Are you OK?'

'Yes.'

'And the baby?'

'Much as before. Where are you now?'

'I've made it nearly as far as the track. I'm going to hang up now and call the police, OK?'

'OK.'

I sat down heavily at the kitchen table and put my hand to my side. I tried to calm my breathing.

Alison had stopped knocking on the door, but I could hear her shuffling about outside.

She pushed open the letterbox.

'Cass, please talk to me.'

Her voice was so flat and strained that I wouldn't have recognized it as hers.

'I can't let you in.'

'You don't understand, I won't hurt you. Anyway, it's all over now.' She began to sob.

'What do you mean?'

'Paul's dead.'

'Stay there.'

I went into the cloakroom on the right of the door. There's a little window almost at head height. I looked out. Alison was standing bathed in the intense white light of the security lamp. She made no move towards me but simply turned to face me, passively submitting to inspection. I examined her closely. Her eyes were red and puffy, and her cheeks were wet with tears. Her hair was dishevelled. Her whole body looked limp and heavy with defeat.

I opened the window.

'What's happened?' I asked.

'This afternoon. An injection. It was very quick and painless. He'd always intended to go before things got too bad. It just came much, much sooner than we expected.'

I was trying to take this in when a new and quite different sort of pain seized me. Beginning at the sides of my body, it flowed into my belly and rose steadily to a peak. I gripped the rim of the little washbasin and closed my eyes until the pain ebbed away. I opened them again to see Alison staring anxiously at me.

'What's the matter? Is the baby coming?'

'No, no, not yet.'

Even as I said it I wondered if it were true. I looked at my watch: twenty to seven. I hadn't timed the last contraction, but the one before that had been at six fifteen. They were getting closer.

We looked at each other in silence for a few moments, then Alison said, 'When did you realize?'

'About five minutes ago, oddly enough.'

'I suppose you found Lucy's thesis on one of Margaret's backup disks. I should have known a lot earlier on that there'd be another set somewhere,' Alison said. 'She was so bloody well organized.'

She didn't sound bitter, just resigned.

'But Alison, how did you think you could get away with it?'

'I nearly did, though, didn't I?' There was no triumph in her voice, only sadness.

'Did you kill Lucy, too?'

Alison looked astonished. 'Of course not! I was terribly upset when I heard about the accident. But then . . .'

She paused. Our eyes met and I was the first to look away. Strangely, what I felt was not anger or fear, but something more like embarrassment, the sort of feeling one gets when one is obliged to comfort someone with their ignorance or bad manners.

'But then. . . ?' I prompted.

'Well, after a bit I did begin to wonder. Lucy's work was so good – she'd done a lot of research before she even came to Cambridge – and some of it was almost in publishable form. It seemed such a pity to waste it.'

'You could have published it under her name.'

'Oh, what would have been the point of that?' she said impatiently. 'She was dead, after all. It couldn't affect her career, could it? Whereas for me – it could make all the difference. I was so desperately worried about losing my job. I knew I wouldn't get another one at my age and with no publication record, and I couldn't see how we'd manage without my salary. Luckily the girl who shared Lucy's room was away in the States for the term, so I borrowed a key to their room from the porter's lodge and erased the article from the hard drive of Lucy's computer. I took her backup disks, too, and all her written notes. I thought I'd got everything.'

'I know what happened next. When you showed Margaret the article, she saw what you'd done. Did she threaten you with exposure?'

'She invited me round to her house and told me that no-one else knew and that she would keep quiet about it, on condition that I didn't submit the article for publication and that I resigned. Otherwise she'd tell Lawrence and I'd be sacked.'

The pain hit me again like a fist clenching and unclenching low in my belly. I groaned and continued to cling onto the washbasin.

'Cass? How are you feeling?' Alison's voice seemed to come from a distance.

The pain ebbed slowly away.

I took a deep breath. 'I'm OK. Go on.'

Alison was too caught up in her story to stop anyway. 'She said she thought she was being generous. Generous! I begged and pleaded with her, but she was adamant. I was so angry! There we were, sitting by that bloody pool, next to that enormous house that her husband's money had bought. How could she understand anything about our struggle to keep going?'

There was a pause.

'Then what happened?'

She cleared her throat. 'I lost my temper. There was a pile of exam papers lying on the table beside her. I grabbed the top one and tore it in half. That got her going all right. She went for me and I pushed her away. She fell into the swimming pool, hit her head on the side and sank like a stone. At first I did think of going in after her and pulling her out, but then . . .'

She looked up and flushed when she saw me gawping at her.

'It just seemed meant to be, somehow. An accident, really, like Lucy's death. After all, I didn't actually *intend* to kill her.'

This time Alison was the one to glance away, and I saw a muscle twitch below her left eye.

'Margaret had been wearing a wrap-round skirt over her swim-suit,' she said. 'I took off all my clothes and waded into the pool and managed to get it off her. I didn't want any doubt about its being an accident.'

The image that this conjured up in my mind was one that I knew I'd never forget.

'I searched the house for Margaret's copy of the thesis. At last I found it, in a little drawer tucked underneath her desk; both a disk and a hard copy. Then I just walked home quickly. Luckily there wasn't a soul about.'

'Did you tell Paul what had happened?'

'Of course not. That was the whole point, don't you see?' she said as though I was being wilfully obtuse, 'I didn't want Paul to be worried. I didn't even tell him my job was at risk. The week after the funeral, I managed to get into Margaret's office and check for anything incriminating. After that I thought I was safe.'

I felt a heaving sensation and a warm wetness between my legs.

I saw my own astonishment mirrored on Alison's face.

'What is it?' she asked.

'My waters have broken.'

I grabbed a towel and stuck it between my legs.

'You'd better let me in. I've been through this myself, remember, and I was with my daughter when she had her baby.'

I looked doubtfully at her. 'The doctor should be here soon. And Stephen.'

'Oh, come on. I won't hurt you – or the baby,' she said impatiently.

'You wouldn't hurt me! What about the cake? You switched it for a piece with cannabis in it! That's what Paul was smoking to relieve his MS, wasn't it?'

She looked contrite. 'I didn't think that it would have such a dramatic effect. I just wanted to get you out of the way for a while.'

'And when you realized that Margaret had another set of backup disks, you searched my house!'

'I'm so sorry about breaking that sweet little bowl.' This seemed to worry her as much as anything.

A wave of pain hit me. Something inside was being pulled tighter and tighter.

'No, no,' I groaned.

I clutched my belly with one hand and thumped the wall again and again with the other. I bit my lip until blood came. Just when I thought that I couldn't stand it a moment longer, the tension relaxed and the pain slowly subsided.

'Cass, please let me in! Please!'

I looked up. Alison's face was at the window. Her eyes were wide with alarm.

I can't do this on my own, I thought.

'Even if I could bear to harm the baby,' Alison said, 'what good would it do me? Think about it. I heard you on the phone; Stephen knows what I've done. So do the police by now. They'll probably all arrive together.'

I thought about it.

'Like something out of a Marx brothers movie,' she added.

At that moment she sounded just like her old self. Perhaps it was that as much as anything that decided me.

'Very well. Put your bag down over there, near the gate. Yes, that's it. Now take your clothes off.'

'What?'

'Just down to your underwear will be enough, but do it, or I won't let you in.'

'But why?'

'I want to make sure that you haven't got a syringe hidden about your person.'

She flushed. I thought she wasn't going to do it. Then she kicked off her shoes and pulled off her fleece, dropping it on the ground. A few moments later, her sweater and jeans joined it. She stood there shivering in her white cotton knickers and bra; a big, pale, Rubenesque woman.

'Socks as well?' she asked.

'No, that's enough.'

I went into the hall and opened the door. Alison walked through into the kitchen and I followed her.

'You can put my coat on,' I said.

She took it off the chair where I had left it when I came in, and slung it round her shoulders. She sat down at the kitchen table. The rope of hair was still lying there. Alison just looked at it at first, then she stroked it.

'I never thought you'd pluck up the nerve to get rid of this. It really suits you.'

'Thanks.'

'How about a cup of tea?'

I thought it over. 'Oddly enough, it's just what I feel like, but I'm not supposed to eat or drink at this stage, am I?'

'Oh, sod that. Your body will tell you what it wants.'

Alison put the kettle on. I watched her moving about the kitchen laying out cups, getting the milk out of the fridge.

'Why don't you sit down?' she said.

I shook my head. I had to keep moving, pacing up and down

231

between the door and the window, the palms of my hands resting on my aching belly.

There was still something I needed to know.

'What about Rebecca?'

Alison poured out the tea. 'She tried to blackmail me. Told me she was finding the work too difficult, but couldn't afford to re-take her final year, so could I fix things for her? She said it would wreck my career if it came out about me and Lucy. I couldn't think how she knew.'

'She didn't,' I said dryly. 'You both must have got the wrong end of the stick. She thought it was you, not Margaret, who'd been having an affair with Lucy. You thought she meant the thesis.'

Alison's mouth gaped. She groped for a chair and sank onto it, her eyes never leaving my face. I struggled not to feel a grim satisfaction as I told her about Margaret and Lucy.

'You didn't know about that, did you? You needn't have killed Rebecca.'

Her eyes were now fixed on the table.

'When you went to the hospital to finish her off, did you inject her with whatever Paul used? Something from the chemistry lab, I suppose.'

Her head jerked sharply. 'I couldn't risk her incriminating me. How would Paul have managed if I'd been arrested?'

The folder from my briefcase was still lying on the table. The flap had fallen open.

'That's my article,' she said, sounding surprised.

'Do you know, I've been carrying it around in my bag for months. I never did get round to reading the rest of it.'

She took the article out of the folder. 'This isn't going to be much use to you now, is it? I'm sorry about that.' She folded it neatly in two. 'What's going to happen to the department, do you think?'

'We'll be OK.'

Alison tore the article in half very slowly and neatly.

'Why did Margaret have to make such a fuss?' she said.

She went on with her work of folding and tearing. A little white mound of torn paper was growing in front of her. I stood on the other side of the table and watched her.

'All this need never have happened,' she continued.

She scooped up the scraps of paper in both hands and tossed them up. They flew out of her hands like startled birds and then floated down with majestic slowness, landing on her shoulders and hair like giant flakes of snow. Some settled in our cups and the tea turned them ochre.

'It's not Margaret. It's you,' I said. 'You're the one. You're the Snow Queen.'

She looked at me, puzzled. I studied her face, taking in her creamy complexion, the slightly ironic set of her lips, the lock of white hair springing up from her forehead.

The anger I'd felt earlier returned. I could hardly speak for emotion, but at last I spat the words out. 'You mustn't try to put the blame on anyone else. Of course Margaret couldn't let you steal someone else's research. Of course she couldn't. Trying to tell the truth about things – that's what academic life is about. If we haven't got that, we haven't got anything. It's more than a job, it's what we *are*.'

Alison and I stared at each other across the kitchen table. She was the first to look away. I watched her eyes slowly fill with tears. Her face softened and relaxed.

'You're right,' she said.

'Why did you want to see me?'

She sighed. 'I just wanted to explain how it all happened, and I had a vague idea that I maybe could protect my daughter and her family. It'll be bad enough for her already that we're dead. I thought perhaps the rest needn't come out. Silly, really.'

'Stephen will be here before too long – and the police.'

She shrugged. 'There's nowhere to run to. May as well wait here as anywhere.'

233

I nodded.

'Paul was so fond of you, Cass,' Alison said. 'He really used to look forward to those chess games.'

I pulled out a chair and sat down opposite her. She smiled at me and stretched out her hand across the table. As I reached to take it, pain tore through me. I sucked in my breath and closed my eyes. A gigantic wave was lifting me higher and higher. Alison's fingers tightened around mine.

I was hemmed in by the table. I struggled to my feet.

'I've got to lie down,' I groaned.

Alison leap up and put her arm around me. Clasped to one another like Siamese twins, we staggered together up the stairs, the narrow space squeezing us close. I sank to my knees on the floor of the study. Alison came down with me as if we were yoked together.

'I can't go any further,' I gasped.

She began working quickly and efficiently, unfastening my clothes, pulling off my sodden tights and knickers. I parted my thighs.

'Yes, yes, take a deep breath. Now push. Push!' she shouted.

She leant over me. I looked up at her face. She was grimacing in sympathy.

'That's it. Grip my hand as hard as you can. Try to breathe slowly. Yes, that's it.'

For a few blessed moments the pain stopped. I relaxed my grip. Then it began again: something bigger, more important and more complicated than pain. I slid to a lying position and drew my knees up. I was dimly aware of sounds in the background, a door banging, voices shouting.

I heard Alison cry, 'Yes, yes! That's it! Yes!'

She was sitting behind me now with her legs spread wide. She pulled me back against her breasts. I gripped her knees and braced myself. The crown of the baby's head appeared between my thighs.

234

I heard thudding on the stairs. I looked up and saw Stephen appear in the doorway, with Jane at his shoulder. They stood for a moment transfixed. I clenched my fists, gritted my teeth and gave a last, great heave. With a final slithering rush, our daughter was born.

Stephen was just in time to catch the blood-smeared baby in both hands.

Epilogue

Futile – the Winds –
To a Heart in port –
Done with the Compass –
Done with the Chart –
Emily Dickinson

'Careful, careful.'

'I am being careful,' said Stephen as he unbuckled the carrycot and eased it out of the back seat of the car. 'I can still hardly believe that they've let us take her home.'

'I know. I was expecting to feel a heavy hand on my shoulder as we walked out of the hospital.'

Stephen and I stood for a moment at the gate to the Old Granary with the carrycot between us. We watched the clouds scudding across the huge expanse of fenland sky. It was a deliciously fresh, sparkling spring morning in early April. After six weeks in the premature baby unit, Grace was coming home on the exact day that she should have been born. It had taken a while for us both to recover from the shock of her early arrival, and then Grace had suffered jaundice. I had stayed in the hospital with her. After all the weeks spent under artificial light, it felt strange to be outdoors. The world was full of movement and energy, and everything seemed too brightly coloured.

There was a sound behind me. I turned my head to see Jane

and Cathy standing at the door of the house. They were both grinning. Jane was holding a bottle of champagne and Cathy was clasping Bill Bailey to her breast. He struggled free, bounded down the garden, and wound himself around my legs in an ecstasy of welcome.

'I know you'll want to be quiet,' Stephen said, 'but I didn't think you'd mind Jane and Cathy. They helped me get things ready.'

'It's lovely to see them.'

Jane came forward and Stephen tilted the carrycot so that she could peep into it. I folded back the white cellular blanket and we admired the little sleeping face. Grace's thumb was in her mouth and her other hand, curled into a fist, was resting against her cheek. Jane put her face close to the baby's and inhaled.

'Oh, God, the smell of small babies! It always make me wish I'd become a paediatrician or had six kids of my own! Isn't she gorgeous?'

'Just perfect,' I agreed.

Up in the sitting-room, Stephen put Grace in her carrycot on the window seat. I sat down beside her. The familiar room seemed different somehow. Then I saw that it *was* different: there was a new rug on the floor. Underneath it, I knew, were stains that hadn't quite come out of the floorboards. But that wasn't all: there was more space. The books had gone from the floor, and the wall by the stairs was covered in new bookshelves.

Stephen was about to ease the cork out of the champagne bottle. He paused and glanced over at me, gauging my response to the changes.

'You don't mind, do you? I know you'll want to sort the books out yourself, but I thought I'd just get them off the floor. Safer for the baby. Plus, I've decorated the little bedroom for her. I took yesterday off work to do it. I wanted it to be a surprise.'

'Yes, that's all right. I mean, yes, of course, it's great!'

Grace's birth and the weeks watching over her in hospital had brought us together in ways I hadn't imagined were possible. We hadn't talked much about the future. We had somehow just taken it for granted that we would live together in the Old Granary when we had brought Grace home. We hadn't talked yet about selling Stephen's flat, nor about getting married. Those were questions for later. Now, there was the round, satisfying pop of a champagne cork being drawn to focus on. Jane held out glasses to catch the froth, and the next few minutes passed in a confusion of toasts and laughter.

When we were all settled in our seats with our glasses, Cathy said, 'There's something else you might feel like celebrating. I heard just as I was leaving college: Lawrence has resigned. He's leaving at the end of the summer term. Merfyn wants you to know that he and Aiden are pushing for new appointments to the department, and then when you get back from maternity leave, there'll be everything to play for. He said he'd ring you when you've had time to settle in.'

'Lawrence is leaving? But why?'

I couldn't imagine him anywhere but in college. In fact, I wasn't even sure that I'd ever seen him anywhere else. I'd wondered if he ever went home.

'The notice that went up on the board said he was taking early retirement because he wanted to devote more time to his subject.'

'Is that the academic equivalent of spending more time with your family?' Stephen asked.

'That's right. But the question is: did he jump or was he pushed?' I said. 'I bet the trustees were furious when all that stuff came out in the papers about his trying to block the inquiry.'

'I've wondered about that,' Cathy said. 'How did the papers get hold of it all?'

'I didn't tell them.' I glanced at Stephen.

He held up his hands in self-defence.

'Not guilty,' he said. 'I do know that certain members of the local constabulary thought you had a rough deal. I really don't know any more than that, but however it happened, it's bloody good news.'

238

He picked up the champagne bottle.

Cathy sighed, 'Much as I'd love some more, I've got to get back to college.'

She came over to kiss me and have a last look at Grace. 'Don't be in a hurry to get back in harness. Enjoy her while you can.'

After Cathy had gone, Stephen asked Jane how Malcolm was coping. 'It must have been a hell of a shock finding out about Margaret and Lucy.'

'Ah, yes,' Jane said slowly. 'I was meaning to tell you about that. You're not going to believe this, but it wasn't all that much of a shock . . .'

I stared at her. 'You don't mean to say that he knew all along?'

'He didn't know *who* it was, he just knew that there was someone. But he let it ride, didn't want to force the issue. He thought if he didn't say anything, she'd get through it and settle back into the marriage.'

'Actually he was right, wasn't he?' Stephen said. 'She *was* getting over it.'

Would I have destroyed the letters, I wondered, if I had known that? And how had destroying them influenced the course of events? Was there even any point in thinking about that?

Jane cleared her throat. I looked at her and saw that she was blushing.

'I might as well tell you. Malcolm and I, we're . . . well, we've become rather close.'

'That's marvellous!' I said. I thought of what Jane had said about wishing she'd had six babies. Well, she wouldn't have time for that, but maybe there'd be time for one? She was only a few years older than me, after all.

Jane was beaming all over her face. 'It's very early days. I mean, we won't be rushing into anything, have to see how things go.' Her face grew more serious. 'And of course, it hasn't been a year yet since . . .'

She didn't finish the sentence. She didn't need to. It was less

239

than a year since Margaret had died. Less than a year, too, since Grace had been conceived. My daughter made a little snuffling sound. I leaned over her. Her hand had fallen away from her face. I stroked her palm. She stirred in her sleep and her tiny fingers closed tightly round mine. Impossible now to imagine a world without her. I thought of the night she had been born. In the bustle and confusion of the moments after Grace's birth, Alison had slipped away. When the fog dispersed the following morning, the police found her parked car in a field about a mile away. Her body was inside it. I was shocked, but not for long. I came to see that while it wasn't exactly a happy ending, it was perhaps for her the best possible one. I had almost come to terms with it, but there was still a sore place in my heart for Rebecca's mother and I didn't think that would ever go away. Marion had come down from Newcastle to see me in hospital, bringing me a beautiful hand-knitted shawl. We would keep in touch.

Jane broke into my thoughts.

'Here's to Grace,' she said. 'Long life and happiness!'

'Not many people have such a dramatic entry into the world,' Stephen said.

I raised my glass. One day I would tell her all about it.